ReShonda Tate Billingsley
Her bestselling novels have been hailed as

"Emotionally charged . . . not easily forgotten."

—*Romantic Times*

"Full of palpable joy, grief, and soulful characters."

—*The Jacksonville Free Press*

"Poignant and captivating, humorous and heart-wrenching."

—*The Mississippi Link*

Praise for
A FAMILY AFFAIR

"Scandalous drama mixed in a story of forgiveness that spans over time. . . . In *A Family Affair*, finding out [about the past] could be a painful thing."

—*The Washington Informer*

"It will tug at your heart. . . . Kudos to this divine writer. . . . It's always refreshing to read one of her novels, and walk away with a message to carry on in your daily life."

—*Rolling Out*

"A heartwarming story that had me hooked."

—*Book Referees*

"A compelling tale."

—*Black Expressions*

THE SECRET SHE KEPT

"Entertaining, riveting. . . . Jaw-dropping, drama-filled. . . . A must-read."

—*AAM Book Club*

HOLY ROLLERS

"Sensational. . . . [Billingsley] makes you fall in love with these characters."

—*RT Book Reviews*

THE DEVIL IS A LIE

"Steamy, sassy, sexy. . . . An entertaining dramedy."

—*Ebony*

"A romantic page-turner dipped in heavenly goodness."

—*Romantic Times* (4½ stars)

CAN I GET A WITNESS?

A *USA Today* 2007 Summer Sizzler

"Billingsley serves up a humdinger of a plot."

—*Essence*

THE PASTOR'S WIFE

"Billingsley has done it again. . . . A true page-turner."

—*Urban Reviews*

I KNOW I'VE BEEN CHANGED

#1 *Dallas Morning News* bestseller

"Grabs you from the first page and never lets go. . . . Bravo!"

—Victoria Christopher Murray

"An excellent novel with a moral lesson to boot."

—Zane, *New York Times* bestselling author

HOLY
ROLLERS

ReShonda Tate Billingsley

POCKET BOOKS

New York   London   Toronto   Sydney   New Delhi

Pocket Books
A Division of Simon & Schuster, Inc.
1230 Avenue of the Americas
New York, NY 10020

This book is a work of fiction. Names, characters, places, and incidents either are products of the author's imagination or are used fictitiously. Any resemblance to actual events or locales or persons, living or dead, is entirely coincidental.

This Pocket Books paperback edition June 2014

POCKET and colophon are registered trademarks of Simon & Schuster, Inc.

For information about special discounts for bulk purchases, please contact Simon & Schuster Special Sales at 1-866-506-1949 or business@simonandschuster.com.

The Simon & Schuster Speakers Bureau can bring authors to your live event. For more information or to book an event, contact the Simon & Schuster Speakers Bureau at 1-866-248-3049 or visit our website at www.simonspeakers.com.

Manufactured in the United States of America

10 9 8 7 6 5 4 3 2 1

ISBN 978-1-4165-7808-6
ISBN 978-1-4165-7817-8 (ebook)

A Note from the Author

When I was a little girl, I used to write my mother long, drawn-out letters whenever I got in trouble. I would eloquently explain why I did whatever I did, and then I'd slip the letter under her bedroom door. I know those letters used to get on her nerves. I had a flair for the dramatic (I guess that's where my daughters get their theatrics from). But my mom would smile (okay, she didn't always smile) and gently tuck the letter away, knowing "that's just how I was." I'd also write poems and make-believe stories and force my little sister to sit and listen . . . again, and again, and again. She'd smile and give me her undivided attention, even though she would much rather have been somewhere watching *Tom & Jerry* (okay, so I had to threaten her sometimes). But the fact remained that even at a young age, I had my family's support.

Then I got married. You hear all the time about spouses who don't support their significant other's dreams. That is so not my story. I would sit and talk with my new husband about wanting to write a book (but I couldn't because I was too cheap to buy a computer—hey, it was 1995). So my husband snuck some money out of our paltry account and bought a computer so I could write (I think he was just tired of my writing him letters, too). And to this day, his support—of my writing, of my travels, of my literary career—remains strong.

The stories like that are endless. It's why, no matter how hard I try, I can't complete a book without acknowledging those who made it happen.

As usual, my first ounce of gratitude is for my God, who continues to bless me abundantly. So much so that sometimes I have to just stop and marvel in all that He's done. The quote at the top is from two of my favorite gospel singers, Mary, Mary. Throughout my literary journey I've had some who judged my relationship with Christ by the stories that I write. To them, I say, "You don't know how much I praise, don't know how much I gave . . ." Not only that, but if I inspire even one reader, if I help even one person on her spiritual journey, then I think my God is pleased.

Now, coming down off my soapbox . . . In addition to my husband (Miron), mother (Nancy), and sister (Tanisha), I have to say thank you to my three beautiful children, who really aren't all that impressed with my books but put up with my writing and greet me like I've returned from war after every single book tour.

I must give lots of love to my girls—who keep me grounded, who support me and have my back no matter what—**DR. CLEMELIA RICHARDSON** (there, I put your Dr. in, put you first, and even put it in bold and all caps, are you happy now?); Jaimi Canady (thanks for being the one to tell me my blacks don't match, and texting me things like "never, ever wear that outfit again." Oh, this is the eighth adult novel, can you hurry up and finish the second one so you can catch up?); Raquelle Lewis (I should put Dr. in front of your name for all the therapy sessions since middle school); and Kim Wright (we sure miss you back here in the States. Thank you so, so much for everything). Kim, I would've put you first but Clemelia would've had a stroke.

To my soul sister, Pat Tucker Wilson. You have truly seen the good, the bad, and the ugly of both the literary and television news world, and you've kept your head up and helped me keep mine held high. Thank you for always being there, no matter what.

To the other side of my support system, Fay Square and LaWonda Young, thank you for loving my kids like they were your own and helping me be able to do what I do. To my nephew's biological father, thanks for the inspiration on how to be a deadbeat dad. My family is keeping you in our prayers.

Of course, many, many thanks to my agent from the very beginning, Sara Camilli; my phenomenal workaholic editor, Brigitte Smith; my publicist, Melissa Gramstad; the best publisher in the world (and I'm not just saying that because she's published all my books), Louise Burke; and everyone else at Simon & Schuster/Gallery Books, thank you for everything! To the most talented editor this side of the Mississippi (make that the world), John Paine, thank you for sculpting my story into a work of art.

To my colleagues in this literary struggle, thanks for being a friend: Victoria Christopher Murray, Nina Foxx, Al Frazier, Kimberla Lawson Roby, Alisha Yvonne, Carmen Green, Zane, Tiffany Warren, Dee Stewart, Pat G'orge Walker, Victor McGlothin, J. D. Mason, and Rhonda McKnight. To Tasha Martin, I'm so glad to have you on my team.

My journey to bring *Let the Church Say Amen* to the screen has been a long (and often frustrating) one. Thank you so much to Regina King and Reina King for never giving up. To Maurice Stone, Charles Debow, Robert Hines, and Robbi Jones, thank you so much for helping to make this dream a reality.

To Bobby Smith, Jr., thank you for believing in my projects so much. I'm looking forward to great things.

I'm always skeptical about this next part, as I know

there are so many book clubs that support my work. But again, it's just too hard not to take a moment and say thanks. This time around, thanks go to Sistahs in Conversation and Sistahs in Harmony for a first-class affair (Donna Moses—you are the bomb!), Sistah-friends (you ladies are awesome, just remind me not to touch that PD drink again), and a special shout-out to Arnesha "SoFly" Foucha. Thanks also to these other book clubs: Cover 2 Cover, Savvy, African American Literature Lovers, Nubian Pageturners, Girls with Grace, Ladies of Literature, Cush City, Black Pearls Keepin It Real, SWAP, Distinct Ladies, Mahogany, Reading Today's Books, Sharp, Novelties, Sisterly Bond, B-Sure, Women of Substance, My Sisters & Me, Pages Between Sistahs, Shared Thoughts, Brag about Books, Sister 2 Sister Brother 2 Brother, Renaissance, Women of Character, Phenomenal Women, 7 Virtues, KC Girlfriends, Sisters at the Roundtable, Nappy Love, Avid Mocha Readers, and Sophisticated Souls. (I'd love to list you all but please know that if you're not here, it doesn't diminish my gratitude.)

Thank you to all the wonderful libraries that have supported my books, introduced me to readers, and fought to get my books on the shelves. Thank you also to Tee C. Royal, Yasmin Coleman, Tammy Smithers, Cale Carter, Joe McGinty, Hiawatha

Henry, Tanisha Webb, Todd Smith, Yvonne Johnson, Candace K, Pam Walker, Curtis Bunn, Sigrid Williams, and Gwen Richardson.

To all my wonderful Facebook friends, especially the ones who comment regularly, even telling me to "get off and go write!" Jackie, Sheryl, Candace, Alisha, Kendria, Cassandra, Denise, Dasaya, Maleika, Christie, Jerrode, Sylvia, Demetria, Apryl, Alana, Lana, Tonia, Sheretta, Jetola, Cindy, Ralonda, Maxsane, Maurice, Cecelia, Deborah, Constance, Martha, and Sherryle. (My name is ReShonda and I'm addicted to Facebook.)

And finally, thanks to you, my beloved reader. If it's your first time picking up one of my books, I truly hope you enjoy it. If you're coming back, words cannot even begin to express how eternally grateful I am for your support. Thank you. A thousand thank-yous. This is the twentieth book, and because of you, I'm hoping for twenty more!

Now that I'm through rambling, let's get to the good stuff . . . turn the page and enjoy, Holy Rollers!

Oh, by the way—join me on Facebook at www.facebook.com/reshondatatebillingsleyreaders.

Much Love,

ReShonda

1

That fool needs to die. I'm talking an acid-in-the-face, burning in-the-bed, slow and painful death."

Audra Bowen's eyes grew wide as she stared at her friend. Juanita Reynolds, or Nita as she was called by those who knew her best, was never one to mince words, and the way she was glaring at Coco, their other friend, in disgust proved she was maintaining her sterling record.

"You need to put some arsenic in his coffee, lace his beer with cyanide, something," Nita continued.

While Audra would never be that graphic, she definitely felt where Nita was coming from. She also knew that she better jump in this conversation, because sensitivity was not Nita's strong suit.

"Coco, no one thinks you need to try and duplicate a Lifetime movie," Audra said, cutting her eyes at Nita. "We are just really concerned about you, that's all."

They were sitting in a booth for lunch at Grooves Restaurant, one of the swankier spots in Houston. Audra should've known something was up. When the hostess had tried to seat them near the door, where they usually liked to sit so they could see and be seen, Coco had all but had a fit and asked to be moved to the back, in a secluded part of the restaurant. As soon as she removed her sunglasses, they saw why.

"A man has one time to put his hand on me," Nita said. "One time." She held up one finger. "Then it's gonna be a lot of hymn singin' and flower bringin'."

"Calm down," Coco began, slipping the dark sunglasses back on. "It's a lot worse than it looks."

"If it got any worse, you'd be dead," Nita snapped.

The sight of Coco's puffy black eye made Audra want to cry. It was especially noticeable because of Coco's light skin. Of the three of them, she was the prettiest. She could pass for Mariah Carey's sister, except there was nothing glamorous about Coco. She wore her golden brown hair straight and parted down the middle. With her petite frame and passive demeanor, she looked like a librarian. Still, she'd never had any trouble attracting men, which was why they couldn't understand why she stayed with that psychopath

Sonny. But it was useless to complain. They'd been down this road so many times, and no matter how many times Sonny hit her, Coco refused to leave. She was repeating a vicious cycle. Her mother was in an abusive relationship, which she, too, refused to leave.

Nita asked the question she always asked. "Coco, you are a smart woman with your own money and your own job as a teacher. I don't understand. How long are you going to let him do this to you?"

"I told you, I'm working on an exit plan if Sonny doesn't get it together," Coco said, giving the answer she always gave. "Sonny has been stressed ever since the Texans cut him. He's been worried about getting picked up by another team. I just don't want to leave him when he's down."

"Go somewhere with that bull," Nita snapped. "Players get cut every day. So you're supposed to let him beat you because he's feeling sorry for himself? I don't think so, and I can't figure why you keep making excuses for him." Nita leaned back in her seat, frustrated.

Audra totally agreed. She had no idea why Coco stayed with her boyfriend of two years. Granted, Sonny had been a gem in the beginning, but over the last year, he'd turned into somebody they didn't recognize, especially in the six months that he'd been cut from the team. Coco was always talking about the good times they used to have, but Audra was like Nita. After the first time, all the good memories would have been gone—along with her. But no matter what Sonny did, Coco stayed. And now that she was three months' pregnant with his child, they knew the chances of her ever leaving were slim to none.

"The bastard hit you while you're pregnant!" Nita said, as if it had just dawned on her. "You're still in your first trimester and he wants to put his hands on you!"

"Can you guys let me handle this?" Coco pleaded. "This is the first time he's gone off in months. He's not going to do anything to hurt me or the baby, okay?"

Nita dramatically rolled her eyes as Audra struggled to find the right words to get through to her friend.

"Just stop judging me, okay? You never know what you'll do unless you're in that situation," Coco said.

"I know I wouldn't let some six-foot-six man who's built like an army tank put his hands on me, I know that much," Nita said, jabbing her finger to emphasize her point.

"Just drop it, please?" Coco said. "Besides, if I had known you guys were going to trip like this, birthday or no birthday, I would've bowed out."

Audra shot Nita a chastising look to get her to

back off. Otherwise, Coco would be out the door in a minute.

"Can we change the subject, please?" Coco leaned back as the waitress set their drinks in front of them. "Audra, how was your date last night?" she asked after the waitress walked off.

"Let's just say his eyebrows were arched better than mine," Audra said, letting Coco change the subject. Nothing they said would make a difference anyway. "And the fact that he knew my Louis Vuitton was a knockoff spoke volumes." She sighed heavily. "I'm never gonna find my son a father. I hate men." Audra spat out the words with conviction, like they resonated from deep within her soul.

"No, you hate your choice in men," Nita remarked drily as she picked up her Crown and Coke and slurped it down like it was just Coke.

"You need to stop being picky," Coco added.

Audra rolled her eyes. "And settle for somebody who beats me up on the first and the fifteenth?" As soon as she said it, Audra wished she could take the words back. The smile faded from Coco's face.

"Coco, I . . . I'm sorry." She motioned toward the empty glass set in front of her. "It's the liquor."

Coco bit down on her lip. "Don't worry about it," she said, shifting uncomfortably.

"No, I shouldn't have said that." Audra covered Coco's hand with her own. "I know you love Sonny. We just hate what he's doing to you. Why don't you let me come over and talk to Sonny?" Audra figured since the conversation had drifted back to Coco's boyfriend, she might as well finish it.

"Why don't you let me come over and make Sonny some hot grits?" Nita scowled.

"For the umpteenth time, can you guys just let me handle this, please? I'm getting a plan together, and I'll be all right."

"You've been singing that song for six months now," Nita said. "And don't hand me that 'I'm staying for the baby' crap. If anything, now you should really want to leave so you don't have to raise your child in an abusive household. Break the cycle, girl."

"Drop it, Nita, okay? Just mind your own business." The force in Coco's voice caused her friend's eyes to widen in surprise.

"Fine, just don't invite me to your funeral."

"Hel-lo," Audra said, waving her hand. "Can we please not fight? We're supposed to be having my birthday-slash-pity party."

"I think it's a pity the way she keeps letting Sonny beat her ass."

"Nita!" Audra admonished.

Nita rolled her eyes but shrugged and crossed her arms to let her friends know she was done talking about it.

"Anyway," Audra said, giving up on further discussion about Sonny, "that date with the metrosexual was a bust, and Jared has been blowing up my phone, trying to tell me that wasn't him I heard," Audra said, referring to her ex-boyfriend and their latest drama. She'd really been hoping things would work out with Jared. Not only was he handsome and sexy but he would make a great father.

"Did you not tell him that his number popped up on the caller ID and it's not like you don't know his voice?" Nita asked.

Audra nodded miserably. Three weeks ago, she was at home putting her six-year-old son, Andrew, to bed when her cell phone rang. She had spent all evening trying to cheer Andrew up. Jared was supposed to take him to a Houston Astros game, but he'd canceled, saying he had to work late. When Audra saw Jared's number, she readied herself for his apologies. But he didn't say anything, and she figured he had called her by mistake, which he'd done numerous times before. She was just about to hang up when she heard Jared say, "Come on, baby. Shake it for Daddy." That had caused her to go sit on her sofa and listen for one hour and fifteen minutes. What she heard had her in tears on the floor all night long. Never in a million years did she think she'd hear her man having sex with another woman. Pure, unadulterated, buck-wild sex. Even though she knew she should hang up, no matter how much it tore her up, she listened to everything. Finally, she had hung up and tried to call him right back. But, naturally, he didn't answer.

"I can't believe he was gon' pull that R. Kelly 'it wasn't me' crap," Nita said, snapping Audra out of her thoughts.

"Yeah," Coco added. "Even when you recounted word for word what he said."

Audra sighed heavily as she bemoaned her luck with men. "That's Jared 'if the evidence doesn't fit, you must acquit' Stevens."

"Well, the evidence fit, so I'm glad you quit his trifling behind," Nita said. "He should've been gone. He's a professional boxer who hasn't had a match in three years, living up with you and your son, using your electricity, talking about how he's gonna be the next Mike Tyson."

"He was just so good with Andrew." Audra struggled not to cry. She'd shed enough tears behind Jared, whom she'd put out the very next day after overhearing the phone call.

"It's not good for Andrew to see his mother so un-happy," Coco said.

"That's why you guys need to come with me to the Rockets party tonight," Nita said.

Audra made a disgusted noise. "I'm tired of the pro scene. It's not working. We're too old to compete with those Pop-Tarts," she moaned. They'd gone to a party for Vince Young last week, and she'd felt more like a chaperone.

"Yeah, I'm tired of parties, too. The last one we went to, you were the only one who walked away with a phone number," Coco added. "And he wasn't even a baller. Just a friend of a friend of a baller. I wouldn't have talked to anyone anyway, but it would've been nice if someone had at least tried."

Audra nodded her head. The pro scene was getting really old. Since college, all three of them had messed with football players, basketball players, all kinds of professional athletes or their friends, and they had gotten nowhere.

"You didn't have any luck because you guys weren't working it," Nita said, snapping her fingers.

"We. Can't. Compete," Audra slowly said. Nita enjoyed the pro scene, not just because she at-tracted the most men but because she logged all of their escapades in her journal, which she wrote in daily. She never let them read it—it had been that way since she'd started writing in the eighth grade. She claimed she might release a book one day, something like *Confessions of a Video Vixen*. So she had reason to stay on that scene, but Audra was tired. "Besides, most of these players are married or in a serious relationship and only looking for a chick on the side," Audra continued. "I'm looking for a husband."

"And a daddy," Nita playfully teased.

"And a daddy," Audra replied. "I'm not ashamed to admit it. It's hard for a single mother. But the pro scene isn't cutting it. The old heads are settled and the young heads want young girls. We're all over thirty, or about to hit thirty," she said, pointing to Nita, who was still twenty-nine. "That game is up."

"So we get a new game," Nita casually responded.

"I don't want a game. I want a good, clean, decent man." Audra sighed.

"Maybe even a nice Christian man," Coco threw in.

"See, now you goin' too far." Nita tsked as she downed the rest of her drink.

"Really, I'm not," Coco lamented. "Maybe if I find me a Christian man, I won't have all of this drama."

"She's right," Audra added, even though she knew

if Jesus himself sent Coco a man, she'd be too blinded by Sonny to give him a chance.

"Well, you guys are by yourselves on that one. Because ain't nothing a Christian man can do for me but introduce me to a bad boy. I need excitement in my life," Nita said.

"Well, I need something different, and I promise you, I'm going to find a way to get it." She didn't know how, but Audra knew, from now on, her search for a man was going in a totally different direction.

"So what, you want to try hockey players?" Nita asked.

Audra turned up her lips. "Don't be silly."

"I'm just saying, you have all these grand ideas." Nita shrugged.

"I don't have an idea yet," Audra replied. "But give me a few weeks, I'll come up with something."

Nita and Coco eyed their friend. She had that determined look on her face. Her mind was churning, and they knew her well enough to know she wouldn't stop until she came up with a plan to snag them all some decent men.

2

"Church. I need to go to church," Audra mumbled to herself as she stood at the counter watching the thirteen-inch television in the kitchen of her small two-bedroom apartment.

"Mommy, what are you talking about? We don't go to church."

Audra snapped out of her daze and glanced down at her son. He was adorable, with curly hair, deep dimples, and butterscotch skin. He looked just like his daddy, and it took everything in Audra's power not to take her anger and frustration at Chris Gipson out on their child.

"Huh, baby? What did you say?" Audra definitely didn't want to start thinking about her triflin' baby daddy, who refused to be in her son's life because he'd "told her from jump he didn't want any more kids."

"I said, why are you talkin' about you need to go to church?" Andrew repeated. "We don't go to church." The wide-eyed, innocent way he said it brought a quick pang to her heart. Audra's mother would turn over in her grave if she ever heard her grandson saying that. Audra had been raised in the church, but when she went off to college, she'd lost her way and never found it again. With all the troubles she had—with men, struggling as a single mother, and trying to pay her bills—she didn't have much faith.

"Ummm, Mama was just looking at the morning news," Audra replied.

"I know, you looking at that Grinning man," Andrew said.

Audra patted his seat at the kitchen table, motioning for him to sit down. "It's Grinan, Jose Grinan, and you know I watch the news every morning. You watch TV in the afternoon. It's Mommy's turn."

He stuck out his bottom lip as he climbed in the chair. "But I wanna watch Power Rangers."

She playfully swatted his head. "Eat your cereal before it gets soggy." She loved her little boy with every ounce of her being. Her friends didn't know it, but her mission to find a man had intensified after Andrew came home last month in tears because he was no good at soccer and "wanted a daddy to help teach him how to play." That wasn't the first time he'd made reference to his daddy lately. He was getting to the age when he was old enough to wonder about his father. Audra had refrained from telling him what a jerk his father was, but Andrew couldn't comprehend his dad not being in his life.

"I don't want Frosted Flakes," he whined.

"Boy, eat that cereal," Audra said as she grabbed the television remote and turned up the volume.

". . . so, is there really a shortage of young ministers?" Jose was asking.

"Absolutely," the handsome man sitting across from him replied. "Unfortunately, we don't have as many young men going into the ministry these days. And while we have plenty of young associate ministers, we want to groom them to become head ministers."

"And you're hoping this conference will change that?" the female anchor chimed in.

"Yes, Melinda," the man replied. "We have over five hundred men under the age of forty registered for the conference. They're coming from all over the country, and many from right here in Houston. They are either in the ministry or interested in the ministry. We'll be discussing a number of issues, as well as ways we can best serve the community. The public is invited to our open forum on Thursday night, as well as all worship services." He flashed a smile, displaying a set of perfect teeth. To Audra, everything about him seemed perfect. His smooth brown skin, chiseled jaw, and immaculate appearance all gave the aura of a powerful man.

"Minister Marshall Wiley, thank you so much for being with us this morning," Jose said, turning to the camera. "To recap, the National Association of Baptists will be holding their Tomorrow's Leaders Conference this weekend at the Hilton Americas hotel in downtown Houston."

Wanting to shout with joy, Audra grabbed a pen off the counter and wrote down the conference information that appeared on the screen. This was the answer she'd been searching for.

"So, you finally turning your life over to the Lord?"

"Nana Bea!" Andrew bolted from his chair and threw his arms around his babysitter's leg.

Bea Ruffin was Audra's angel. She lived across the hall, and since she was retired, she'd become a lifesaver, stepping in when Audra had to take Andrew out of day care because she could no longer afford to pay for it. Miss Bea, as everyone affectionately called her, offered to babysit while Audra worked her job as receptionist at a local hair salon. Over the years, Miss Bea had become a member of the family, which explained why she had let herself in without knocking.

"Hey, sugar dumpling," Miss Bea said, ruffling Andrew's curly hair. "How are you this glorious morning?"

"Bad." He stuck out his bottom lip. "Mommy won't let me watch Power Rangers. She's watching that Grinning man."

Bea chuckled as she shook her head at Audra. "I saw your nose all up in the TV. I was watching that minister earlier. You finally getting back in the church?"

"I was just watching him talk about that church conference," Audra said, not giving away the reason why. "I was thinking about going."

Miss Bea threw up her hands. "Hallelujah! I knowed there was a God," she said, imitating Sofia from *The Color Purple*.

"Oh, you got jokes this early in the morning."

Miss Bea winked as she nudged Andrew back to his chair. She had been after Audra for years to develop a better relationship with God, and although she had stopped openly pressuring her, Miss Bea always let her know that she was staying "prayed up" on Audra.

"I'm talking about going to a church conference, not church," Audra protested.

"Chile, wherever you praise the Lord is fine with me, long as you praising him," Bea said as she walked over and stood next to Audra. Her wavy salt-and-pepper hair was pulled back into a bun, and she wore her usual white cotton dress with her white nurse shoes, even though she'd hung up her nursing duties ten years ago.

"Well, I'm going to this conference for a different reason." Audra lowered her voice and glanced back at her son, who was drinking the milk from his bowl. "It's a young ministers' conference. Ought to be some good men there."

Bea shook her head in disgust. "Lord Jesus. The girl goin' on the ho stroll at a religious event."

Audra wasn't fazed by Miss Bea's disapproval. "You're the one always telling me that I'm looking for love in all the wrong places."

"Yeah, but I also said you need to stop looking for love, period, and let love find you."

They'd had this discussion numerous times, and Audra knew that they would never see eye to eye. She silently cursed herself for even bringing the issue up.

Miss Bea wagged a bony finger in Audra's face. "You and your girlfriends always on the hunt for some men. It's shameful."

If Miss Bea weren't like family, and such a big help to her, Audra would have told her where to go. But she bit her tongue instead.

"You're a good mother, Audra," Miss Bea said, her tone softer. "You've just had some bad luck with men. So stop trying so hard. Focus your attention on Andrew."

"I am, but there are some things I can't do, like teach him how to be a man," Audra whispered. "So I don't think there's anything wrong with me trying to find him a daddy."

"Men don't want to be chased. They want to do the chasing."

Audra walked over and flipped the TV to the cartoon channel. She wasn't about to have this conversation again. "Okay, Miss Bea. I gotta go. Are you still taking Andrew to the park?"

Miss Bea looked like she wasn't quite done with their talk, but then she let it go. "I sure am. He's out of school for a teacher in-service. Those teachers have more out-of-service in-service days," she grumbled. "Seems like to me there ought to be more servicing these kids. I think that's just another fancy way to take a day off."

"I agree." Audra grabbed her keys and headed toward the door. She knew anything short of agreeing with Miss Bea would prolong the conversation, and she only had an hour to get to work. Audra glanced at her watch as she got into the car, deciding that she was just going to have to be late today because she had a very important stop to make first.

As she drove, Audra found herself singing along with the Mary J. Blige tune blaring from Majic 102. She hadn't been this excited in a long time. She'd called in to work, left a message on her bosses' phone, and detoured over to Nita's house.

She walked up to the doorstep of Nita's exclusive Galleria area condo, compliments of one of her NBA exes. "Nita, it's Audra. Open the door!" she yelled as she banged on the door. Audra knew her friend was inside asleep because Nita was not a morning person.

She grinned widely as she heard the locks on the front door turn.

"Have you lost your mind?" Nita said, rubbing her eyes. Her satin scarf was wrapped tightly around her head, and she wore a sexy satin burgundy pajama set. "It's seven in the morning."

Audra pushed past her as she made her way inside the spacious three-bedroom condo.

"And the day is passing you by. Where's Coco?"

Their friend had moved in with Nita the day after Audra's birthday dinner at Grooves. Sonny had flown into a fit of rage over her staying out late. Coco had left and went to Nita's that night, but the next day she started having cramps. Nita had rushed her to the hospital, but it was too late. She lost her baby. The doctors said it was probably stress, and Coco agreed, saying Sonny hadn't hit her—that time. Audra didn't know if she believed that, but losing the baby finally made Coco leave, and that was good enough for Audra. They all had expected Sonny to come terrorizing Coco until she took him back, but so far he'd left her alone. Maybe that was because Coco had threatened to go public with the abuse if he ever contacted her again.

"Coco is asleep, like everybody else with any sense," Nita groaned as she closed the door.

"Like everybody else with no job," Audra replied. Nita used to work for Continental Airlines as a flight attendant, but she'd quit, saying the whole "work thing" wasn't for her.

"I beg your pardon. I have a job," Coco said, appearing in the doorway. "It may be teaching bratty third graders, but it's a job. We have in-service today, and I don't have to go in, so I was hoping to sleep late. What are you doing here so early?"

"Girl, somebody better have died for you to be coming over here this early," Nita snapped.

Audra planted her hands on her hips and grinned widely at her friends. "Are you ready to meet your soul mates?"

"What?" both women asked simultaneously.

"You heard me. Are you ready to meet your husbands?"

"I've been ready. That's why you woke me up?" Nita said, dragging herself into the kitchen, where she began making coffee.

Audra followed her. "Well, if you're ready, I have just the spot for us to go."

"You came over here at seven in the morning to tell us about some new club?" Nita asked, pressing the Start button on her Tassimo coffee machine.

"Not a club." Audra paused as she waited for Coco to take a seat at the table. She looked back and forth between the two women. "Church."

Nita seemed confused, but Coco blurted out, "Excuse me?"

"Not church exactly, but a church conference," Audra said excitedly. "We can meet our husbands at a church conference."

"You came over here at seven in the morning after a night of smoking crack?" Nita quipped.

"Okay, Miss Funny Lady," Audra said. "I'm serious."

"You're crazy, that's what you are." Nita flicked her hand at Coco, then removed her cup of coffee.

Audra turned to Coco, knowing she'd be a lot easier to convince than Nita. "You said you wanted a good Christian man."

"Well, yeah, but . . ."

"Well, I have the perfect place to meet them."

"Yeah, you told us. Church," Nita said.

"Not exactly church, but a church conference, where they're grooming young, new pastors. It's taking place this weekend in Houston. Over five hundred of them are registered. There is bound to be someone there for us."

Nita shook her head like she was trying to make sense of what Audra was saying. "So let me get this straight. You want us to seduce some preachers?"

Coco was extremely doubtful as well. "I ain't goin' to hell playing around with no preachers."

"We're not playing," Audra protested. "Think about it. Yeah, we used to be out there just looking for a good time, but these days all of us are looking to settle down. We want to find husbands, and there is nothing wrong with us looking for those husbands at this preachers' conference."

"Are you crazy?" Nita said. "I am not trying to be a preacher's wife."

"Why not?" Audra asked.

Nita held up a finger. "Ummm, number one, 'cause I think a preacher husband would want me to go to church, and unless they got an evening service, I'm not goin' to be able to do that. Sundays are sacred sleep time for me. Number two, I can't be a first lady with these," she said, pointing to the paw print tattoos on her ample cleavage.

"Just cover them up. The tattoos and the breasts," Audra said. Nita was more classy than ghetto, but the paw print tattoos didn't exactly point that way. "You can do that, can't you?"

Nita pushed up her breasts. "Girl, please, women pay top dollar to get boobs like this. I'm flaunting these babies."

Before Audra could respond, Coco spoke up. "Audra, I'm not feeling this plan. I can't see myself being all holy."

"Just hear me out." Audra was animated as she continued explaining the benefits of pursuing the preachers at the conference. On the drive over, she'd thought about Gloria Smithers, the first lady of New Glory Baptist Church. Gloria came into the beauty shop every single week and got top-of-the-line service. She didn't work, drove a Range Rover, had a nanny for her kids, and was always dressed to the nines. She never had a care in the world. She just had to be the first lady. That was the life Audra and her girls were looking for.

Audra told her friends about Gloria, then reminded them about a *20/20* story about how churches were the new big business. "And if you saw the preacher that was on the news, you would definitely be on board. He was too cute," Audra concluded.

"I don't care if he was Denzel, Will, and Kobe all rolled up into one," Nita said. "He's. A. Preacher. And I'm already on the path to hell. I ain't about to speed up my trip."

Audra turned to Coco for support. "I know it's only been a month since you and Sonny broke up, but you've been trying to leave him for a lot longer than that." At the mention of Sonny's name, Coco shifted uncomfortably. "You said it yourself, you want to find a good man. What better type of man to find than a man of God?"

"Audra," Nita began, leaning forward, trying to reason with her friend, "a whole lot of those preachers are the worst ones of them all, womanizing anything with a uterus."

"That is not most preachers," Audra said defensively. Like she really knew. But she had to convince them that her plan was a good idea. "You're going to run into that problem anywhere. I'm just saying, you can get it all—a good man, money, power, and respect—by hooking up with a preacher."

"I'm going back to bed." Nita stood and headed toward her bedroom.

All at once, Audra had a brilliant inspiration. "Wait," she said, eyeing Nita's laptop on the bar countertop. "Let me show you something." She raced over and turned on the laptop. "Just give me a minute," Audra said while she waited for the computer to power up.

Nita huffed like Audra was getting on her nerves. But she waited in the doorway.

"I want you to see what I'm talking about," Audra said as she logged on to the Fox 26 website. She found the clip she was looking for. "I'm glad they post this stuff so fast. Here. Come see the minister I was telling you about."

Nita didn't move, but Coco walked over for a look. "Oooh, he's cute. Who's that?"

"That's who I was talking about. Reverend Marshall Wiley. He's the one I watched." Audra stood back and smiled while Coco leaned in to see the clip.

"Nita, he looks like your type," Coco called.

"If he's a preacher, he ain't my type," Nita said, but she walked over, too. "I don't care what he looks li——. Whoa, he is cute," Nita said, squinting at the computer screen. "And he has big feet."

"He's the new pastor of Higher Elevation Baptist Church," Audra said, very pleased by their reaction. "I've heard people talk about him and the fact that he's very much single, but I had no idea he was that good-looking. And just think how many more like him are going to be at the conference."

"Okay, tell me about this conference again," Nita said, finally showing some interest.

Audra grinned widely as she laid out her plan. Her friends didn't seem convinced, but they didn't interrupt her.

"Okay, I'm still not feeling this idea," Nita said once Audra finished. "But I do think he is too cute. So let me do some investigating."

"That's right, girl. Put those PI skills to work," Audra said. Nita really could be a private investigator, because if something had to be found out about anyone, Nita could find it. But between the money she got from her exes and some money from her mother's life insurance policy, she wasn't stressed out about working.

Audra nodded excitedly. "All right. I have to get to work." She winked at Nita. "And so do you. I'll call you later to see what you find out."

Audra could tell by the new fascination in her friend's eyes as she watched the computer screen that the plan to find a preacher was in motion.

3

For Nita Reynolds, there was no bigger challenge than finding information on people. Her friends were always joking that she must've been a private investigator in another life, because she could find out any- and everything about an individual with nothing more than a name. If there was dirt to be found, Nita could find it. There was just one problem. Minister Marshall Wiley didn't appear to have any dirt.

He'd expanded his flock from four hundred to seven thousand in less than three years. He was thirty-five, widowed—his young wife had died of cancer two years ago—and he had no kids. That flawless slate raised Nita's eyebrow.

"Ain't nobody that squeaky clean," she muttered as she logged on to another website. She'd been hunting on the Internet since Audra left, three hours ago.

She'd stopped briefly when her ex-lover Neil called, hoping for a midnight rendezvous tonight. As much as she'd wanted to—sex with Neil was always mind-blowing—she'd bowed out. She had fallen hard for Neil, a basketball player with the Houston Rockets, but once she realized he was lying about leaving his wife, she'd had to let that relationship go. Nita wasn't trying to play the mistress role.

"Are you still using the computer?" Coco stretched as she walked into the living room. She'd gone straight back to sleep after Audra left.

"Yeah, I've been trying to find out more about this preachers' conference Audra is talking about."

"Is it legit?"

Nita shrugged. "Yeah, apparently there's like this major shortage of young ministers, and so there's this push in the National Association of Baptists to groom future ministers. That's what this conference is all about."

"Ministers. I just can't get with that idea," Coco said as she headed to the refrigerator.

"You know I'm not feeling it either. Shoot, just reading about this Marshall dude, he's too good to be true. He probably has women left and right. He's worth over a million dollars."

Coco stopped short as she removed a bowl of cut-up cantaloupe. "What? How do you know that?" she asked as she pulled out a slice.

Nita turned up her lip. "Girl, please, you know I can find out anything."

"Well, if he's worth that much, then he's scamming the church members."

"No, he was an only child, and his parents left him a lot of money when they died. According to all reports, he lives modestly and remains devoted to his church."

"He sounds too good to be true," Coco said.

"I know. But I have a feeling that this guy is on the up and up." She was watching a video of Marshall preaching. He reminded her of the preacher at her church when she was a little girl.

Coco headed determinedly over to the coffeepot. "So, I guess that means you're on board with this whole idea?"

With those words, Nita shook off her childhood memory. She looked up from her laptop. "I think so. I mean, what do we have to lose?"

"Count me out," Coco said, opening the cabinet and grabbing a coffee cup. She held one toward Nita. "You want some?"

Nita shook her head and motioned toward her empty one. "I'm good. I've had three cups already.

Seriously, Coco, you need to get on board. I mean, what, are you waiting on Sonny to come back around?"

The mention of Sonny's name caused Coco to tense up. "No, I'm done with him."

"You know that fool," Nita replied, seeing her opening. "He's going to come back and wreak havoc on your life. Yeah, he may be leaving you alone for now, but at some point, you can believe he's gonna come running back to you. If you have a new man, a new life, you'll be less tempted to go back to Sonny."

"I'm not going back to Sonny," Coco said with conviction.

"Especially not if you're with some cute, powerful minister." Nita stood and walked over to her friend. "Look, I wasn't feeling this idea initially, but if you think about it, moving on makes sense. We can't compete with the baller groupies anymore, but this, this is level playing ground."

Coco bit down on the side of her cheek. When she'd shown up on Nita's doorstep, teary-eyed and distraught, Nita had stepped aside and, without a word, let her in. The pathetic expression across Coco's face that night had shut off all of Nita's usual smart remarks. And when Coco had collapsed in her arms, Nita had just held her and offered comfort.

After nearly an hour, Coco had finally said, "The baby . . ."

"What about the baby?" Nita had gently asked.

"I . . . I lost my baby," Coco had sobbed, burying her head in her hands.

Nita had felt her heart drop. Even though she didn't like the fact that Coco was pregnant by Sonny, she knew how much joy the baby had already brought to her friend.

In the end, Nita was relieved that losing the baby was the final straw. Coco had left that night and never gone back to Sonny. She wouldn't press charges, but at least she'd been firm about staying away from him.

"So do you really think this is the answer?" Coco asked, snapping Nita out of her thoughts.

"I do. I think we should change up."

Coco hesitated, then said, "Okay, fine. Whatever."

Nita smiled. "I guess we should call Audra and tell her that we're in."

Coco returned her friend's smile. "I guess we should. This news is bound to make Audra's day."

Nita smiled in approval. She was going back to church. She caught herself before she started to thinking on her childhood. Yes, she was going back to church, but this time she was on a mission to find a man.

4

Those preacher men ain't ready for me." Nita wiggled her hips in the full-length mirror. She wasn't trying to be vain, but she looked good. Real good. The miniskirt hugged her size 10 frame in all the right places. She'd taken Audra's advice and covered up her 38 triple Ds, but she still wore a form-fitting white ruffled jacket. As always, her honey brown curls cascaded down her back.

"If you say so," Coco responded. "But what's with the white suit? I know you're not going for a virginal look."

Nita placed her hands on her hips. "And if I were?"

Coco and Audra exchanged looks, then burst into laughter. They were in Audra's bedroom, where they'd all gotten dressed for their night of "holy rolling," as Audra had dubbed it.

"I have the red shoes to give a hint of bad girl," Nita said, sticking out her leg to reveal the high-heeled, strappy pumps.

Both Audra and Coco shook their heads. Nita waved them off and leaned into the mirror to check her reflection one more time. After licking her thumb and running it over her eyebrow to smooth it down, she turned to face her friends. "Laugh all you want. I'm going for the pure look, if you must know. And when I have all these preachers falling all over me, you'll wish you hadn't worn that demon red," she said, pointing at Audra, "and that library navy blue," she added, pointing at Coco.

"What's wrong with what I'm wearing?" Coco said, glancing down at the navy knee-length dress with a white lace collar.

"You look like a schoolmarm," Nita deadpanned. "We're supposed to lure with bait, remember?"

"I thought this was a look ministers would like—you know, kind of first ladyish," Coco said, motioning toward her outfit.

"Girl, I know I haven't been to church in a long time, but I don't think that's what first ladies dress like. Maybe the first ladies' grandmas," Nita said.

"Yeah, Coco," Audra chimed in. "It is kind of old and homely looking."

"Whatever," Coco said with an edge. "I think I look cute."

"If you say so." Nita walked over to her purse, which she'd left on Audra's nightstand, pulled out a Bible, and tore the plastic off. "Let's go. We've got some men to snag," she said, slipping the Bible under her arm.

"Shameful. Just a shame fo' God," Miss Bea said when they walked into the living room. She was sitting on the sofa watching *Wheel of Fortune*. Andrew was asleep next to her.

"What's a shame, Miss Bea?" Coco asked. While Miss Bea gave them a hard time, all of them loved the cantankerous old woman. Nita would never admit it, though. The two of them were always going at it, and Audra swore it was because they were exactly alike.

"Y'all actually goin' hoing rolling?"

"Holy rolling," Audra corrected.

"I said it right." Miss Bea tsked. "Blatantly going after a man of God." She eyed Nita's five-inch heels. "And you're even wearing hooker shoes."

"Operative word, *man*," Nita replied. She held out her foot and wiggled it. "And I'll have you know, these are Christian Louboutin."

"Christian Lou-booty who?"

"Christian Louboutin," Nita snapped. "Designer, seven hundred and eighty dollars."

Miss Bea looked outraged. "That don't make sense. That's my rent for two months." She eyed the heels again. "And ain't nothing Christian 'bout them hooker shoes."

"They were a gift," Nita said lightly. "I didn't pay for them."

"Oh, you paid for them, all right," Miss Bea replied, shaking her head. "You paid one way or another."

"Okay, on that note, we're going to go," Audra said.

Of course, Nita couldn't let the issue drop. "Don't start judging us."

"I'm not judging. I leave that to God. But I'm tellin' you, this ain't the way to find a man. Hawaiian luau," she suddenly called out, solving the *Wheel of Fortune* puzzle.

"Well, I guess you would know how to find a man, seeing as how you've been married four times." Nita chuckled.

Miss Bea didn't see anything funny. "If I've been burned enough, it seems you'd listen to me when I tell you to stay out the fire."

Nita always enjoyed getting under Miss Bea's skin. "Maybe I like it hot."

"Then you'll fit in just fine in hell," Miss Bea said

before turning the volume up even more. The way her lips pursed, Audra knew she was mad.

Audra pushed Nita toward the front door. "Why must you insist on getting her riled up?" she hissed in an undertone.

"Why must she insist on getting all up in my business?" Nita responded. "She needs to be figuring out how to get her a set of teeth that fit."

Audra couldn't help but giggle at that. Miss Bea wore a full set of false teeth, and she hated them. She was always pushing them around with her tongue.

"Anyway, let's go. I got a good feeling," Nita said, doing a little shimmy.

Audra walked over and kissed Andrew. "We'll be back, Miss Bea," she said. "I'm assuming you're going to take Andrew over to your place and let him spend the night?"

Miss Bea simply grunted.

"I'll take that as a yes."

"Come on, Audra," Nita said, standing with the door open. "Let's go so I can find my Samson."

That remark caught Miss Bea's attention. She wagged her finger at Nita. "You're just a modern-day Jezebel, seducing the saints into the sin of sexual immorality."

Nita waved her off. "Don't go trying to scare me

by quoting Revelation. I'm just a woman with a plan. Nothing more. Girls, let's go."

Audra looked at Coco in awe. They both watched Nita strut down the hall. "I don't know what's scarier. The fact that she's so excited about all of this, or that she's actually familiar with a book in the Bible." They both started laughing as they followed Nita out to the car.

It took less than thirty minutes to get to the downtown hotel. Audra was shocked over how psyched Nita was. She'd talked about Marshall the entire drive.

They made their way into the hotel's foyer, where all three of them stopped in their tracks. The NBA scene didn't have anything on this.

"No freakin' way," Coco muttered, her mouth dropping open.

Audra couldn't believe her eyes. They could see women everywhere. In every hue, shape, form, and fashion. Some were dressed conservatively, but the majority of them looked like they just stepped out of a 50 Cent video, with one exception—they were carrying Bibles.

"Okay, I thought the pro scene was bad. This is ridiculous," Coco said as she scanned the room. Women, who outnumbered men four to one, were holed up at tables, some looking desperate, some looking like they were playing hard to get, others flirting like their lives depended on it. There was a whole lot of eyelash batting and fake giggles.

Nita quickly gathered her composure. "Well, that just means we have to work a little bit harder." She glanced down at the souvenir booklet.

"I'm not even going to ask how you got that," Audra said.

Nita flashed a sly smile. "A determined woman knows no boundaries. I've circled some of the power players. That way you don't hook up with a broke, struggling, or wanna-be pastor."

Audra and Coco looked at each other in amazement as Nita continued. "Now, according to their schedule, they will be having this networking mixer for the next hour and a half."

"Networking mixer?" Coco humphed. "More like a happy hour."

"Girl, don't let all these skeezers intimidate you," Nita said. "You just need to find you one of these nice, cute preachers and work your jelly." She slowly scanned the room. "Bingo. I found my target." She smoothed down her jacket as a tall, butter-colored man walked their way.

"Excuse me, Rev . . ." Nita gently reached out

and took the man's hand, stopping him. "Reverend Adams," she continued, eyeing his name tag. "I'm sorry to be a bother, but my friends and I were looking for the praise and worship program."

It took everything in Audra's power not to burst into laughter. Nita was batting her eyes and displaying her best innocent expression.

The man flashed a warm smile. "Well, Mrs. . . ."

"*Miss.* Miss Nita Reynolds," Nita stressed.

"Well, Miss Reynolds. You're a tad bit early. The praise and worship service isn't for another hour and a half."

Nita put her hand to her chest. "Well, dagnabit," she said in a slow southern drawl—even though she was straight out of Brooklyn. "We don't know anyone here, so our timing is off."

"Well, that's what the networking is all about." He held out his hand. "I'm Reverend Lester Adams."

Nita took his hand and seductively shook it. "Well, Reverend Adams, I hope everyone around here is as friendly as you."

Lester shyly displayed a gorgeous smile. "Oh, you'll find we're a very hospitable group."

Nita stepped closer, leaned in, and whispered something in his ear that caused him to chuckle and blush.

She giggled as she stepped back. "Pardon my forwardness, Reverend Adams. I just had to share that." Nita looked around the room. "Thank you for the information. I don't want to take up any of your time."

Lester definitely was enjoying the attention. "Oh, I'm just networking myself. It's always a pleasure to meet new people."

She licked her lips seductively. "Maybe we can get to know each other a little better over a drink. Non-alcoholic, of course."

"Maybe not."

Nita and Lester both turned their heads toward the angry-sounding woman standing behind Lester. She looked like she was two seconds from ripping Nita's hair out.

"Excuse me?" Nita said, offended that this woman was all in her conversation.

Lester's already light complexion brightened as his eyes grew wide.

"I didn't stutter," the woman said, marching closer to Nita. "Reverend Adams won't be picking up any strays today."

"Why don't we let Reverend Adams decide what he'll be picking up?" Nita draped her arm through his. He immediately jerked it away.

"Uh . . . ummm, Rachel. Th-this is, ummm, these

nice young ladies were just . . ." Lester stammered, unable to get his words out.

Rachel folded her arms across her chest and glared at him. "Just what? Just trying to sink their claws into a preacher."

"You don't know nothing about me," Nita said, losing the southern drawl.

"And you betta ask somebody about me. I'm his wife," Rachel hissed. "But don't let the first lady title fool you."

"Rachel, please," Lester whispered. "You've been doing so well."

"Don't please me," she snapped. "This hussy is all over you, and you just hee-heeing all over the place."

Lester looked beyond embarrassed as people started glancing their way. Audra definitely didn't want to get caught up in any drama before they even got started.

"Nita, let's go," she whispered, grabbing her friend's arm.

"Yeah, *Nita,* you might want to go," Rachel snapped.

"Look here," Nita began. But before she could finish, Lester was ushering his wife away.

"Good grief," Audra said once they were gone. "Can you find out if a preacher is married before you start making your move? I didn't wear my fighting shoes."

"For real," Coco added. "That woman looked like she doesn't mess around."

"Whatever," Nita said, irritated but also embarrassed. "I didn't want him anyway."

"I couldn't tell." Audra chuckled.

"Naw, I was just warming up. I'm looking for someone a little more refined." She scanned the room again, settling on the man taking the podium up in front. "Someone like him."

"That's the man who was on TV," Audra exclaimed. "That's Reverend Marshall Wiley."

"Good evening, ladies and gentlemen, brothers and sisters in Christ. We hope you are enjoying your alcoholic-free evening." Laughter rippled through the room. "The National Association of Baptists is so glad you decided to join us. We are on a mission to bring more young men into the ministry, and your support will help that to happen. Praise and worship service will begin in just over an hour in the main ballroom. I hope all of you can make it. In the meantime, mix, mingle, and enjoy yourselves. God bless."

He flashed a warm smile before stepping down.

"See, God *is* in the house," Nita said.

"Why do you say that?" Coco asked.

"He didn't want me wasting my time with Reverend Adams. *That* is the man He put on this earth for me," Nita said in a brisk, businesslike tone, as she fluffed her hair out. "Gotta go. Got to go do the Lord's work."

Nita left Audra and Coco and sashayed over to claim her man.

5

This wasn't any better than the club scene, Audra thought gloomily. Just like at the club, she found herself sitting at a table by herself while her girls were off chatting up men. Nita had immediately clicked with Reverend Wiley, and the two of them had been talking for the last forty-five minutes. Audra could only imagine all the things Nita was telling him. And Coco had caught the attention of a young minister that looked like he was still in college.

Audra sat at the small table near the ladies' restroom. This no longer seemed like a good idea. What was she thinking when she suggested they come here? All her life, she'd been the girl left sitting at the table. Even in her own family, her sister was the smart, cute, personable one who excelled at everything and got all the attention. To this day, her sister was still the shining star. She lived in Canada, in a mansion with her billionaire husband and two little perfect kids, while Audra was a single mother still struggling to find her Prince Charming.

Audra let out a heavy sigh, then checked her watch. The praise and worship service started in a few minutes. No way would Nita want to go to that, so they could use it as their chance to escape unnoticed.

Bored, Audra decided to flip open Nita's Bible, which she'd left with Audra. She'd barely glanced down when she heard someone say, "Now, that's my type of woman—one who will sit at a social event and read her Bible."

It took a moment to register what the man was saying, since she wasn't actually reading. "Oh," Audra replied, looking up at the tall, handsome stranger. He had to be six-foot-two, with smooth, Hershey Bar–colored skin, strong features, and a body that was too sexy to be standing in a pulpit.

"Do you mind if I have a seat?"

Audra extended her hand toward the chair. "Be my guest." No way could this man be a preacher.

He held his hand out. "I'm Lewis Jackson."

"Hi, Lewis," Audra replied, shaking his hand. "Are you a minister?"

He sat down across from her. "Yeah, an assistant

pastor really. From Atlanta. Faith First Missionary Baptist Church. But I'll be taking over as pastor at the end of the summer. And who would you be?"

Audra noticed that he wasn't wearing a wedding ring. "I'm Audra Bowen. I'm, ummmm, I just came for the praise and worship service."

"Well, you came to the right place. Have you ever been to a NAB conference?"

"A what?"

"National Association of Baptists conference. You know, the place where you are right now."

Audra released a nervous laugh. "Oh, I wasn't thinking. No, I haven't."

"Are you from Houston?"

"I am."

"What church do you attend?" he asked.

Audra's mind began racing. She hadn't been to a church in years. *What was the last church she'd visited?* It was for a wedding. "Ummm, I attend Windsor Village United Baptist Church," she said, recalling seeing a story about that church on the news last week.

Lewis frowned, confused. "I thought Windsor Village was a Methodist church."

Audra tried not to look frazzled. "That's what I meant. We were talking about the Baptist convention, and I guess, um, that's where the mix-up came from."

He smiled like he knew she was lying, but the way he was looking at her—as if she was a pork chop on a platter—told her he didn't really care whether she was or not.

"If I may say so, you are the most beautiful woman in the room," he said, running his eyes up and down her body.

Okay, so even pastors run game. "Thank you," Audra responded. So much for Nita's theory that "the demon red" would turn the ministers off.

"You know, it's a little noisy in here. Maybe we can go someplace quiet and talk," Lewis said.

Audra raised an eyebrow because of the seductive look in his eyes.

"I'm not being forward," he replied, quickly plastering on an innocent expression. "I mean someplace like out by the pool or something."

She smiled, relaxing a little. "What about the praise and worship service?"

"I'd much rather talk with you."

Audra felt a quick flutter in her heart. She knew she was way ahead of herself, but what if this was her Prince Charming? She'd just been sitting here thinking about it. What if this was God's way of answering her prayers? She took in Lewis's appearance. Judging from his expensive cuff links and tailored suit, he had money. Add to that his good looks, and he was a dream come true. Her sister would never believe she'd been able to snag a man like this.

Audra inhaled long and deep to calm herself down. The man just wanted to go outside. He hadn't said anything about marrying her. "I'd be happy to go outside and talk."

Lewis scooted back from the table, then rushed around to pull her chair out.

"If you'll give me a minute, I want to tell my girl-friends not to wait on me for the service," Audra said.

"Of course. I'll be anxiously waiting right here."

Audra tried to contain her excitement as she walked across the room to the table where Nita was hemmed up with Marshall Wiley.

"Excuse me," Audra said as she approached the table. Nita was in full-fledged flirtation mode. She stopped midlaugh. "Audra, sweetie, please meet the dashing, handsome Minister Marshall Wiley. Marshall, my dear friend Audra Bowen."

Oh, Nita was laying it on thick.

"How are you?" Marshall asked, standing and shaking Audra's hand.

"I'm g——, I mean, blessed and highly favored," Audra responded.

Nita nodded her approval. "Audra and I have

been friends since elementary school, when I spent my summers in Houston with my grandmother," she said. "After I graduated, I moved from Brooklyn to go to TSU with her."

"Well, it's so nice to meet you, Audra," Marshall responded.

"You, too." Audra knew her friend. Nita was in prime mack mode and didn't want Audra around blocking, so she got straight to the point. "Nita, I was just letting you know to go on to praise and worship service without me. I'm going to, ummm, I'm going to . . ."

Marshall chuckled. "Just because I'm a man of God doesn't mean I don't know what's going on in here."

"No, no," Audra countered. "It's nothing like that. We're just going to talk."

Marshall held up his hands. "None of my business." He turned to Nita. "I do hope this lovely young lady will accompany me to the praise and worship service."

"I'd be honored," Nita said, taking Marshall's hand and pulling herself out of her seat. She leaned in to Audra's ear and whispered, "Girl, go handle your business. Because you'd betta believe I'm handling mine."

"Nice to meet you," Marshall called out over his shoulder as he led Nita away.

Audra waved good-bye and then glanced around the room for Coco. She was nowhere to be found, and Audra didn't want to keep Lewis waiting, so she hurried back over to him. He smiled as she approached.

"Shall we?" he asked, holding out his arm.

"We shall," Audra said, draping her arm through his. Her heart was fluttering. She had a good feeling about Lewis. Maybe her luck with men was about to change, after all.

6

"God, you're good."

Lewis released a pleasurable sigh as he pulled himself up off of Audra and rolled over on his back. She managed a smile, even though she had a sickening feeling in her gut. *What in the world had she done?*

"What's wrong?" Lewis asked, gently nudging a strand of hair from her face.

Audra sat up against the headboard of the queen-size bed, pulling her legs up close. "I . . . I . . . This wasn't a good idea," she stammered, trying to figure out how she could have been talking out by the hotel's pool one minute and up in Lewis's room the next. They'd actually talked for several hours before going to his room, but the point remained the same. She'd fallen into a man's bed in less than twenty-four hours.

"Aaaw, that's sweet. You're feeling guilty." He

leaned in and kissed her cheek. "But I told you, we are two consenting adults. And God knows we are not without sin." He took her hand. "Come on, let's say a prayer and repent."

Audra frowned. She hadn't been in church for a while, but she didn't think you could just blatantly have wild sex and then simply say, "God, forgive me," and everything would be all right.

Lewis didn't notice her apprehension as he bowed his head and began praying. "Oh, most merciful Father, we humbly come before you, children of your Kingdom. We know that one sin is no greater than the next. But we beg your forgiveness for succumbing to the cardinal lust that consumed us. We know you are a forgiving God, so we know you understand. These and other blessings we ask in your name. Amen." Lewis looked up and grinned. "There, all is forgiven. Now let's get something to eat. Girl, you wore me out."

He threw back the covers and jumped out of bed. "I'm gonna jump in the shower."

Once he was gone, Audra closed her eyes and leaned back against the headboard. She still didn't feel right. If she wanted things to be different with Lewis, she had to do things differently. How could she expect him to respect her when she jumped right into bed with him? But he'd talked such a good game. He told her how lonely he was and how he just wanted to hold her. She knew it was a bunch of bull, but she went back to his room anyway. He was intelligent, funny, and rich. Audra didn't want to risk losing him by refusing to go to his room.

"Let it go," she muttered as she reached over to the nightstand and picked up her cell phone. She punched in a number. "Hey, Miss Bea," she said after her neighbor answered the phone.

"Don't hey me. Where are you? It's eight in the morning."

"How do you know I'm not at home?"

"Because I didn't hear you come in. You know that floorboard creaks right outside your apartment."

"Look, I was just calling to check on Andrew," Audra said.

"Andrew is fine. Now where are you? Or shall I say *who* are you with? Lord Jesus, please tell me you are not somewhere laid up with a preacher man."

Audra shifted uncomfortably, as if Miss Bea could see her through the phone.

"You *are* laid up with a preacher man," Miss Bea said when Audra didn't respond. "Jesus, forgive this poor, horny, man-desperate child, for she know not what she does."

"Bye, Miss Bea," Audra said. "I was just checking in. Kiss Andrew for me. I'll be home in a few hours."

Audra ended her phone call, then jumped out of the bed as well. She had to go to the bathroom, but no way was she about to do that in front of a man she just met.

"Are you coming in?" Lewis called from inside.

"You go ahead. I thought I'd order room service. We still have an hour and a half before you have to get to your first workshop."

She heard the water cut off. Lewis stepped out of the shower, dripping wet and without a stitch of clothing on.

Audra tried not to admire his firm body, but he must've known how sexy he was, because he did nothing to hide himself as he walked around the room.

After getting dressed and ordering room service, Audra and Lewis spent the next hour sitting on the balcony talking. She told him about Andrew and was thrilled when he told her how he would love to have a son, especially if he could skip the whole diaper-changing thing.

Lewis had told her all about his life back in Atlanta. After graduating from Clark Atlanta University, he threw himself into helping his mentor build their church. Now they were positioning him to take over. He explained that he had been involved in a serious relationship, but it wasn't "right with God," so he had to let her go.

"Oh, wow, look at the time," Lewis said as he glanced at his watch. "I'm a moderator on my panel—'Can You Be Hip and Holy?'—so I can't be late."

"I would love to come sit in, but since I'm still in yesterday's clothes, that is probably not a good idea," Audra said.

"Yeah, probably not," he replied as he planted a kiss on her lips.

Audra slowly got up, grabbed her purse, and followed him out of the room. She felt warm and tingly as he took her hand and led her down the hallway toward the elevator.

After pressing the Down button, Lewis gently pushed Audra against the wall. "So, sexy lady, when am I going to see you again?" He nuzzled her neck.

Audra threw her arms around his neck. "Whenever you want."

"I want to see you tonight, and every single day for the next three days that I'm here."

"Your wish is my command." Audra giggled just as the elevator doors opened. Three women stood looking at her with utter disgust. They obviously had come for the church conference, as each of them was dressed in her Sunday best.

"Umph, umph, umph," the first woman mumbled as Audra and Lewis stepped onto the elevator.

"Good morning," the shortest of the ladies said. "Are you two here for the conference?"

Audra looked at Lewis, hoping he would say no. "Good morning to you fine ladies, too," he said, oblivious to their disdain. "We sure are. Reverend Lewis Jackson here. From Atlanta." He extended his hand.

Neither of the women took his hand.

"How are you this fine morning, *Mrs.* Jackson," the short lady asked.

"Oh, I'm not M——." Audra caught herself. "I'm fine," she said instead.

"Umph," the woman muttered.

Lewis chuckled as Audra turned her back to the women. She could feel their glares X-raying her from behind. She breathed a sigh of relief when the elevator door opened on the second-floor meeting rooms. Audra had to go down one more floor to the lobby, so she stepped aside to let the women pass. "Is this your stop?"

"So you two aren't coming to the meetings?" the short woman questioned as they exited the elevator.

"Yes, ma'am. We'll be there in just a minute," Lewis said.

The woman turned her nose up as she followed her friends.

"I'm not sure," Audra said after the doors closed again, "but I think they know where I was coming from."

Lewis leaned in and kissed her. "Who cares?"

Audra pulled herself away as the elevator doors opened again. She stepped out into the lobby.

"Go home, get changed," he commanded. "I want to do my workshop, then come spend the day with you. Then I want to take you and your son to dinner." He smiled and blew her a kiss. "I'll call you later," he said, just as the elevator door closed.

Audra wasn't so sure about that plan. She was wary about introducing yet another man to her son, especially so soon after Jared. Any man she was with had to understand that she and Andrew were a package deal. She crossed the lobby, telling herself she had to think with her head right now, not her heart. And her head was telling her to slow down. She might be footloose and fancy-free with her own feelings, but she had to protect her son. As bad as she wanted a father for Andrew, she had to get to know Lewis better.

As Audra stepped out into the sunlight, though, she had a good feeling. Somehow, she was sure that Andrew and Lewis would get a chance to meet—and sooner rather than later.

7

The debriefing had begun. Coco and Nita sat in the living room of their apartment. They'd tried to wait on Audra, but since she wasn't answering her phone or their texts, they could only assume she'd hooked up with the guy she'd told Nita she was going out by the pool to talk to.

"So you didn't meet anybody for real?" Nita asked her roommate. "All those good-looking men and you didn't meet a single one? What about that young guy?"

Coco waved away the look of pity on Nita's face. "That guy kept talking about 'Am I saved?' When I told him I wasn't sure, all he wanted to do was 'pray for my soul.' He spent an hour trying to introduce me to Jesus. Then on top of that, he wasn't but twenty-two."

Coco had known all along that searching for men at a religious conference was a bad idea. Besides, she didn't need to be rejoining the dating game so soon anyway. Sonny would have a fit if he caught her even talking to another man. Though Sonny was out of her life, she hadn't managed to let that fear go.

"After I got rid of that guy, I didn't try to talk to anyone else. It was like a meat market in there," Coco continued, shaking off all thoughts of Sonny, "and I didn't feel like competing."

Nita tsked as she cocked her head and studied her friend. "Girl, what is wrong with you?"

"Nothing's wrong."

"Tell that to someone who doesn't know you," Nita scoffed. "Please don't tell me you're still bummed out about Sonny. Because if you wanna know the truth, you leaving him was the biggest blessing you could've ever gotten."

It was Coco's turn to study Nita. "One night with a pastor and you're suddenly a religious authority?"

That shook her a little. "Whatever, I'm just speaking the truth. And for your information, I didn't spend the night with Marshall. I went to Praise and Worship, had coffee afterward, then we went our separate ways."

"What?" Coco said.

"Yes, ma'am. I'm dealing with a good, clean Christian man, as y'all say. I can't throw all of this on him up-front," Nita said, motioning toward her body.

"I can't believe you, the master freak, is saying that."

"I'm a freak who knows when to get her freak on." Nita laughed, knowing that Coco saw right through her. "Speaking of freak, you know Audra hooked up with a real cutie pie?"

Coco was about to respond when the doorbell rang. The way Nita pulled the blanket up on her lap told Coco that she was going to have to answer it.

"Well, speak of the devil," Coco said after opening the door.

Audra walked in, her skin glowing. "Hey, y'all."

Nita raised her eyebrow as she studied the newcomer. "Don't hey us. Why do you still have on your clothes from last night?"

Audra grinned mischievously. "That would be because I haven't been home to change."

"I know you did not sleep with that man," Nita said, all but bouncing out of her seat. Audra sashayed over and plopped down in the chair, looking very content.

"You *did* sleep with him," Nita said when Audra didn't reply.

"Oh, Audra, why'd you go and do something like that?" Coco said, closing the door and joining Nita back on the sofa.

The tone of Coco's voice wiped the smile right off Audra's face. "What is that supposed to mean?"

"It means, I thought you were trying to find a husband," Coco said. "You don't snag a man—especially a preacher—by sleeping with him on the first night you meet him."

Audra looked offended. "First of all, I'm grown, and he's grown. So there's no need to play games. If it's something we both wanted, there's nothing wrong with that."

"Is that the line he fed you?" Nita asked, smirking.

"Whatever," Audra replied. She'd never tell Nita that it was.

"So you didn't go home at all last night?" Coco asked.

"No, I didn't. And for your information, Lewis wants to spend the day with me, then take me and Andrew to dinner."

"So now you have this dude meeting your kid?" Nita asked. That had always been her biggest complaint about Audra. Her friend was a good mother but was always thinking some man was "the one," so she would introduce them to her son.

"No, I am not," Audra corrected her. "I said, *he* wanted to. I decided not to let Andrew meet him yet, but I have a good feeling about Lewis, Nita," she added, like she was exasperated that they'd spoiled her good mood. "I told you guys I was going to be more discerning after Jared. But just the fact that he wants to meet my son speaks volumes. He has to go to his workshop this morning, but he said he's going to skip the rest because he wants to spend the day with me. So, so much for your theory that he wouldn't want me if I slept with him. If anything, that just made him want me more."

"No, that just made him want *some more*," Nita said.

"Come on, Nita," Coco said, trying to check her friend's abrasive nature.

"Okay," Nita said, throwing her hands up. "Did you at least use protection?"

"Of course. Do you think I'm stupid?"

Nita cut her eyes at Coco.

"Shut up, Nita," Audra warned.

"I didn't say a word."

Audra took her compact out of her purse. "Anyway, I just came by to get the scoop on you guys," she said, checking her reflection.

"There's no scoop on me. I didn't meet anybody," Coco said.

"She's too busy mourning Sonny," Nita replied, getting comfortable on the sofa. "I told her she needs to be down on her knees thanking God that he found him another woman to go beat up."

Audra shot Nita an angry look. They'd heard that

Sonny was dating someone else, but nobody had broached the topic with Coco.

"What?" Nita shrugged. "Y'all know I'm not gonna bite my tongue."

"It's okay. As my grandmother used to say, I'll meet my prince. Not on my time, but on God's time," Coco said.

"Well, come to church with me tomorrow," Nita said grandly. "Maybe your prince is there."

Both Audra and Coco spun their heads toward Nita. "You're going to church?" Audra asked.

Nita shrugged. "If I'm gonna be a pastor's wife, I need to get in the habit of going to church."

"So you're for real about the wife thing?" Coco said. "I thought you were just looking for a sugar daddy."

"Well, Reverend Marshall Wiley just might make me change my mind. Now, are you coming or what? You, too, Audra."

"I can't," she replied quickly. "Lewis has already said he wants all my time today and tomorrow."

Coco nodded her head, appreciating the irony of a preacher not going to church. "I guess you can count me in. I think I need to go say a prayer. Because the day Nita Reynolds is urging people to come to church is the day the world just might be coming to an end."

8

Nita could not believe she was back in church, at the early service at that, and sitting in the front row.

She'd attended church probably ten times in the last ten years. Not that she didn't come from a spiritual background. Shoot, Nita had been the one who got her mother, Queenie, involved in church. But then Queenie had taken worshiping to a whole other level, hooking up with some Jim Jones jackleg preacher when Nita was thirteen. Queenie became so obsessed with that church, she would often abandon Nita and her younger brother to fend for themselves. Watching her mom take the money they had to spend for groceries and give it to the church had soured Nita on religion. Eventually she stopped going to church altogether.

But sitting here was reminding her how, even at a

young age, she used to feel so at peace when she went to church. Nita shook off her thoughts. She was here on a mission to find a man, not the Lord.

And the man she wanted was smiling down at her from the pulpit right now. Marshall looked so sexy and powerful, standing up there like he was the king of the world. Nita licked her lips as she imagined herself blowing his mind in the bedroom.

"Stop thinking dirty thoughts," Coco leaned over and whispered.

Nita slyly grinned. Coco knew her so well.

". . . and at this time, we'll ask all of our visitors to stand," Marshall announced.

Nita smiled and lightly waved at him as he looked her way. He motioned for her to stand up, and the smile quickly left her face. She was hoping to be left out of this part. The elderly man sitting next to her must have noticed the exchange, because he patted her arm and whispered, "Stand up, little lady. Your friend, too."

Nita gritted her teeth as she stood. She hit Coco's arm to get her to stand as well. Nita so hoped this was not one of those churches that you had to announce your name, church, family history, et cetera. If that was the case, she was definitely going to leave—right in the middle of service.

Fortunately, someone just came and gave her and the other visitors a card.

"At this time, we'd like for our members to take a few moments and greet our guests," Marshall said as the choir began playing an upbeat tempo.

Nita shook a few hands, hugged a few people, then sat back down, despite the mixing and mingling still going on. No sooner had she returned to her seat in the front row than four women appeared in front of her. All of them had gray or graying hair tucked under pillbox hats. They were dressed in their Sunday best, looking like a box of M&M's in an assortment of bright colors. Nita assumed they were the welcoming committee.

"Here you go, baby," one of the women said, handing Nita a purple afghan. "We keep these at the church for situations like this."

Both Nita and Coco stared at the afghan in confusion. "Excuse me?" Nita said.

"I said, this is for you." The woman thrust the afghan toward her again.

Nita wasn't sure what she was supposed to do with a blanket. It had to be eighty-five degrees in the church.

"What should I do with this?" she asked.

All four women looked at her like she couldn't possibly be that stupid.

"Cover yourself up," one of the taller women said. "What do you think it's for?"

"I don't need to cover myself up," Nita replied, offended.

"Really you do," the first woman replied. "You're sitting in the front row in that teenybopper skirt. Pastor don't need those types of distractions."

"Umph, not to mention I think I smell you," one of the other woman snidely added, turning up her nose.

"Lucy, please," the first woman said. She turned back to Nita. "Honey, we're just trying to tell you, in this house of the Lord, it's common practice that we ask the ladies sitting in the front row to put the throw over their legs."

Coco had on a miniskirt, too. Why were they giving only Nita a hard time? Nita wondered. Granted, Coco's skirt may not have been as short as Nita's, but still. Nita took a deep breath, calming herself down. She didn't need to be acting a fool on her first visit to this church. She decided the faster she took the throw, the faster these women would get out of her face. And since the music was winding down and people were returning to their seats, she didn't want extra attention.

"Thank you," she said, accepting the afghan.

The women shot her fake smiles, then returned to their seats.

Nita was so mad she couldn't even pay attention to anything Marshall was saying. If she weren't so embarrassed, she would've gotten up and marched right out of that sanctuary.

Coco leaned over and whispered, "You still think you're cut out to be a first lady?"

Nita glanced back at the women, who were sitting in the pew across the aisle. All four of them were looking at her with disdain.

"These biddies don't know who they're messing with," she whispered back. "I'm the wrong woman to punk. But I can show them better than I can tell them." She let the afghan fall on the floor and, ever so slightly, gaped her legs open. She tried not to laugh as she caught all four women clutching their chests in horror.

"You know you're wrong," Coco said after the service had wrapped up. They were standing in the foyer, waiting on Marshall to finish speaking to people.

Nita glanced over at the four women, who were standing a few feet away, like sentinels. They were obviously talking about Nita, snarling and glaring at her.

"Whatever," Nita said, rolling her eyes at the

women. "I get sick of people judging me. Ever since I was a little girl, these hypocritical church folks have had something to say. Back then it was because my mama wasn't saved. Then, when she got saved and caught up in that stupid church, it was because my brother stole some money out of the offering plate. Only nobody stopped to ask why he stole it. He was trying to get some money for food since Mama was giving dang near every dime we had to the church."

Nita caught herself when she noticed Coco's stunned look. Although they'd been friends for years, neither Coco nor Audra knew how bad things had been for Nita at home.

"I'm sorry. I didn't mean to go off," Nita said, composing herself. "I just get so mad at how judgmental these people can be."

"Maybe you're reading too much into it."

They stopped to speak to an old man who wanted to shake their hands and invite them back.

"I mean, all they did was offer you a blanket," Coco said after the man walked off.

"Please, you saw the way they were looking at me." Nita motioned behind her. "The way they're still looking at me."

Coco nodded like she knew Nita was right.

Nita's mood quickly brightened as Marshall made his way over to them.

"Thanks for waiting around," he said, gently hugging Nita.

"I'm just happy you invited me. The service was really nice." She pointed toward Coco. "This is my friend Cosandra, but we call her Coco."

He extended his hand. "Pleased to meet you, Coco. Thank you for visiting Higher Elevation."

Coco shook his hand, admiring how fine he was. "My pleasure."

"Juanita, I'd love to take you ladies to dinner," Marshall said.

Nita smiled tightly as she glanced at Coco. She hoped that her friend could read her mind. Luckily, Coco knew exactly what Nita was thinking, and she said, "You know, thanks for the offer, but I have another appointment."

"Are you sure?" Marshall asked.

"She's sure," Nita said, draping her arm through his. Everything in her wanted to turn and see the looks on those old biddies' faces.

"So, Coco, you can go on. I'm sure Reverend Wiley will drop me off at home after dinner."

"Of course I will," he replied. "And it's Marshall."

"Marshall," Nita corrected.

"Well, you all enjoy dinner," Coco said. Marshall smiled as he turned to speak to someone who had just walked up to him.

"See you at home," Nita said as Coco walked off. She glanced over to see the four women had moved closer. They were still whispering like they were trying to figure out what was going on between Nita and Marshall. "Or maybe I won't see you at home—at least if I'm lucky," she said in the women's direction.

"Did you say something?" Marshall asked, turning back to her.

"No, sweetie," Nita quickly replied. "I was just saying good-bye to Coco. I'm ready whenever you are."

He smiled as he took her hand and led her out of the foyer.

9

Coco had forgotten how entertaining church could be. Not only had Reverend Wiley delivered a soul-stirring sermon but Nita had definitely made the trip worth her while. Those old women were furious that Nita had all but flashed Marshall in the pulpit. Yeah, Nita was definitely going to have her hands full if she planned on sticking around.

Coco wasn't mad at Nita for dumping her to go eat with Marshall. In all their years of man-hunting, that was an understood rule—a girlfriend could be dumped for a good-looking man at the drop of a dime.

On her way to the car, Coco decided to duck into the Family Dollar store next to the church. She needed to pick up a few personal items, and stopping here would save her a trip to CVS later.

Coco picked up the items she needed, then found herself near the children's rack. She slowly browsed through the clothes, trying not to get depressed. "After you've done all you can, just stand," Coco softly sang as she picked up the cutest pink baby outfit. The choir had sung one of her favorite gospel songs by Marvin Sapp, and the lyrics had been stuck in her head since the service. She continued singing it softly, and stopped only when she noticed a man staring at her.

"Oh, I'm sorry," Coco said. "I didn't realize that I was singing so loud."

He wasn't the most handsome man she had ever seen—he was about five-nine, medium build, a cropped fade, thick lips, and a complexion that looked like it had seen its share of acne—but his cool demeanor and immaculate attire made him look distinguished.

"No," the man said with a wide smile. "Please don't stop on my account. I've actually been listening for a few minutes to your beautiful voice."

Coco felt her cheeks flushing. Even though everyone told her what a beautiful voice she had, she still always had a hard time accepting compliments. Sonny had told her one harsh night that her singing got on his nerves, so she had pretty much stopped.

"Thank you," she bashfully replied.

The man seemed to shake himself out of a trance as he stared at her. "I'm sorry," he said, shifting the package of diapers he was carrying from his hand to under his arm. "I promise, I'm not a stalker or anything. I just, your voice . . . Wow. Are you a professional singer?"

"No, I, ummm, I just love to sing," she said.

"Well, God has definitely blessed you with a beautiful voice." He smiled again and extended his free hand. "I'm Davis Morrison," he said. "Your voice is angelic."

"Please."

"No, seriously," he replied. "I don't think I've ever heard anything so beautiful."

"Thank you." She paused, not sure how to end this chance meeting. "Well, it was nice to meet you, Davis."

They stood in awkward silence for another few moments before Coco nodded. "Okay, I guess I'd better get going. Thank you again for the compliment." She flashed another smile before walking off.

"Excuse me. Excuse me." Coco turned around to see Davis hurrying to catch up with her.

"I don't mean to be forward, but are you married?" he asked. His gaze went to her left hand. "I mean, I didn't see a ring, but you know modern women. You just never know. A lot of women today don't feel it's necessary."

Coco wiggled her fingers. "Oh, no. If I ever get a ring on this finger, you'd better believe that it's going to be necessary for me to wear it."

They both laughed.

"My sentiments exactly." Davis paused briefly before continuing. "So, I, uh, there's . . . there's a coffee shop next door, and I was just wondering if you'd like to have a cup of coffee with me. I mean, I know you're probably busy, but a cup of coffee won't take long."

"Are *you* married?" she asked. The pointed question came out before she even realized she had had the courage to say it.

"Nope. I wouldn't be in the Family Dollar asking you out if I was."

She eyed the diapers under his arm.

"Oh, this is for one of my church members," he said, holding up the small package. "She's a single mother, and I'm always trying to help her out."

Coco hesitated. She didn't doubt that he was telling the truth, but something made her hold back. "Ummm, I don't know. I don't drink coffee." When she saw how dejected he became, though, she changed her mind. "But I will have a cup of tea."

They walked to the cashier, paid for their items, then headed to the coffee shop.

Coco glanced down at her watch. She couldn't believe she'd been sitting and talking with Davis Morrison for two hours. She had learned so much about him in that time. He was a teacher at KIPP Polaris Academy for Boys, a charter school on the city's north side. He attended Higher Elevation and had just left church when he'd bumped into her. Davis was single, although he had joint custody of his five-year-old daughter. Coco told him that she'd recently broken up with her boyfriend, but she didn't give out any more details.

They'd had a stimulating conversation, about everything from their childhood to whether President Obama was doing an effective job to their current relationship situation.

"Do you mind if I ask how old you are?" Coco asked. She could tell he was older, but she didn't know by how much.

"I'm forty-four," he replied.

"Oh."

"What about you?"

"Now, you know I'm not gonna give you my age. You never ask a lady that."

"Wait, you asked the question first!" He waved his hands in protest. "Anyway, as Aaliyah said, age ain't nothing but a number."

Coco cocked her head playfully. "What do you know about Aaliyah?"

They continued talking, laughing, and getting to know each other. Coco hadn't felt this close to a man since Sonny, and she was intrigued.

"So, tell me again why you're not married."

He scratched his head. "I guess I don't believe in going out and trying to find a wife. I believe that she'll come when God sends her to me, and so far she hasn't shown up on my doorstep."

Coco was surprised. She definitely wasn't one to wait on God. She'd been searching and searching for a husband, which explained how she'd ended up—and put up—with Sonny. She'd always felt like she could change Sonny. After all, in the beginning he was the most loving, kindest man she'd ever met. But Sonny had some evil ways, and every time they surfaced, she excused them, brushing them off. Coco's mother had suggested they take their troubles to church, but Sonny didn't want any part of a church, and she'd never pressed the issue.

"Coco, that's not your real name, is it?" Davis said.

"No, actually it's not. It's Cosandra. But I hate that name, so I've been called Coco since I was a little girl."

"I think Cosandra is a pretty name."

Coco lowered her gaze. Normally, the way he was looking at her would've made her uncomfortable, but now she actually liked it. He gave off a warmth that made her feel at ease.

"Well, Coco, would it be possible for me to see you again?"

She forced a smile as she finally met his gaze. Even though she'd had a wonderful time talking to him, she couldn't get involved with a man right now. She had some major issues to work out.

"It's probably not a good idea," Coco gently said.

Davis was taken aback. "Why? I mean, you didn't enjoy our conversation?"

"No, it's not just that. I'm just not ready to get into a relationship."

"I didn't ask you for a whole relationship. I just want to see you again," he said playfully.

She chuckled. "Well now, I guess I'll just pick my face up off the floor. I didn't mean to be presumptuous. It's just . . . that relationship I told you about that I just got out of? Well, it was pretty bad."

"Again, it's just dinner," he said, not pressing her with questions like she expected. "You do have to eat, don't you?"

Coco didn't respond. Today it was dinner, tomorrow it would be violent outbursts. No, the more she thought about it, the more she didn't want to travel down that road again.

"Or better yet," he said, "why don't we meet at church next Sunday?"

"What?" Coco had been invited to a lot of places in her life, but never to church, at least never by a man.

"Come as my special guest," he said.

"Wow, I don't know about that."

"It won't be a date."

After the moving spirit that she'd felt during the hymn, Coco decided to take him up on his offer. She wouldn't mind returning to Higher Elevation. Plus, Nita was right. She had to get over Sonny and stop living in fear of what he might do.

"Okay, I can do church."

"Great! But . . . would it be possible for me to get your number? You know, so we could talk before then?"

"Sure," she said, taking out a piece of paper and writing her phone number down.

"Thank you." He tucked the paper into his pants pocket.

Coco tried to calm the butterflies in her stomach. This would be the first man she had talked to since she started seeing Sonny. But it was time to move on, and Davis Morrison seemed like the perfect man to help her do that.

10

This was the man God had sent her. Miss Bea always said that Audra had such bad luck with men because God hadn't sent her the man she was supposed to be with.

That was about to change. Reverend Lewis Jackson was signed, sealed, and delivered direct from God. After their past two bliss-filled days, Audra believed that with all of her heart. Now, watching him sleep so peacefully, she knew that her prayers had finally been answered.

The doorbell rang, snapping Audra out of her love-induced trance. She jumped from the bed, knowing it was Miss Bea being nosy. Letting Lewis spend the night had been a huge step, because even though she'd brought men around her son, she'd never let them spend the night until Andrew got to know them well. But Lewis had checked out of his hotel and at the last minute decided he wanted to spend one more day with her. So she felt obligated to let him stay the night. Of course, Miss Bea had protested when Audra asked that she keep Andrew overnight.

Audra gently cracked the door open. "Miss Bea, why are you ringing the doorbell?"

Her neighbor stood with her arms folded across her chest. "I didn't want to walk in on you and your guest." She didn't hide the disgust in her voice.

"Where's Andrew?"

"In my bed, still asleep. So leave the door open," Miss Bea said, marching past Audra and into the living room.

"Well, why don't you go back over there to him? I'll get him later today."

Miss Bea spun around to face Audra. "Now you know I don't have any problem keeping Andrew, but I do have a problem with that strange man being up in your house."

"I'm sorry, last I checked, I was grown," Audra protested. She held up her hand as Miss Bea was about to say something. "And before you start, Andrew is my first concern, hence the reason I asked you to keep him last night."

Miss Bea shook her head. "Didn't you tell me that

man was a minister? What kind of minister will lay up with a woman he just met?"

"Okay, Miss Bea," Audra said, grabbing her hand and pulling her back toward the door. "Thank you for your concern. I will be there to get Andrew a little later." Sometimes Audra just wanted to give her neighbor a piece of her mind, but as usual, she let it slide.

"Have you asked yourself if maybe you're just a one-night stand? Didn't you say he was from out of town?"

Audra rolled her eyes. Miss Bea was definitely ruining her euphoria. Yes, they'd made love, a few times, but Lewis didn't make her feel like a one-night stand.

"Miss Bea, I can handle myself, okay? Thank you for watching Andrew." Audra eased the door closed.

"I hope you know what you're doing," Miss Bea called out.

Audra leaned against the door and sighed. She spent several moments shaking off Miss Bea's negativity. For once in her life, she had no doubt that she was doing the right thing, and Miss Bea would just have to trust her.

Audra made her way into the kitchen and started fixing breakfast. She'd laid the bacon on the griddle when Lewis appeared in the doorway, shirtless. "Good morning," he said.

"Good morning to you, sleepyhead," Audra said, leaning over to kiss him.

"I'm sorry for conking out on you so early, but this conference wore me out. Then our day at Kemah sealed the deal."

Audra smiled warmly. They'd spent yesterday on the Kemah Boardwalk, eating, playing miniature golf, even Jet-Skiing. Lewis was like nothing she'd ever imagined. He was fun, had a great sense of humor. He was affectionate and doting. And not that she had any money to spare, but he wouldn't let her spend a dime of her own money. She'd been pleasantly surprised to find that he didn't beat her over the head with his religion. In fact, if he hadn't told her, she would've never known he was a preacher, especially because of his sexual appetite. But she liked that she didn't have to figure out his game. He made no qualms about wanting her sexually, but he also showed that he was interested in more than just her body.

"I enjoyed myself as well," Audra said.

"I can't tell you the last time I had so much fun," Lewis said. "I felt like a kid again." He stretched, rippling his torso, then leaned against the kitchen wall. "Besides, it's not often that I get to just relax."

She poured flour into a mixing bowl. "I'm glad you were able to get some rest. You seem to work hard."

"That's the understatement of the year." He peered in the bowl. "What's that?"

"I'm making you some homemade biscuits."

"What? You're beautiful, fun, and you can cook?" He clasped his hands together and looked up toward the ceiling. "Thank you, Jesus."

"Ha-ha," she said, though she was flattered. "Breakfast will be ready in about twenty minutes. Go get dressed before my son wakes up and decides to come home. The last thing we want is for him to find a half-naked man in his kitchen." Lewis had been completely understanding when Audra told him she wasn't ready for her son to meet him yet.

Lewis kissed her again. "I guess you have a point. I can't wait to meet Andrew. I'll go get dressed and watch ESPN until breakfast." He stopped in the doorway. "Audra," he said, turning back toward her. "I had a great time yesterday. I'm so glad we met."

He was so nice. "Me too, Lewis. Me too."

He blew her a kiss before heading out of the kitchen. Audra sighed dreamily. Even though she'd decided she would wait for his next visit—he said he'd come back in three weeks—Audra couldn't wait for Lewis to meet Andrew. She hoped the two would hit it off, and she and Andrew could finally live the life she dreamed of.

11

So, did you enjoy it?"

Nita flashed an appreciative smile at Marshall. "I did. Thank you so much for bringing me here." She was still having a hard time believing that she'd not only sat through a Broadway musical, but actually liked it. When Marshall had first asked her to go see *Aida,* she had balked. She had no desire to watch a bunch of people dancing and singing in loud choruses onstage. But she'd really enjoyed the show.

"It's my pleasure," he said. "I hope that it's the first of many more dates." As usual, Marshall was looking impeccable, in a gray sweater and tan slacks.

"I think it will be," Nita replied. She was amazed at the feelings that were running through her. She had braced herself for a Bible-touting, self-righteous man, but Marshall was so far from that. Being with him was refreshing. For once, she didn't have to figure out what game a man was running. He was open and forthright, and she especially liked that he didn't judge her.

Marshall stopped and turned to face her. "Look, Nita, I know this is a little forward, but I really like you and I would like to explore a relationship with you."

Nita was speechless. Of course, this had been her goal, but she'd never in her wildest dreams imagined the conquest would be this easy or this fast. She'd only been seeing Marshall for three weeks. But they had talked every day, and she'd even been to church three weeks in a row. That in itself was a sign that it was serious.

"I'd like that, Marshall," she said sincerely.

He paused, apprehensive about what he would say next. "But I have to be honest. Being with me comes with its problems," he finally continued.

She raised an eyebrow. "How so? You're not bipolar or anything?" She knew it was a little crass, but Nita had dated a guy who had an extreme case of bipolar disorder. He played professional football, and he was a straight maniac. One minute he would be telling her how much he liked her, the next he would flip out and call her all kinds of names. Yeah, behavior like that would positively be a deal breaker.

"No." Marshall laughed. "I assure you, I'm not bipolar. But as a young pastor, I have a lot of people in my church who feel they know what's best for me. And after my wife died, well, they became even more protective."

She nodded knowingly. "And let me guess, they won't like me?"

He laughed again, like she already knew the answer. "That's not my concern. Because as long as I like you, that's all that matters. But they may make life difficult for you."

Nita waved him off as she continued walking. "My friend Savannah had that same problem when she started dating a pastor at Lily Grove. Trust me, I can handle the Holy Rollers."

"The Holy Rollers? Who are they?" Marshall asked, walking alongside her.

"Those old biddies who have appointed themselves your guardians and my judge and jury," she said with a chuckle.

"Oh, you must mean Vera and her crew. Yeah, people like them." Marshall shook his head. "It's one of the downsides of this job. Ever since my wife died, they keep a close guard and all but run off anyone who I am even remotely interested in."

"Why do they want you to stay single?"

"That's not their aim. It's just that, in their eyes, no one can measure up to Katrina, my late wife."

Nita had no desire to compete with a dead woman's memory, and she was determined to be with Marshall. Besides, she'd never been one to run from a challenge. These women made her even more determined to prove that she could snag someone like Marshall. The more she thought about it, the more annoyed she became. They were the same types of hypocritical women as those at her childhood church that had turned their backs on Nita and her brother when they tried to get help as their mother became wrapped up in her cult.

"Well, sweetie, I assure you, I can handle a bunch of old women," Nita said.

"Somehow, I don't doubt that you can." He laughed as he took her hand in his and walked toward the car.

His touch felt good. Too good, in fact. Nita couldn't believe how attracted she was to Marshall. She wanted to make this work, and the reaction of those women at church made her even more determined. She refused to be judged by anyone, especially those old hags. So if she could get her man *and* put some hypocritical holy rollers in their place, that would make everything worthwhile.

12

Coco heard the annoying shrill of her cell phone, but she couldn't find the small pink Razr in her over-size purse as she tried to make her way inside the apartment. She finally located it just before the call was set to go to voice mail.

She smiled when she saw who it was. "Hey, Ma."

"Hey, baby."

Even though she was thirty years old, Coco still loved hearing the sound of her mother's voice. Despite the madness that had often visited their home during her childhood, her mother's warm voice had always made her feel safe.

"What's up?"

"My utility bill," her mother joked.

"You are so not funny." Coco plopped down on the sofa and kicked her feet up on the coffee table.

She immediately removed them when she thought of Nita going off about her shoes on the expensive table.

"Well, I was just calling to check on you since you can't call me."

"Mama, I just talked to you two days ago."

"So? I could've died of a heart attack between now and then, and you wouldn't have even known."

"I'm sure someone would have told me." Coco hesitated, feeling a flush of apprehension. Her mother was being dramatic, but just the mention of something bad happening to her sent Coco's heart racing.

"I talked to your brother."

"Cool," Coco said, glad that was why her mother had called. "He sent me an e-mail and I sent him a care package."

"I just don't understand why he had to go to war," her mother bemoaned.

To escape the war going on in his house, Coco wanted to say. Instead, she asked, "So, did you give any thought to my offer?" She had been trying to get her mother to come visit from Tyler, Texas, where her parents had moved the day Coco graduated from high school.

The joy that had been in her mother's voice moments ago faded away. "Well, ummm, you know, your father, he . . . he just doesn't think it's a good idea," she stammered.

Coco groaned at the mention of her father. Howard King was the reason Coco had turned away from the church. Her father, as deeply religious as he claimed to be, was the biggest tyrant she'd ever met. He made Sonny look good. Coco had prayed many a time that he would just die in his sleep, because, after years of watching her mother be abused, she knew death was the only way her mother would become free. Her older brother, Carlos, had joined the army, and Coco knew it was because he couldn't stand seeing his mother get abused.

"Mama, it's just for a few days." Coco sighed. As a teen, she had been too scared to talk to her mother seriously about escaping, but after she'd moved out, she'd tried several times to convince her mother to leave her father. She was hoping if she could just get her mother away from Tyler, she'd be able to get through to her. "I'm your daughter, for Christ's sake. Daddy can't understand that?"

"Cosandra, you know how your father is. I brought it up, and he got all upset and told me we weren't discussing it anymore. You know I just try to create as few problems as possible, so I let it drop."

The defeated sound in her mother's voice caused Coco's stomach to sink. Not because she wasn't used to it but because she knew her mother had resolved that being unhappy and living in fear was the way she was going to spend her life.

"Mama, let me talk to him," Coco said, knowing as the words left her mouth, they would be useless.

"Baby, just let it go, okay? Your dad has been in a good mood lately, and all this talk of me leaving, even if it's just for a short visit, has him all sour again. I'd rather leave it alone."

Coco swallowed the lump in her throat. She loved her mother with all of her heart, but she hated this submissive, accept-anything trait of hers—a trait that Coco had unfortunately inherited. But unlike her mother, Coco wouldn't spend her life trying to fix a broken man. True, she had tried, but her getting stressed to the point of losing her baby, well, that was the final straw. She wondered what her mother's snapping point would be.

"Sonny called here and told me you broke up with him," her mother said, changing the subject.

Coco should've known that was coming. Sonny had a way of working his charm on all women—including her mother.

"He told me that you left for good and he's just devastated. He said he'd even bought you a ring," her mother continued.

Yeah, right. Marriage was the last thing on Sonny's

mind. Even when she found out she was pregnant, Sonny had said they could raise the baby without being married.

"Mama, it's over. I told you what Sonny did." While Coco hadn't shared the full extent of the abuse with her mother, she had told her a little, including the last argument, the one that caused her to say enough was enough. She'd left off the baby part.

"I know, sweetheart. But Sonny's a good man."

"By whose definition, Mama?"

"He's a provider. He's not out there running women. He makes good money and he shares it with you, and you two aren't even married. He's like your daddy. Underneath all of that anger and pain is a good man."

Coco let out a heavy sigh. She couldn't believe her mother. "Mama, I can't do it anymore."

"He said he's sorry and it would never happen again," her mother continued. "Maybe you can try a little harder at not making him mad."

Okay, it was definitely time to go. As sweet as her mother was, this was another trait Coco couldn't stand. She wanted to tell her mother maybe if she had stood up to her father, Coco would never have been involved in an abusive relationship. She would never have felt it was okay for a man to put his hands on her in a violent way. But telling her mother any of that wouldn't change anything. She would only leave her mother in tears.

Coco decided to switch tactics. "It's a moot point now, Mama. I've met someone else, and I want to see where that goes."

"Coco!" her mother exclaimed. "You're already involved with someone else? I didn't raise you like that."

"It's not even like that, Mama." Coco sighed. "We're just friends. But I really like him."

"Getting back with Sonny is one thing. Getting involved with someone else so soon is another thing entirely," her mother said.

Coco debated telling her mother how different Davis was, but right about now, she didn't want to hear her mother try to convince her why she needed to give Sonny another chance. "Mama, I gotta go."

"Cosandra Chanel King. Don't you dare rush off this phone with me."

Coco felt a lecture coming on. She didn't want anything spoiling the good feeling she had about Davis. "Seriously, Ma. My other line is ringing. It's work. I love you. I'll call you later, okay?" Coco hung up the phone before her mother could protest any more.

She had hardly punched the End button when

the phone rang again. "Mama, I told you I'll call you later," she answered.

"Hey, baby."

Coco froze at the sound of Sonny's voice.

"You cooled down yet?" he asked.

She took a deep breath and remembered her promise to herself not to let Sonny back in her life—no matter what he said. Keeping that vow had been easy because he hadn't tried to contact her, until now. "Sonny, I told you I'm not playing. There is no cooling down. It's over. We're done," Coco said forcefully.

Sonny laughed like she had said something funny. "Baby, we're never gon' be done," he said casually. "I want to see you."

Coco began nervously pacing across the living room. "Sonny, aren't you seeing somebody?"

"Naw," he said, easy as could be. "I'm gonna be honest, I tried. But I can't get you out of my system. I love you, girl, and I want us to work out our problems."

"Sonny, what part of 'it's over' do you not get?" she said in exasperation. "I'm done being your punching bag."

"Aaaw, why you gotta say it like that? We just had a few little lovers' spats."

The sad part was that Sonny actually believed

that. Shoot, for a while he'd had *her* believing that craziness.

"Sonny, please. Just let it go. You can have any woman you want. So leave me alone."

Silence filled the phone. She could tell the charmer's smile was no longer on his face. "Naw, babe. I'm not goin' to be able to do that," he finally said.

Coco debated telling him that she was seeing someone else, even if that wasn't exactly what she would call her three dates with Davis. But the last thing she wanted to do was set Sonny off. She made a mental note to just change her cell phone number. Fortunately, he didn't know where Nita lived.

"I'm goin' to give you a little more time to cool down," Sonny said. "But I'm not goin' anywhere. You can believe that. You and me, baby. We were meant to be together. Until death do us part."

He laughed menacingly as he hung up the phone. Coco couldn't help but notice the goose bumps that had crept along her arm.

13

Hey, pretty lady. Can I come over?"

Audra groaned at the sound of her ex's voice. No matter how many times she cursed him out, he would wait a few weeks, then call as if nothing were wrong.

"Chris, the only way you're coming over here is if you're bringing a check for Andrew," she snapped.

He released an exasperated sigh. "Can I call you one time without you griping about money?" he asked, all the flirtation gone from his voice.

"No, you can't." Audra couldn't believe him. From the moment she'd revealed she was pregnant, Chris had been a total jerk. "Now, for the thousandth time. Don't call me until you're ready to be a man and do right by your son."

"I told you I don't have a job. Ain't too many people trying to hire an ex-con."

Audra rolled her eyes. She'd met Chris at an NBA All-Star after-party, but he wasn't a professional player. He was the friend of a friend of a baller. Still, she'd gotten involved with him. They were going strong until he got arrested for selling drugs. He'd served his time, but now he blamed everything that was wrong in his life on the fact that he'd been to prison. Miss Bea had once asked her why she would've gotten involved with someone like Chris, a high school dropout who liked to boast that he specialized in "pharmaceutical sales." Audra didn't have an answer for that. When they'd met, Chris had been rolling in dough and had no problem showering her with nice things. But then he'd gotten arrested, served two years, and when he came out, she'd made the horrible mistake of sleeping with him. Nine months later, much to his dismay, she'd given birth to Andrew.

Chris had gotten out of the drug game because he hated prison. That didn't help matters, though. Now he just spent his days hanging out with his friends and living off some woman.

"Chris, I'm sure you can find something to do. Shoot, go be a day laborer," Audra said.

"Are you crazy?" he replied, offended. "I ain't goin' and standin' on a corner, hoping someone comes along and hires me. I told you before you had Andrew, you were on your own. You made that decision to have him by yourself, so don't trip with me."

Audra knew having this argument again was totally useless. She had been begging him for years to do better by his son, but her words always fell on deaf ears.

She glanced down at the overdrawn notice from her bank, lying on top of a stack of overdue bills on the kitchen counter. She was surprised they hadn't closed her bank account, she was always so overdrawn. Lewis had shocked her by discreetly leaving a check for five hundred dollars when he'd returned to Atlanta. He said he'd seen the past due notices and was hoping it would help. It had. She'd offered to send the money back, but he insisted it was a gift, and she had used the money to buy groceries and pay her electric bill before they cut her lights off. She still had to figure out how to pay all the other bills, though. Lewis's generosity just hammered home how trifling Chris was.

As if she didn't have enough problems, today her boss had told her they were going to have to let her go at the end of the month for financial reasons, so her situation didn't look like it would become better anytime soon. The only saving grace was at least she'd make it through the holidays.

"While I have you on the phone, I need some

help, Chris," Audra said. "I'm having a hard time financially. I'm behind on all my bills, and my car is about to be repossessed."

"And that would be my problem because . . . ?"

"Because you haven't given me one dime for your child, that's why!"

"You act like I haven't done anything. I gave you five hundred dollars."

"Yeah, when Andrew was two!" she shouted. "Christine is coming up and I need help."

"Look, we had an understanding from jump. Neither of us wanted kids. I have two already. I told you I wasn't having any more for a long time, and you agreed with me. So you can come with that guilt trip all you want. I ain't trying to hear it," he said with finality.

Audra didn't know how she could hate someone so much. If not for her doe-eyed son, she would simply pretend Chris was dead.

"Does it not bother you at all that Andrew will grow up without a father?" Audra said, hoping to appeal to his sensitive side, or at least the sensitive side he used to have once upon a time.

"Nope. Shoot, my dad wasn't there and I turned out all right." He had the nerve to laugh.

"Really, you didn't," she said before slamming the

phone down. She was tired of letting him get to her. Talking to him never made one bit of difference.

Audra sat down and started sorting through her bills, trying to figure out what she could pay now and what she could stave off until later. She was resigning herself to the fact that they'd all have to wait when her phone rang again.

"Yeah?" she snapped.

"Ummm, Audra?" Lewis's voice was filled with concern. "Is everything okay?"

Hearing him made her shoulders crumple. What she wouldn't give to have him hold her right now and forget all her troubles.

"Baby, seriously, are you okay?" he asked when she didn't respond.

Audra nodded as if he could see her. "I'm sorry, Lewis . . . it's just . . . it's . . . ." Before she could finish her sentence, a wave of tears overtook her.

"Audra, what's wrong? Is Andrew okay?"

"Yes," she said, sniffing. "It's just everything is going all wrong. I got laid off today. Then Andrew's father called here trippin' and he's refusing to help and the bills are just piling up and it's just . . . it's just too much for one person to have to handle."

"Baby, God doesn't give us more than we can handle."

Audra wanted to tell him to go somewhere with all that faith-filled talk, but that would show him how far apart they were on the spiritual spectrum. God had abandoned her a long time ago.

"I'm sorry. I'm just stressed. I know you didn't call to hear me complain," she said, recovering herself.

"No, you can talk to me about anything." He paused. "Why didn't you tell me you needed some money?"

"Are you serious? I mean, I never expected you to leave that five hundred dollars." She added, trying to explain, "You don't know how much that helped me, but I'd never feel comfortable asking you for money."

"I don't understand why not." He tsked. "Audra, I need you to understand that I'm here for you. I'm not wealthy or anything, but I do pretty well, and any way I can help, I'd love to. I can't believe that jerk, what's his name?"

"Chris."

"Chris. I can't believe he could live right there in the same city with his son and not do right by him. Man, if I had a son, I'd spend every moment I could with him."

Audra closed her eyes and inhaled. *Where had this man been all her life?* "Thank you, Lewis."

His voice took on a more professional tone. "Okay. How much money do you need?"

Audra shook her head. "No, seriously, we'll be okay." She didn't want to start off their relationship by constantly taking money from him.

"I'm not going to force you, Audra, but know that I'm here for you. Are you sure you're okay? You don't sound too good."

"I don't feel too good either." She rubbed her temple. She'd had a small headache before Chris called, but now her head was throbbing.

"I wish I was there to make you feel better."

That brought a smile to her face. "Me, too."

"Hey, I have an idea," Lewis continued. "Why don't you come here? Since I couldn't come there like I planned, you come here."

That came out of the blue at her. "What?"

"Yeah, I'll get you a ticket today," he said excitedly.

"Do you know how much a last-minute ticket to Atlanta costs?" she asked, but she was starting to feel excited. Several years ago, a dentist she was dating had spontaneously flown her to Miami, but that had been the extent of her jet-setting.

"Don't you worry about the costs. I'm paying for it. Come to Atlanta and we can have a great time. I can show you around my wonderful city."

Audra hesitated, even though she wanted to do a dance. "But I can't leave Andrew."

"Come on now. You told me your neighbor treats him like her own grandson. I'm sure she'd be more than happy to watch him for the weekend."

Not if she knows where I'm going, Audra thought. She closed her eyes and processed what he was saying. She knew Lewis's offer was exactly what she needed. "Okay," she finally said.

"Great!" he sang. "I'll make the arrangements. I'll give you a little time; you can come tomorrow evening."

Audra wanted to catch the first flight out in the morning, but she said, "Sounds like a plan." Her heart warmed at the thought that this time tomorrow she'd be laid up in Lewis's arms.

"Bye, baby. I can't wait to see you," he said.

Audra smiled as she placed the phone back on the hook. She couldn't believe it—her day had gone from horrible to happy with one phone call. She raced to the bedroom to pack her bags. "Take that, Miss Bea," she sang as she pulled her suitcase out of the closet. "I guess this proves that Lewis sees me as more than a one-night stand after all."

14

Coco squeezed Nita's hand. She knew exactly what Nita was thinking and wanted to calm her down. They were sitting in the second pew at Higher Elevation. Davis, whom Nita had met when he came to the house to pick up Coco on their second date, was on one side of her and Nita was on the other. But next to Nita was an oversize woman in a gigantic hat with bird feathers, singing loudly and banging a tambourine. The feathers poked Nita every time the woman jumped around.

"Service is almost over," Coco whispered.

Nita gritted her teeth. "I'm about to take this tambourine and stuff it up this woman's—"

"Ssshhh," Coco said, holding a finger to her lips. "She can hear you."

"And?" Nita snapped.

"And, I ain't always been saved," the woman hissed as she rolled her eyes.

Nita rolled her eyes right back. That woman better be glad Marshall was standing up there grinning at her so proudly, or else she would knock that incredibly ugly hat off the woman's head.

Nita could barely make it through the rest of the service, she was so ready to go. She knew she had told Marshall she could deal with the women in his church, but now she wasn't so sure. She'd learned the Holy Rollers were a quartet of longtime troublemakers—Addie, Hazel, Lucy, and Vera, who seemed to be the ringleader. Last week Vera had tried to arrange a dinner between Marshall and a widow who attended the church. Marshall said he politely declined, and then officially introduced them to Nita, but his efforts hadn't done any good. They still looked at her like she was crap and even now were giving her the evil eye. Nita couldn't understand how they were getting anything out of the service, since they spent so much time worrying about her.

Nita knew she could still deal with them, but she was starting to question whether it could be done in a way that wouldn't bring Marshall a world of embarrassment.

Nita was grateful when Marshall finally dismissed the service.

"Let's go," she said before the first person was out of the pew.

"Dang, what's the rush?" Coco asked.

Nita rolled her eyes at the tambourine lady before she nudged Coco to get moving. "I need to get out of this place. It's suffocating. Plus, I want to call and see if Audra made it to Atlanta." She wasn't happy about Audra making the trip at all, so maybe if she focused her attention on that, she wouldn't dwell on the hateful attitudes of these so-called Christians at Higher Elevation.

"I'll meet you out in the lobby," Davis said to Coco. "I need to speak to a friend."

Coco smiled, then followed Nita out of the sanctuary. "Aren't you going to tell Marshall you're leaving?"

"I'll send him a text. I'm not in the mood to deal with the drama." Nita had reached the foyer when Vera and the crew stepped in front of her.

"Hello, Nedra," Vera said.

"It's Nita," Nita calmly said.

Vera shrugged like she could care less. "I was just wondering if you would like to come by for dinner today."

Nita frowned. She knew they weren't trying to be nice to her, so they had to be up to no good.

She eyed them skeptically. "You don't want to break bread with me, so what's up?"

"We want to know your intention with Pastor," Addie bluntly replied.

"Yeah, it's obvious you're a loose woman, and we're sure Pastor is only with you for one thing," Lucy added, her eyes slowly roaming up and down Nita's body. "We would rather you do what you got to do and move on."

Nita inhaled deeply. "You don't even know me." So much for trying not to embarrass Marshall. She was about to lose any semblance of religion she did have. "Look—"

Coco once again reached up and squeezed her arm. "Let's just go," she whispered.

Nita ignored her and took a step in Vera's direction. "If you and these Holy Rollers don't get out of my face . . ."

"Holy Rollers?" Vera asked.

"You say that like it's a bad thing. I ain't ashamed to be rolling for Jesus," Addie proclaimed.

"And if anybody is a Ho . . . I mean, a Holy Roller, it's you," Lucy added. "Rolling after anything that's holy, hoping to use your Jezebel ways to snag him."

"Oh, I can show you some ways, all right," Nita said, removing her earrings.

Coco grabbed her arm more forcefully this time. "Come on, Nita." She dragged her friend toward the door.

"You'd better listen to her, 'cause just as the Blood of Jesus is in this church, so shall be your blood." Vera looked like she was getting worked up. "See, what you don't realize is that Pastor got his armor on, and we're his armor bearers."

"Bring it on, old lady," Nita growled.

"Come on, it's not worth it," Coco said.

Nita was about to jerk free when she noticed everyone in the foyer was staring at her. She saw Marshall peeping over the crowd to see what was going on. One of the few sensible things her mother had ever said to her rang in her ears: *Kill your enemies with kindness.*

Nita gave Coco a look to let her know she was calm, then eased her way back toward Vera. The woman stepped back, like she was ready to start swinging if need be.

Nita leaned in close to her ear and whispered, "You wanna know my intentions? To be your first lady. And when I make that happen, you will be the first person I get rid of." She stood back, calmly put her earrings on again, and then sashayed out of the church.

"You are so out of order," Coco said once they made it to the parking lot.

"Whatever," Nita said, frowning as her phone started vibrating. She pulled it out of her purse. "These women don't know who they're messing with. But I can show them better than I can tell them."

Her frown was transformed into a smile as she read the text: *Hey, Sexy Lady. I'm all alone in this great big bed. Wish u were here. Would luv to feel your naked body next to mine. N.J.*

"What?" Coco said, eyeing Nita suspiciously.

"Nothing." Nita pulled the phone close to her chest.

"Who sent you a text?"

"Nobody." Nita tried to stuff the phone back in her purse.

"Unh-unh. Don't nobody me," Coco said, reaching for the phone. She quickly snatched it away and read the text. "Neil?" she asked in astonishment. "Girl, what are you doing?" She looked back toward the church. "You're not still fooling with him, are you? I thought you liked Marshall."

Nita snatched her phone back. "I do. And I'm not fooling with Neil. But that doesn't mean he doesn't keep trying."

Coco shot Nita a warning look. "Neil is trouble."

"Bye, Coco." Nita pulled her keys out.

"I'm just saying."

"Just saying nothing." Nita wiggled her finger in Coco's face. "I got enough people trying to judge me as it is. Don't you start, too."

"It's just—"

"I can handle Neil," Nita said forcefully. "Shoot, at this point maybe I need to go back to Neil and leave all these church folk alone."

"You don't mean that."

Nita made a shooing motion. "Bye, Coco. Go get your man. I need to get out of here before I lose my mind."

Nita didn't give Coco a chance to say anything else as she climbed in her car. She'd just been mouthing off about going back to Neil, but right about now, that was an option that looked more and more appealing. Neil, she could handle. These church folks? She wasn't so sure.

15

Audra still couldn't believe she'd come to Atlanta to visit a man. And not just any man, but the man who could be her husband. Even though Lewis had given her no indication that he was ready to get married, he had asked her last night if they could be in an exclusive relationship. He said he knew they were moving fast, but he'd never fallen for someone so soon and he couldn't stand the idea of her being with anyone else.

Audra pulled out her phone as she stepped off the tram. She wanted to check on Andrew, whom she'd left with Miss Bea for the weekend. After touching base with him, and dodging Miss Bea's barrage of questions, Audra darted over to the carousel to catch her luggage as it made its way around.

After retrieving her bag, she glanced about the

baggage claim area, looking for Lewis. She immediately spotted him waiting by the north entrance door. He looked so handsome standing there in jeans, a white shirt, and a tweed blazer. He waved when he saw her and immediately began speed-walking toward her.

"Hey, you," he said as he approached.

Audra reached up to hug him. She meant to kiss him passionately, but he turned his head so quickly, her lips met his cheek. Audra was startled, and when he noticed, he said, "Oh, I'm sorry. I didn't mean to offend you. It's just with me being a pastor and all, I'm always cognizant about public displays of affection."

She frowned. He sure hadn't been worried about displaying affection when they were in the elevator in Houston, but she let it drop.

"Don't worry, baby," he said, taking her suitcase. "I have a great weekend planned, and you'll have a chance to show me all the affection you want." He winked at her.

Audra smiled at the thought, her apprehensions quickly disappearing.

"Let's go get something to eat," Lewis said as he led her out to the car. "Anything in particular you want?"

"No, I'm just happy to be here," Audra said, settling into the front seat of his BMW 750. "Nice car," she remarked, running her hand along the soft leather armrest.

"Yeah, I roll in style," he responded.

She took in the scenery as they drove. Atlanta wasn't as pretty as she'd imagined, but it seemed up and coming, a place where she wouldn't mind living and raising a son. "So where are we going?"

"It's a nice little quaint restaurant in Conyers," he replied. They chatted as they rode for what seemed like over an hour. Audra wanted to ask why he didn't pick a place closer, since he told her he lived only about twenty minutes from the airport. But when they pulled up to the little bistro, she understood why he wanted to come here. It was secluded and romantic. She couldn't have dreamed of a better place to enjoy dinner with her man.

Over their meal they talked about everything from world affairs to what type of music they liked. Audra loved that they had so much in common. But her favorite part of the night was when he started talking about his plans for the future—plans that included her.

They'd just finished their main course when Lewis said, "I'm ready for dessert."

"You still have room for dessert?" she asked. He'd downed a sixteen-ounce steak and large baked potato.

"Oh, no. The dessert I want isn't on the menu." He licked his lips seductively.

Audra had fallen for that their first night. Since then she had wondered if their connection was purely physical, but the wonderful conversations they always had convinced her that the attraction was more than that.

Lewis paid the check, and they made the hour-long drive back to his place, all the while continuing to talk. He told her how he'd been called to preach and his dreams for his church, which he was slated to take over in July.

They pulled into a private parking garage and entered the high-rise condo. Lewis's place was a true bachelor pad. With the exception of a print of a man leaning over a cliff to help another man up, there was no artwork on the wall. The chocolate leather sofa looked worn, and the glass coffee tables looked like they were about to drop a leg. But the entertainment system with the fifty-four-inch television and stereo system was top-of-the-line. Several cardboard boxes were stacked up against the wall in the dining room.

"Been here six months and yet to unpack," he said when he noticed her eyeing the boxes. He pulled

Audra away from her inspection of the place. "So, now can I have my dessert?"

She smiled, stepped back, and began unbuttoning her blouse. "Dessert is served."

Audra was still in a state of euphoria when they rose the next morning. Lewis fixed omelets for breakfast, then told her to get dressed. She didn't ask any questions when he once again drove for more than an hour. This time they ended up in Buckhead, an upscale area of Atlanta. Lewis took her shopping and bought a few presents for her to take back to Andrew. She had a wonderful time, and before she knew it, they were wrapping up the day—in bed again.

Sunday morning, Audra rose first because she wanted to fix breakfast for him before they left for church. She was flying back late that day and was actually looking forward to going to church with Lewis.

"Wow, it smells good in here," he said, stretching as he walked into the kitchen. He was barechested, wearing only his boxers.

Audra set his plate of pancakes, bacon, and eggs on the table. "A meal for my king."

He kissed her gently, then sat down. "I could get used to this," he said, grabbing a fork.

"I was just wondering what time we need to be at church," Audra said, pouring him some orange juice.

Lewis kept chewing as he mumbled something she couldn't understand.

"What?" she asked.

He swallowed his food. "I said, we're not going to church today."

"What?" she asked. She didn't have an overwhelming desire to go to church, but she'd just assumed that, if she was going to be with Lewis, that meant she'd be going to church every Sunday.

"Yeah, I'm trying to enjoy some time off before I take over as pastor," he explained. "Besides, I told you, I want to spend the day with you. I want to cherish every minute of our time together."

Audra was torn. A part of her wanted to go to Lewis's church. She wanted to know more about his world, see what she hoped she would one day be a part of. "I was kinda hoping to meet the people at your church," she said.

He pulled her onto his lap. "There's time for that, baby. I want you all to myself this weekend." He stuffed a piece of bacon in her mouth, at the same time biting the other end until their lips met.

Audra smiled, no longer disappointed.

"I assure you, babe, you'll get sick of church before

it's all said and done, because I have a feeling you'll be around a long time," he said.

"That's just what I want to hear," she said, kissing him again.

"I know," he said, running his hand over her leg. "So why don't you come show me why I made the right choice?"

He didn't give Audra time to respond as he jumped up, grabbed her hand, and once again led her to the bedroom.

16

Coco stood in the background as Davis gingerly stroked the little boy's head. He couldn't be more than eight years old, and the way he looked—lying on the hospital bed, tubes coming from everywhere, his face bandaged—was heartbreaking.

The boy's mother stood on one side of the bed, desperately clutching his arm, as if sheer strength could will him back to health. He'd been innocently riding his bike when a drunk driver came out of nowhere and knocked him careening into the air. They'd called Davis because he was the closest thing to family the woman had. Like the woman he bought diapers for, this woman turned to Davis for help with her son.

Coco and Davis had been preparing to go out on a date when the phone rang. She had wanted to go on home, but he'd asked her to accompany him to the hospital. Now Coco almost felt like she was intruding. But both Davis and the boy's mother had asked that she come on in.

"How you doin', Jacob?" Davis asked.

He couldn't respond, but the pain was evident in the little boy's eyes.

Davis continued to smile reassuringly. "Well, you know what? You just hang in there, because you're going to be fine. I know it feels pretty crummy right now, but I promise you, it'll get better."

The boy's eyes glittered with hope as his mother continued to fight back tears.

"Baby, Mr. Morrison just came by to say hi." She took one of her son's hands while Davis took the other. He then stretched his other hand out for Coco to join them.

"And if you don't mind," Davis said, "we're going to say a little prayer for you."

Coco hesitated but knew now wasn't the time to refuse, so she stepped forward. Davis bowed his head and began praying. It was a sad prayer that had Coco herself fighting back tears.

Afterward, Davis leaned down and whispered something in the boy's ear that brought a small smile to his face. He then hugged the boy's mother and told her, "You call me if you need anything."

"Thank you so much, Davis," she said before turning to Coco. "I'm sorry for ruining your evening."

"Oh, no. It was no problem," Coco said sincerely.

They bid Jacob and his mother good-bye, then headed out to the car. Both of them were silent as Davis navigated onto the freeway.

"Thank you for coming with me," he finally said.

"No, it was my pleasure."

He glanced over, pleased by her response. "I like having you by my side," he said. "I think we make a great team."

Coco didn't mind being on a team that helped children.

"I know I'm jumping ahead, but . . ." He paused as he kept his eyes focused on the road. "Is that something you'd like—I mean, I know it's soon, but is that something you can see, you know, us being together?"

Images of Sonny bursting into Sunday morning service and wreaking havoc suddenly filled her mind. No, thanks, she wasn't about to put Davis through that embarrassment. She knew without a doubt that Sonny would ruin any chance at happiness she ever hoped to have.

"Let's just take it one day at a time," she said cautiously.

Davis frowned like he couldn't understand her apprehension, but he let the issue drop. "So, you still feel like dinner?"

"Nah, it's kind of late, and I have to work tomorrow."

"Well, let me make it up to you. Let me cook for you next weekend. I would do it this weekend, but I have my daughter." Davis had told Coco all about his pride and joy, Crystal.

"Do you have a picture of her?" Coco asked.

"You know I do." He held on to the steering wheel with one hand as he reached in his back pocket with the other and pulled out his wallet. "This is the most recent one," he said, flipping the wallet open to the photo flap. Crystal was an adorable little girl with thick black ponytails that hung to her shoulders. She had Davis's skin color and his cheekbones.

"She's beautiful. How old did you say she was?"

"Five." He glanced down at the photo. "That's my heart right there," he said, turning solemn. "Not the most ideal situation, raising a child out of wedlock, but you make the best of things."

"Do you and Crystal's mother get along?"

"We do, we have a really good relationship. But don't worry," he added, when he noticed the flicker of doubt in her expression, "there's no chance whatsoever of us getting back together. I had to learn that the hard way." He took the wallet, closed it, and stuck it back in his pants pocket.

Coco wanted to ask more, but she was scared her questions might lead to him asking in return questions she didn't want to answer.

"So, tell me some more about yourself. Not the generic stuff. I want to know about Cosandra the woman."

"For starters, Cosandra the woman hates her name. So it's Coco."

He laughed. "Okay, Coco." He paused, taking in her beauty. His scrutiny made her blush. "Tell me why you're single."

She took a deep breath. They'd been talking on the phone almost daily, and he'd already asked her this twice, but she'd dodged the question. She really should be honest. But how do you tell someone you let yourself be abused? No, she was too ashamed to admit that. "Well, I was involved with a man named Sonny Fuqua, but it didn't work out."

Davis straightened up. "Sonny Fuqua, where do I know that name?" His eyes suddenly grew wide. "Sonny that used to play for the Texans?"

"Yeah, that's the one."

"Wow, talk about big shoes to fill."

"Trust me, you've already filled his shoes and then some." They'd only been out a few times, but Davis had already shown her more respect and compassion than Sonny had in their entire time together.

"So why didn't you guys work out?" Davis asked.

"Let's just say Sonny has a lot of issues to work on, and I got tired of trying to help him."

"So it's over?"

"It's beyond over."

"So you're free to be all mine," he said, draping his hand over hers.

She smiled thinly. He didn't waste any time. "I told you, one day at a time."

"I can accept that because Cos——, I mean, Coco King, I have a very good feeling about us, and my intuition is almost never wrong. And more than anything, I'm a very patient man."

He winked as they continued the ride home.

17

God was testing her. That was the only way Nita could explain why she was standing in line at Starbucks behind the man she'd long ago deemed her weakness.

Nita took in Neil's form. He was still in tip-top shape. The tight black Nike tank and warm-ups hugged his 220-pound body in all the right places. He looked every bit the athlete that he was, and as always he made her body temperature rise.

But Nita's attraction to Neil wasn't all sexual. Neil had been one of the few men she'd absolutely loved. For months he fed her lines that he was leaving his wife. When she found out it was all a big lie, she'd been devastated, although she'd never let anyone know how much.

She shook herself out of her Neil-induced trance.

She decided to turn and leave before he spotted her. She'd ignored his recent texts and avoided his calls, so it was cruel punishment that she would end up behind him in Starbucks. She'd made it to the door when she heard Neil call out, "Nita?"

She paused, her hand on the door handle. *Just walk away,* she told herself.

Instead, she turned around. "Neil? What a surprise."

He glanced down at her empty hand. "Were you leaving without getting your coffee?" He smiled sexily, like he knew she'd seen him and was trying to bail out.

"Ummm, I left my wallet in the car," she said, quickly thinking of a lie.

"Well, let me buy you some coffee," he offered.

Nita took a deep breath. *Lord, give me strength.* She had confronted Neil when she found out he'd bought his wife a new eight-carat wedding ring. He'd finally admitted that he wasn't getting a divorce "just yet."

"What would your wife think of you buying me coffee?" The smile vanished from her face. As much as her body wanted him, her head needed to prevail. Neil was nothing but trouble.

"She wouldn't think anything. That's over."

"So you finally divorced her?"

He paused. "Ummm, not quite, but—"

"Bye, Neil," Nita said, turning back toward the door.

"Wait!" he said, grabbing her arm. "I miss you, Nita. I think about you night and day. Please come see me."

That stopped her in her tracks. Neil was one of the top players in the NBA, and he didn't have to beg any woman. The fact that he was begging to see her took her breath away. She took a deep breath as memories of their times together came rushing back. He must've known he was getting to her because he lovingly ran his finger along the inside of her arm, sending chills up her body.

She shuddered inside. "Umm, Neil. I . . . no."

He put his hand on his chest. "You're breaking my heart, baby. Why?"

"Number one, because you're married," she huffed.

"In name only."

"But married nonetheless." She took a step back. "Number two . . . I'm seeing someone. Seriously seeing someone."

At first Neil looked shocked. He finally broke into a grin and leaned in to her ear. "Bet he can't make you feel like I do."

Nita struggled to contain the excitement running through her at the feel of his breath on her neck. She wanted to tell Neil that she had no idea how Marshall could make her feel, that she'd yet to do anything but French-kiss Marshall. But Neil didn't warrant an explanation. Besides, if he knew Marshall was so proper, he wouldn't stop until he wore Nita down. No. Nita needed to pretend that she'd never bumped into Neil.

She took a step back again. "It's wonderful that you're full of yourself, but I'm not interested."

He smiled like he knew better. "Aaw, baby. You'll always be interested," he said confidently. "I'm in your blood. It's just a matter of time." He quickly kissed her on the lips, then made his way out of the coffee shop before she could say another word.

18

"You heifers gon' eat without me?" Nita stood over her friends, who were sitting in a booth at Checkers Restaurant.

Audra and Coco stopped eating their cheese sticks and exchanged glances before both of them started giggling like schoolgirls.

"These men have your noses wide open. Have some self-respect," Nita joked as she eased into the booth next to Audra. She was grateful her girls had called her to meet for lunch. She'd been thinking about Neil nonstop since seeing him yesterday. It was one thing for him to just text or call, but to be that close to him was really messing with her mind.

"Okay, I'll admit it, my nose is wide open," Audra replied. She'd been back from Atlanta for a week, and she couldn't stop talking about the wonderful time she'd had. "Me and Lewis have called each other every single day since I got back, at least three to four times a day."

"You're flying off to spend time with another man in another city," Nita said to Audra. "And you," she continued, pointing at Coco. "I don't know what to say about you. One minute you're mourning that psychopath Sonny, the next you're like 'Sonny who?'"

"I would think you'd be happy," Coco said. "You were always the one saying the only way I would get over Sonny was another man."

Nita picked up a cheese stick, then dipped it in marinara sauce. "I did say that, didn't I? There's nothing that can help you get over one man like another man." She couldn't help but note the irony of that statement, because Marshall wasn't helping her get over Neil. She popped the cheese stick in her mouth before motioning for the waiter to come take her drink order.

"Hey, cutie pie," Nita said when he approached their table.

"How are you?" The young man grinned widely at Nita. "I've taken your friends' orders. What can I get for you today?"

"Waiter on a platter," Nita joked, leaning back and checking out his behind.

"Excuse me?" he said.

Audra cut her eyes at Nita.

"What?" Nita shrugged. "The brother is fine. And he's a working man, which makes him even more attractive."

Nita continued to scan his backside. "How old are you, baby?"

"Nineteen," he said proudly.

"Whew, Lord," all three women exclaimed.

He smiled. "So, I'm suddenly not so attractive because of my age?"

"Naw, you're still fine," Nita said. "But I can't go to jail messing with no babies. So just bring me a grilled chicken salad."

He looked offended as he reached down and took the menu. Nita wasn't fazed, though. She leaned in on the table.

"So, Audra, has Coco let you meet her new man?"

"Nope. You?"

Nita nodded. "Yep. And he seems nice, but there must be something wrong with him. Why is he in his forties and still single?"

"Why is Marshall single? Why is Lewis single?" Coco said defensively.

"Lewis is single because he has yet to find his perfect woman. He was waiting on me," Audra said matter-of-factly.

"And I told you, Marshall's wife died and he wasn't in any hurry to find another one," Nita said.

"Well, for your information, Davis was in a serious relationship."

"And let me guess," Nita said, "he cheated on her and she dumped him."

Coco shrugged. "I've never gone into details with Davis on his relationship with his ex, Angie. I sure don't need him asking me a bunch of questions about Sonny. But they do have a daughter."

"Wow," Nita replied. "So you'd be a ready-made mama."

Coco smiled. The thought actually warmed her heart.

"What about Marshall? Does he have any kids?" Audra asked.

"No," Nita groaned, "and he's made it clear that he wants a bunch of them. And you know this body wasn't made to be birthin' no bunch of babies." Nita ran her hands down the sides of her torso.

"Excuse me. Weren't you the main one trying to get pregnant from Neil?" Audra asked. About two years ago Nita had been desperate to get knocked up by Neil.

"Baby, that's because Neil had just gotten a thirty-six-million-dollar contract. That was security." She sighed. "But I guess it just wasn't in the cards."

"And you had better be glad it wasn't," Audra replied. "Because you said it yourself—his wife, Joann, is crazy."

Nita flicked her hand. "I don't know why he's still married to Joann. Obviously she doesn't make him happy."

"Or maybe Neil is just a dog," Audra said.

"Or maybe it's the three kids? Shoot, with all those kids, I'd stay married to her, too," Coco said.

"Whatever, it doesn't even matter. Neil is history. I'm all about Marshall now."

Audra picked up on the slight tremor in her voice right away. Narrowing her eyes at her friend, she remarked, "Well, that didn't sound very convincing."

"It sure didn't," Coco added. "And if you are all about Marshall, then why were you sitting here flirting with the waiter?"

Nita shrugged nonchalantly. "Old habits die hard, I guess." She leaned over to sip some of Coco's drink. "Seriously, I was just having some fun. You know ain't nothing a waiter working at Checkers can do for me but introduce me to the man that owns Checkers."

"Well, you know if you become first lady, you'll have to change some of your ways," Coco said.

Nita rolled her eyes. "Don't remind me." The thought of the changes she'd have to make in her life was enough to make her wonder if she was cut out to be a preacher's wife. But she wasn't getting any younger. And while she had no intention of having a bunch of kids, she definitely wanted one.

"Seriously," Coco continued, "I thought you really liked Marshall."

"I do like him. A whole lot actually," Nita said, surprising herself with her declaration. "But I told y'all, this love stuff is for the birds. My mom was married four times before she died." Nita held up four fingers, one after the other. "Do you hear me, four?" she repeated as if they didn't already know this story. Until the day she died of a heart attack, Nita's mother was searching for the right man to love her. Even when she'd gotten wrapped up in the church, she stayed hopeful that "the Lord would send her a man."

"None of those fools she married brought anything to the table," Nita continued. "If anything, when they left she was worse off than when she met them. So not only did she never find love, she never got anything out the deal. That's not going to be me."

"But Marshall seems like a really good guy," Coco said.

"He is, and I think he'd make a great husband, but hear me when I tell you, I'm not falling head over heels in love with him. I want someone who has money, will respect me, treat me nice, and we enjoy each other's company. But that love stuff? Get real. I'm not even trying to go there. Why get my hopes up?" Nita debated telling them the other part of her problem with Marshall—his abstinence from sex— but she didn't feel like having them ask a bunch of questions.

Both Audra and Coco looked at her pityingly.

"Don't weep for me," Nita scowled. "You heifers are goin' to be the ones sick when me and Marshall are married and I'm living the good life."

Audra took a long sip of her drink. "So what are you goin' to do, whip it on him or something and make him propose?"

"Please, I wish." Nita groaned. Since Audra had brought it up, she decided to share her frustrations, after all. "Considering the fact that Marshall doesn't believe in premarital sex, whipping anything on him is unlikely."

"Get out of here," Audra said.

"Yep, he's serious about it, too. But it's cool. For now, anyway." Nita paused to collect her thoughts. "He makes me laugh, and I enjoy being with him. I tell you what, though, I'm going to have to get him to marry me quick, because I think this is the longest I've ever gone without sex," Nita joked.

"Yeah, and we all know there's only so long you can go without getting your itch scratched," Audra said, smiling slyly.

Nita blew off her comment as the waiter, who now had an obvious attitude, set their food and her drink down in front of them.

"Does he know," Coco asked, "you know, about your history? Have you told him?"

Nita shot her a crazy look. "Why in the world would I do that?"

Coco shrugged. "I was just asking."

Nita was pensive for a moment. "I mean, he did ask. But I told him I'd only been with a few guys, and had three boyfriends."

Both Audra and Coco tried not to laugh. "Try thirty-three," Audra giggled.

"Okay already with the jokes," Nita said. "He doesn't need to know all my business. All I know is this better pay off."

"It will," Audra replied.

Nita dug into her salad. Audra was right: this would pay off. She just had to get Neil out of her mind and focus on Marshall. This plan was better than going after pro players and it had taken half the time and even less effort. Nita had resigned herself to the fact that if she was ever lucky enough to permanently snag a professional athlete, she was going to have to deal with a lifetime of infidelity, something she was willing to do as long as she got paid. This way, she'd still have the money and she wouldn't have to worry about her man cheating on her.

"Let's have a toast," Nita said, raising her glass. "To my girl Audra."

"What are you toasting me for?" Audra asked as she lifted her glass also.

"For coming up with this brilliant idea," Nita replied. "Maybe you two can find the true love you're looking for and I can find my happiness."

"May we all toast to finding true love," Coco said.

Nita sucked her teeth. She could live without the love. As long as Marshall was spending his money on her, she'd be happy. After a lifetime of broken hearts, that was more than enough.

19

Coco was on cloud nine, despite the fact that she was trying her best not to fall for Davis. After all, she'd been on cloud nine with Sonny, and look how that ended up.

Coco stopped herself from going down that road. Her relationship with Sonny was over, and she was not going to let its ugliness spoil what she had with Davis. She needed to wipe Sonny and all memories of him out of her head.

"A dime for your thoughts," Davis said, waving his hand in front of her face. They were sitting at the dining room table in his quaint three-bedroom home in Bellaire, enjoying a meal that tasted like it had been catered from the finest restaurant in Houston. Coco couldn't believe that Davis had cooked everything himself.

"I'm sorry. I guess my mind wandered off," she said.

"I guess I'm not a very good date if your mind is wandering off."

"On the contrary, you're a great date." The best date I ever had, she wanted to add.

"Well, you've hardly touched your food," he said, motioning to the tilapia on her plate. She'd taken a few bites and then become lost in thought. "You don't like it?"

"Oh, I love it. It's better than I've had at most restaurants," she replied. "I just got lost in thought, you know, taking everything in." She took a bite of the fish, savoring the taste in her mouth. "Ummm, I love that you fixed this meal for me. I love this place. I love being here with you." As soon as she said it, her hand went to her mouth and she wished she could take the words back.

"I love being here with you, too," he said, trying to make her feel more comfortable. They ate in silence for a few more minutes before he said, "So, how's Nita doing—you know, after that disaster at church last Sunday?"

Coco was grateful that he had changed the direction of the conversation. "Nita's doing okay," she said. "She doesn't do well with people judging her, and she gets it quite a bit."

"It seems like she has a wall up as a defense mechanism."

Coco was struck by that observation. She'd never thought of it like that, but that's exactly what Nita had. Underneath her rough, abrasive exterior, Nita had a heart of gold. She'd just been through the wringer so many times with men and women that she had gotten to a place in her life where she had a get-them-before-they-get-me mentality.

"Yeah, she really likes Reverend Wiley," Coco said, "and he really likes her, it seems. But boy, those women in the church . . ."

Davis chuckled. "Yeah, you don't have to tell me. I've seen them firsthand. Rumor has it that Reverend Wiley was interested in this other young lady at our church last year. He never asked her out, but Vera and her friends made that woman's life miserable because she had two kids, and Heaven forbid their beloved pastor would marry someone with kids. She ended up moving to another church."

"Well, they can forget it if they hope to run Nita off. My girl has a spine of steel, and she's not going to go down without a fight."

"Oh, so you mean we could have some serious drama in the church?"

"If there's drama to be had, Nita's the one to bring it." Coco laughed. "But hopefully, it won't come to that."

They made more small talk as they finished up their dinner. They had just put the plates in the sink when his doorbell rang.

"Who could that be?" he said, glancing at his watch.

Coco followed him back into the living room. Davis opened the door to reveal a pretty, petite woman with long, jet-black hair. She was dressed in light green hospital scrubs. Standing next to her was the little girl from the picture in Davis's wallet.

"Davis, I've been trying to get in touch with you."

"Angie? What's going on?" he asked.

"Daddy!" the little girl exclaimed as she jumped into his arms.

"Hey, sweet pea," he said, picking her up and kissing her on the cheek.

Angie finally noticed Coco, who had taken a seat on the sofa. "Oh, I am so sorry," Angie said. "You have company."

"No, come on in." Davis stood aside for her.

Coco braced herself for the drama. She'd yet to hear a civil baby mama story.

"Hi," Angie said, offering a meek wave.

"Hi," Coco replied. She wasn't sure how to gauge the woman's seemingly friendly demeanor.

"I am so sorry to interrupt your date," Angie said, turning back to Davis. She appeared frazzled as she continued talking. "I've been trying to get in touch with you for two hours."

"Oh, my cell phone is off. What's up?"

"I got called in to work tonight, and I have no one to watch Crystal. Her usual sitter had a death in the family today. I would've taken her with me, but I'm working the ICU tonight, and it would've been a nightmare having Crystal there. Since you were on the way, I just took a chance that you were home." She turned to Coco. "I didn't mean to disturb your night."

"Oh, it's no problem," Coco said, finally relaxing, since it didn't seem like any drama was about to jump off.

"My on-call is mandatory, and I'm already on thin ice, so if I don't go in, I could lose my job." Angie glanced around the room, taking in the ambience of the light jazz and dim lights. "But you know what? I don't want to ruin your evening, so I'll just take her to my aunt in Galveston." She reached for her daughter.

"Don't be ridiculous," Davis said, pulling Crystal back. "That's an hour away. You go on to work, and Crystal will just stay here with me and my friend, Coco."

"Your name is Coco?" the little girl asked. "Like the hot chocolate?"

Coco smiled. "Yes, like the hot chocolate."

"Are you sure?" Angie asked. "It's not your night."

"Now, you know better than that," Davis said. "I love spending time with my baby." He tickled Crystal, and the little girl broke out in a fit of giggles.

Angie turned to Coco. "No, let me ask her. Are you sure? You're not going to think badly of Davis by having your evening ruined by our daughter, are you?"

With all the baby mama horror stories she'd heard, Coco was pleasantly surprised at how nice Angie was being.

"No, seriously, it's no problem," she said. "We were just about to watch a movie, and Crystal can sit right in the middle of us and watch, too."

"Yay!" Crystal exclaimed. "Can we watch *The Princess and the Frog*?"

"We'll see what's in there, baby," Davis replied, pointing to his DVD shelf. "Why don't you go and check out what we have?"

Crystal wiggled out of his arms and dashed over to the entertainment center.

Angie sighed in relief. "Thank you guys so much. Please don't hold this against him," she told Coco. "He really is one of the good ones."

Coco wanted to ask if he was so good, why they'd broken up. As if Angie knew that was the question on Coco's mind, she said, "I'm the reason we're not together." She paused, smiling at Davis like they shared a secret. "I just discovered something about myself, like I'm not cut out for marriage—to a man anyway."

Davis shook his head as he nudged her toward the door. "And on that note, you better get going before you're late."

She giggled. "Thanks again. You guys have fun. Bye, baby," she called out to her daughter.

"Bye, Mommy!" Crystal didn't look up from the DVDs.

"You have fun with Daddy and his friend," Angie said.

"The hot chocolate lady!" Crystal exclaimed.

"Yes, the hot chocolate lady." Angie kissed Davis on the cheek. "As usual, you're a lifesaver." She reached over and hugged Coco. "And it was so nice to meet you. You seem like a very nice woman, so I hope to see you again."

Davis gently took Coco's hand. "I hope you will, too."

As soon as Angie walked out the door, Coco turned to Davis, her eyes questioning. "Was she saying what I think she was saying?"

He sighed. "Yes, out of all the women in the world for me to get with, I had to pick one who was *confused* but didn't figure it out until three weeks before our wedding."

"Wow," Coco said.

Davis looked off into the distance, like he was taking a trip down memory lane. "Yeah, she left, and I found out she was four months' pregnant two months after that. But I'm just glad I found out before we got married, because I don't believe in divorce under any circumstances."

Coco was taken aback by that comment. "So, you mean you would've stayed with her if she told you she was gay after you were married?"

He shrugged. "I don't know. She would've had to get over it or something. Divorce is never an option. You work through any problems you may have."

Coco didn't think that theory applied to domestic abuse as well. Surely if she and Sonny had been married, Davis wouldn't have expected her to stay in that relationship. She wanted to ask him further about that, but, again, wasn't ready to open the door for more questions, so she let the issue drop.

"Well, your luck with women is almost as bad as my luck with men," Coco said instead.

"Yep, but hopefully, all that is about to change. Maybe our past relationships failed because God was saving us for each other." Davis smiled as he took her hand and they sat back on the sofa.

20

Audra sniffed the floral arrangement for the fifteenth time. She smiled as she held the card close to her chest. In all her years of dating men, with all the professional athletes she'd pursued, nobody had ever sent her flowers.

Audra removed the card and read it again. "Just because I miss you." She ran her fingers over the Tiffany bracelet that had accompanied the flowers. Lewis had truly made her day. She'd been out job searching all day long and was absolutely exhausted. She'd had a parent-teacher conference earlier with Andrew's teacher, who said he'd been acting up in class. That was totally out of character for Andrew, who was as close to angelic as a child could get. She'd have to watch him closely to see what was prompting that behavior.

Audra's thoughts were interrupted by her doorbell

ringing. She looked out the peephole to see a UPS deliveryman.

"Hi," she said, opening the door.

"Sorry to bother you, ma'am," the man said, as he pointed to the door next to her, "but your neighbor in Unit Twenty-four left a note that you could sign for her delivery."

Audra nodded. "Yeah, she's expecting this."

He smiled as he handed her the form to sign. She quickly signed her name, then handed it back to him.

"Okay, *Mrs.* Audra Bowen," he said, reading her signature.

"It's Miss," she said.

His eyes lit up like that was exactly what he wanted to hear. "Miss Bowen. Thank you very much. By the way, I'm Greg." He extended his hand.

"Hi, Greg," she said, shaking his hand. He was flirting with her, and he was definitely cute enough— with his mocha-colored skin, curly hair, and muscular frame. And the way the brown uniform hugged his body was equally attractive. But she wasn't interested.

"I'll take that now," she said, holding out her hand for the package, which was nestled under his arm.

"Sorry." He handed the package to her. "Say, ummm, I don't usually do this, but I'd love to take you out. You know—"

"I'm involved with someone," she said, cutting him off. "But I'm flattered. You have a nice day."

He smiled in defeat. "Okay, you take care."

He had just walked off when Miss Bea's door swung open. She leaned against the doorway, shaking her head.

"What?" Audra asked.

"That could've been your knight in shining armor, and you just blew him off," Miss Bea said.

"Were you standing there spying out the peep-hole?"

"I was inside my apartment, minding my own business. It ain't my fault these walls are paper-thin," Miss Bea protested. She looked down the hallway where the deliveryman had just left. "The Lord coulda sent that man to your doorstep, and you wouldn't even give him the time of day."

"The deliveryman?" Audra asked incredulously.

"Girl, them UPS drivers make lots of money. Besides, if he didn't make but a dollar an hour, it would be more than you make." Miss Bea smirked.

"Whatever, Miss Bea," Audra said, turning up her lip. "Besides, I have a man."

"Oh, yeah, the freaky minister."

"He is not freaky!"

Miss Bea shook her head again. "He sho ain't no

man of God, I can tell you that much. And you better be sure about it while you out here blocking your blessings."

"And on that note, bye, Miss Bea."

"Andrew home yet?"

"Not yet."

"You need to find a job," Miss Bea said. "I miss him coming over here after school."

"Okay, Miss Bea, since you put it like that, I'll go find a job today," Audra responded as she headed back inside.

She set the package down and began adjusting the arrangement on her coffee table one more time. She chuckled as she thought of Miss Bea saying she should've given the UPS man a chance. Audra didn't have anything against a hardworking man, and she did know they could make good money, but why settle for someone like Greg when she had Lewis— handsome, powerful, sweet, and rich?

Thinking about Lewis reminded Audra that she hadn't called to thank him for the flowers. She reached for the phone, then punched in Lewis's number. Her heart fluttered when he picked up.

"Hey, you," she said softly.

"Hey, baby. Did you get the flowers?"

"I did, and the bracelet. Thank you so much."

"I wish I could've been there to see the smile on your face."

"I wish you could've been here, too." Audra couldn't believe how giddy she felt—like a schoolgirl with her first crush.

She and Lewis talked for ten more minutes before he told her he had to go. She hung up, feeling satisfied. The two of them had so much in common. And he seemed to love the fact that she was open to trying anything, like skydiving. He'd told her he wanted to do that the next time they got together, and Audra was all for it.

Audra was still grinning long after she'd placed the phone back on the hook.

"Mommy, why are you smiling so much?"

Audra spotted Andrew standing in the doorway. She hadn't heard him come in from school. "Mommy's just very happy," she said, reaching down to kiss her son on the forehead.

"Why?" he asked, dropping his backpack in the middle of the floor.

"Because I have the best son in the world."

"Unh-unh." He looked at her suspiciously. "That's a boyfriend smile."

Audra waved her son off and scooted him toward the kitchen. "Okay, Mr. Smarty-pants. Let's get you something to eat."

Andrew giggled as he darted over to the kitchen table. "It's okay, Mommy. I was hoping Mr. Jared came back. I like him, a lot. I hope he can be my daddy."

That stopped Audra in her tracks. "Sweetie, I told you, Mr. Jared isn't coming back."

Andrew stared at her like he was hoping she would say she was joking. "He's gone for real?"

She took his hands. "Baby, he's gone for real."

"So I'm never gonna have a real daddy to be with me all the time?" He looked like he was about to cry. "Ryan and Michael have daddies. Why can't I have one?"

Audra cringed at the desperation in her son's voice. She also couldn't help but bemoan her luck. With all the grim statistics on the number of boys growing up without fathers, her son's two best friends had to have father-of-the-year type dads.

Audra knelt down and hugged her son tightly. "Don't you worry, sweetie. Mommy has a feeling that you'll get a daddy soon. But in the meantime, I want to be your mommy and your daddy."

Andrew looked like he wasn't pacified, but he sat down at the kitchen table anyway. Watching her son's disappointment made Audra even more determined. She would make her relationship with Lewis work by any means necessary.

Even if she had to turn proactive.

21

"Okay, this is getting really old," Nita said, fluffing out her spiral curls. "I mean, I'm really feeling Marshall and all, but this is ridiculous."

"Nita, please explain to me what's ridiculous about going to church," Coco said as she peered into the mirror and applied another layer of mascara to her eyelashes.

"Every single Sunday?" Nita huffed in frustration. "I mean, I don't understand what the big deal is. Why can't I just stay home and watch one of those ministers on television?" Marshall had made it clear from the start that he didn't ask for much, but he did expect her to attend church on a regular basis.

"It's not the same. The Bible says . . ."

Nita spun around and stared at her friend. "Good Lord, Davis has converted you?"

Coco smiled tenderly. "Nah, I'm just enjoying my newfound relationships, that's all."

"Relationships? As in plural?"

"Yeah." Coco beamed. "My new relationship with Davis and with God."

Nita rolled her eyes. "Good grief, we've created a monster."

"Nah, I'm not like that. I just can't remember the last time I've been this happy," Coco said as she slipped her stockings on.

Nita was about to respond when her cell phone rang. Her heart began racing when she glanced at the number.

"Hello," she sang sweetly.

"Hey, Sexy."

"You definitely have Sexy on the phone. May I ask who's calling?" She knew exactly who it was, but she wouldn't dare let Neil think he was in the forefront in her thoughts.

"Oh, so, now you don't know my voice?"

"Who is this?" Nita said, toying with him.

"Dang, one minute you love me, and the next, you don't even know my voice?"

Nita sucked her teeth. "Who said I love you?"

"Your body," Neil said.

Coco shook her head when she realized who was

on the phone. Nita ignored her friend's chastising glare as she slipped out on the balcony.

"Since you don't seem to be getting the message that I'm not interested, do you mind telling me what you want?" Nita asked. She was hoping he didn't detect the smile in her voice.

"Just laying here, thinking about you," Neil said. Nita envisioned him, laying across his bed, shirtless, his rippled abs glistening after a hard day on the court, his head freshly shaved, and his light brown eyes beckoning her as usual. "I know you've been thinking about me."

All the time. "Please. I have better things to do."

"I want to make love to you," he said, cutting to the chase.

She didn't respond. *This man was married. And she was working on getting married. But Neil could scratch that itch that Marshall won't touch.* The good and the bad voices in her head started doing battle.

"Don't you want to see me?" Neil asked.

Do I ever, she thought. Just the memory of the good times they'd shared sent shivers up her spine.

"Come over. Please," he begged. "Do you still stay in the same place? If so, I'm not that far from you. I can give you directions and you can come now."

She wanted to tell him she'd be there in ten minutes. Just as the words were about to tumble from her mouth though, she remembered Marshall. Nita took a deep breath, closed her eyes, and said, "I can't."

"You gonna make me beg? Because I will. There's no shame when it comes to you. I just want to be with you. I miss you so much. We don't even have to do anything."

Yeah, right. Shoot, if Nita went over there, you'd better believe she wanted to do something. "I can't," she repeated, envisioning Marshall once again.

"Why not?"

Coco knocked on the balcony glass door and motioned toward her watch.

Nita waved her off, turning her back to the door. *Just tell him you're seeing someone.* "I have to go to church this morning," she finally said.

Silence filled the phone before Neil burst out laughing.

"Do you mind telling me what's so funny?" she asked, getting an attitude.

"I thought you said you couldn't come over because you had to go to church," he said, still laughing.

"I did say that."

Neil fell silent again, the laughter dying down when he realized she was serious. "Oh, wow. Did you get saved or something? Because I have a hard time imagining you as some sanctified churchgoer."

"Now, why does the fact that I decided to go to church mean I'm saved and sanctified? Why can't I just be going to church?"

"Well, if that's the case, I'll TiVo one of those church programs for you, like Joey Olsteen or Creflon Dollar."

Nita laughed. "Whatever, Neil."

"I'm not playing, baby. I need to see you."

"Nah, I'm not going to be able to do that. I told you I have to go to church." She wondered if he could hear the quavering in her voice. Coco waved to Nita again through the balcony window. She held up a finger.

"Come see me after church." Neil always was persistent, and he didn't like being told no. "I promise I'll make it worth your while."

Nita inhaled deeply. Neil was a player who never had any intention of settling down with her, and anything with him would be all about a good time. And a good time only. But anything with Marshall, well, that was long-term.

"Come on, baby," Neil said. "Don't make me beg. You know you want to see me."

He knew her so well. "Don't get beside yourself."

"I want to see you. I got some tricks I wanna show you."

Nita felt her temperature rise. She was so sexually

frustrated. And who knew when she'd get any relief. *Just one last time,* the bad voice told her. *Just one last time to satisfy your urges and get Neil out of your system.*

Nita eased down onto the patio chair, squeezed her eyes shut, and finally said, "Okay."

"Okay?" He sounded surprised. "So you're on your way now?"

At least go after church, the good voice said. "I'll come by later," Nita whispered. She was going to try to be good after this one last time. Right now Nita wanted to make Nita happy, and Neil was just the man to do that.

Nita hung up the phone, then went back inside.

"What?" she asked when she noticed Coco glaring at her.

"I'm not going to say a word," Coco said, spinning around to head toward the door.

"Good," Nita said. "Because I do know what I'm doing."

"I hope so."

Coco let the issue drop, but Nita could tell she wanted to say something.

They rode to church in silence. Nita knew Coco was itching to give her two cents, but she wasn't providing any openings. During church Coco barely looked Nita's way, and once the service had wrapped up and they were waiting outside Marshall's office, Nita finally said, "What is your problem, Coco?"

"I don't have a problem," she said nonchalantly. "I'm just waiting for you. Davis isn't here today, so you're my ride."

"Obviously you have a problem. You haven't said two words to me since we left the house. I know you're not trying to judge me," Nita softly hissed.

Coco stared at her friend before saying, "I'm not judging you, Nita. I just think you have a good thing going with Marshall, and I don't want you to mess it up."

Nita rolled her eyes. "I'm not going to mess it up, okay?" She glanced at Marshall's office door. He was inside talking with a member. The door was closed, but she still lowered her voice. "I know I have a good thing with Marshall. It's just, well, I have some unfinished business with Neil."

Coco's mouth dropped open. "What does that mean?"

"It means what it means. I'm going to wrap up this business, and Neil won't be a problem anymore."

"Nita . . . ," Coco sadly said.

Nita was about to respond when Marshall opened his door.

"Hi, sweetheart," he said, walking toward them.

"I'm sorry, but I'm going to have to take a rain check on dinner. It seems there's a problem with last Sunday's offering."

Nita had been trying to figure out how to get out of dinner, and here fate had worked it out. "Aaaaw," she said. "Well, duty calls. You can call me later." She put her arms around Marshall's waist. "Nice sermon." She leaned in to kiss him, but he immediately pushed her back. Uneasiness blanketed his face. "Juanita, we're in the middle of the hallway. I can't be standing up here kissing my girlfriend in church."

Nita stepped back, feeling scolded. "Excuse me?"

He sighed. "I told you about public displays of affection in church. Until we're officially married, we can't be carrying on here."

Nita stared at him in disbelief. Since when did kissing her man constitute "carrying on"?

"I'll call you later," he said. Then he had the nerve to pat her cheek like she was his junior-high-age cousin. Marshall strode back to his office.

Nita spun toward Coco, fuming. "Did you see that?" She stomped down the hall, Coco right behind her. "He freakin' dismissed me." Suddenly, Nita stopped and spun toward Coco. "I got this ex over here begging to be with me, and my so-called boyfriend won't even kiss me because someone might think we're carrying on?"

She huffed in frustration as she got out her cell phone. "Hmmph, gon' blow me off?" she said, pulling the small jeweled phone out of its case. "I bet I know someone who won't." She started dialing numbers. She really had been unsure about taking Neil up on his offer, but Marshall had just made that a whole lot easier.

"Nita, wait," Coco said, grabbing the cell phone.

Nita narrowed her eyes. "Coco, don't play with me."

Coco's expression was serious. "Nita, hear me out, okay? As your friend I'm asking you not to do this—"

"No, I'm sick—"

Coco held up her hand to cut Nita off. "Trust me, okay? Just wait. At least through the weekend, and if you still want to go see Neil, I won't say a word."

Nita looked at her suspiciously. "Wait? For what?"

"Just trust me, okay?"

Nita sighed, looked at the church, then back at her friend. "Coco . . ."

"Just trust me."

"Whatever." Nita shrugged. Coco didn't want her acting out of anger, and Nita agreed with her—to an extent. She'd chill for now. But she knew, at this rate, it was just a matter of time before Marshall drove her right into Neil's arms.

22

Audra taped the last of the balloons to the railing in Marshall's five-thousand-square-foot house. She and Coco were supposed to be helping him get ready for Nita's surprise birthday party, but they'd spent the last thirty minutes marveling over his incredible brick and stucco house. He tried to play down the beautiful and spacious home, saying his late wife had wanted such a big place.

Marshall had gone into the kitchen to talk to the caterers, and Audra and Coco were finalizing the decorations in the foyer.

"So do you think Nita would want them to move into another house?" Coco whispered as she stuffed the leftover streamer into a box. "You know, since his wife picked this out and all."

Audra looked around the living room. The place

definitely showed a woman's touch. The oversize tile had intricate designs. The ivory sofa blended into the Berber carpet and was set off by the custom rust-colored curtains, which hung before the floor-to-ceiling windows. "Girl, you know your friend. It won't bother her that another woman lived here, but she's going to want a bigger place, I can tell you that much."

"Bigger than this?" Coco asked.

Audra gave her a what-do-you-think look.

"Yeah, I guess this is Nita we're talking about." Coco chuckled. "I think it's so sweet that Marshall would throw a surprise birthday party for her."

"Yeah. Can you believe we kept it a secret?"

"I know. It was hard, especially because of how frustrated she's been with him. I almost had to tell her the other day just to keep her from going to see Neil."

"Well, I'm glad you got through to her." Audra checked out the spread on the table. Marshall had made sure to have all of Nita's favorite foods on hand.

"I *hope* I got through to her," Coco replied. "Yesterday she was moping around the house, talking about Marshall was acting like her birthday was no big deal." Coco checked the room to make sure he was nowhere around, then leaned in and whispered, "Do you know she was considering letting Neil fly her to Jamaica for her birthday?"

"What?" Audra scoffed. "I don't understand why she's messing with him."

"Well, hopefully after she sees all that Marshall has done, she'll get him out of her system."

"Good, because Marshall is a good catch," Audra whispered.

They turned toward the dining room entrance when the door swung open. "All done, ladies?" Marshall asked.

"Yep, ready for the guest of honor," Audra replied, eyeing Coco and hoping Marshall hadn't overheard them.

"It looks good. Juanita is going to be so surprised. Ladies, I can't thank you enough," he said, taking in the decorations. "I think Nita will really like it. I want this night to be special."

"Well, I can assure you it will be because she's totally not expecting it. What time will she be here?" Coco asked, straightening out the "Happy Birthday" banner.

Marshall checked his watch. "In an hour. The driver should be headed her way. She thinks she's coming for a quiet dinner."

The doorbell rang, interrupting their conversation. "Well, that's probably the first of the guests." He motioned for the doorman to answer. "Coco, is Davis going to be able to make it?"

At the mention of Davis's name, Coco's eyes lit up. "He's on his way."

"Great. Davis has been a hard worker at Higher Elevation, and he's one of the good guys."

"I know," Coco said, grinning bashfully.

Marshall flashed a warm smile before darting off to greet the guests who had begun arriving. He'd gotten a list of some of their friends, some of Nita's old co-workers, and a few people from the church who didn't really know Nita but came so they could meet her.

Forty-five minutes later, most of the guests had arrived, and Marshall gave the announcement that the driver was pulling up with Nita.

He cut off the lights, and a hush fell across the room. Audra was closest to the door, so she could hear the click of Nita's stilettos as she approached.

Audra could only imagine the irritated expression on her face. After all, this was her thirtieth birthday, so Nita had wanted to do it up big. Both Coco and Audra had bailed out, pretending they had something else to do, so she'd been hot with them as well.

Nita pushed the doorbell several times. Marshall hushed everyone in the room and stood in front of the door for a long moment.

"Would you stop making her wait?" Coco whispered. "You know she's already in a foul mood."

Marshall chuckled and tightened the belt on the bathrobe he'd thrown over his clothes. "Hey," he said, finally opening the door.

"What took you so long? Didn't you hear the doorbell?" Nita snapped.

"Yeah," he answered, stretching. "Sorry, I dozed off."

"On my thirtieth birthday, you were 'sleep? It's bad enough you send a driver instead of coming to get me yourself. I thought you were trying to be romantic or something, but it was so you could stay at home and sleep?" Her voice was laced with disbelief.

Audra hoped they jumped out and yelled surprise real soon, before Nita started going off.

"I'm sorry, sweetheart." Marshall leaned over and lightly kissed her. She moved out of the way and brushed past him into the foyer.

"And why is it so dark in here?"

Even in the dark, Audra could see the outline of Nita's lips poked out.

"Oh, let me cut on some lights." Marshall flipped the light switch, and everyone jumped out.

"Surprise!" they all yelled.

Nita's mouth fell open as chatter filled the room.

"Oh, my God. I can't stand you guys," Nita said as Coco and Audra came over and hugged her.

"We bet you can't, you old grouch."

Marshall came up behind Nita and wrapped his arms around her waist. "Happy birthday, sweetheart."

Nita swatted him. "I can't believe you let me think you were blowing my birthday off."

"I would not be at home asleep on your birthday, which you've only reminded me of every day for the past three weeks."

One of Nita's friends, her former trainer, named Raheim, walked up to her. "Hey, Nita."

"Hey, you, what's going on?" she replied, reaching over and hugging him. "This is my boyfriend, Reverend Marshall Wiley."

"How are you doing?" Raheim said, shaking Marshall's hand. "I've visited your church a few times. I enjoyed it."

"Please come back anytime," Marshall replied.

"Will do," Raheim said before turning back to Nita. "Girl, you look good," he said, pointing to her body. She had on a black wrap dress that hugged her just right but wasn't too tight or too revealing. "You're bad for my business. Looking so good after leaving me."

"I do look good, don't I?" Nita said, twirling around.

"Yes, you do," Marshall said. "Now, if you all will excuse us, I have some more people I want Nita to meet."

Nita smiled at her friends before following her boyfriend.

After an hour of mixing and mingling, Marshall marched up to the middle of the staircase. Nita stood at the bottom of the stairs in front of him.

"Everyone, please grab a glass of champagne from one of the waiters," he said, pointing to the men and women walking around the room in black vests, carrying trays with drinks on them.

"What, preacher man is drinking champagne?" Raheim called out.

"Hey, they had wine in the Bible," Marshall playfully retorted. "What they didn't have is that Hennessy in that cup there. You ain't fooling nobody. I saw you walk in here with a flask."

Raheim laughed as he put his glass behind his back. "Hey, you know some of us are still a work in progress."

Marshall grinned and turned his attention back to the crowd. "First of all, let me thank each of you for coming out for such a special occasion. Now, some of you have had some things to say about me finding such a beautiful woman and falling in love so quickly.

But this isn't quick for me. I've been waiting for a long time."

Nita's face filled with pride as he spoke.

Marshall's expression turned solemn. "When I lost my wife, I thought I'd never know happiness again. But God is an on-time God. He may not come when you want Him . . ."

"But He'll be there right on time," several people in the crowd chorused.

Marshall nodded in agreement. "I have been blessed," he continued, "to have met Juanita Reynolds. And she's everything I want in a woman." He paused, looking directly at her. "But there is one thing that I don't like about her."

Nita's eyebrows arched. As did Audra's and Coco's. Marshall must have lost his mind, Audra thought, because no way was Nita going to let him embarrass her like that.

"What is he doing?" Coco whispered.

Audra shook her head. "I don't know, but I hope this is heading somewhere. I would hate to see Nita act a fool in front of all these people."

Marshall rubbed his forehead like he was deep in thought. "There is just one thing that's really been bothering me, and I would like for Nita to change."

Several rumbles reverberated throughout the crowd. Nita's head had tilted to the side, the first step in her I'm-about-to-go-off mode. Marshall stared at her as he slowly descended the stairs. He stopped right in front of her, stone-faced. "I don't like your last name." He broke out in a huge smile as he slowly knelt down on one knee. "I think Juanita *Wiley* sounds so much better."

"Oh, my God," Coco said.

It took a moment for Nita to register what was happening. But when Marshall pulled a small black box out of his coat pocket, she almost dropped her drink. Audra quickly took it, trying to contain her own excitement.

"Juanita Denise Reynolds, will you do me the honor of taking my last name?" Marshall said as he held the four-carat marquis ring out to her. Nita's hands went to her mouth as tears formed in her eyes. "I want you to be my helpmate, my lover, my first lady, my friend," Marshall continued. "I want you to be my wife until death do us part."

"Oh, Marshall," Nita said through her tears.

"Is that a yes?"

"Yes. Yes, it's a yes," Nita said as he slipped the ring on her finger. She threw her arms around his neck as she squealed in delight.

Coco leaned over to Audra. "Mission accomplished."

"I guess it is," Audra said, holding up her drink to toast to her best friend's happiness. Marshall was good for Nita. He may have been a little slower pace than she was used to, but he was exactly what she needed. Audra just hoped Nita realized that.

23

Coco squeezed the phone tightly in her hand. Her mother couldn't possibly be saying what she thought she was saying. "He did what?"

Mrs. King let out a long sigh. "I'm so sorry, baby. I can't believe your father would do something like that, but you know he's enamored of Sonny."

"But I'm his daughter!" Coco exclaimed. She had to grip the steering wheel tighter to keep from running the car off the road. She'd been driving back to Nita's place when her mother called with the news that Sonny had managed to worm her new address and cell phone number out of her father.

"I know, but Sonny gave him some sob story about wanting you back." Her mother paused. "I thought about telling him about, you know, about Sonny hitting you, but I know you didn't want your father to know. Plus, it wouldn't have made a difference because he'd already given Sonny the information, which he got out of my address book. All telling him would have done was sent your father into a rage about us not telling him in the first place."

Coco let out a heavy sigh. It amazed her that her father would get upset about someone being abusive when he was abusive. But that was a taboo subject—always had been. As children, Coco and her brother were supposed to stay in their room and pretend like they didn't hear their dad beating the crap out of their mom. Coco's brother had come to their mother's aid once when he was a teen, and both of them had ended up with black eyes.

"Honey, I told you only because I want you to be careful," her mother said, snapping Coco out of her thoughts. "I don't think Sonny is going to do anything, but I just wanted you to know."

"Okay, Mama." Coco had to get off the phone. She shouldn't get mad at her mother. It wasn't like *she'd* told Sonny. And to tell the truth, however she felt about her father, he didn't know how bad things were with Sonny.

"Coco, be careful, okay?"

"Okay, Mama," Coco repeated. "I'll talk to you later."

Coco hung up the phone and said a silent prayer that Sonny wouldn't come around. But somehow she knew better.

Her worst fears were realized when she pulled up to Nita's condo and saw Sonny leaning against his black Mercedes. She debated flooring the accelerator and peeling out of there, but she knew the sooner she dealt with Sonny, the better.

"You can run, but you can't hide," he said as she got out of the car and made her way toward him.

"Sonny, what do you want?" she asked.

"I want you to stop trippin' and come home."

"What part of 'I'm not coming back' do you not get?"

He shrugged her off. "So, you're not happy to see me?"

"Sonny, would you go and don't come back?" She tried to walk past him. *Lord, please just let him leave,* she thought.

Sonny grabbed her arm. Coco's eyes widened as she glared at his hand. He instantly released her and raised his hands in mock defense. "I'm sorry, babe." He stepped in front of her, putting on the charm. "Look, Coco, I came back here to say I'm sorry. You know I love you. I'm sorry for hurting you, but you know I was under a lot of stress. I mean, my career was coming to an end, and instead of being there for me, you were just stressing me all the time."

She glared at him. "So, it's my fault you hit me."

She could tell he was getting frustrated, but he took a big, long breath. "Of course not. I just . . . You know football makes us aggressive, and I have to learn not to bring that aggressiveness home. But baby, I need you. I'll go to counseling, talk to a preacher, whatever it takes."

Coco closed her eyes, searching for the right words to say. There was no part of her that wanted Sonny. She'd finally managed to break free, and she didn't want any empty promises to lure her back.

"I can't. I can't do it," she said matter-of-factly.

He started fumbling with his jacket. "Look." He pulled a small box out of his pocket. "This shows you how serious I am." He popped the box open and held it out toward her. Her jaw dropped at the sight of the large princess-cut diamond. It had to be at least five carats. So he wasn't lying about having a ring. "Coco, marry me, and I'll show you I'm a changed man."

She stared at him, at the ring, then back at him. "Sonny, what are you doing?"

"I'm asking you to marry me."

Coco's heart sped up. Not because she was remotely considering his offer but because she was scared of how he would react when she said she wouldn't marry him.

"Here," he said, grabbing her hand, "put it on. I know you'll love it." He started forcing the ring onto her finger.

Coco struggled to pull her arm away. "Sonny, stop!"

"Just put it on, baby." He was trying to push the ring on. The crazed look growing in his eyes scared her.

"Sonny, you're hurting my arm!"

"Coco? My dear, are you all right?"

Coco had never been so happy to see Nita's nosy neighbor, Mrs. Warren. The elderly lady was walking her toy poodle, which began barking viciously at Sonny. "Ssssh, Pepper," Mrs. Warren said.

Luckily, the interruption caused Sonny to drop her hand.

"Do you need me to call for help?" Mrs. Warren said, frowning at Sonny.

Coco was speechless as Sonny forced a smile. "Naw, she's fine," he said.

"Coco?" Mrs. Warren repeated.

"I . . . I'm fine," Coco stammered. "He was just leaving."

Sonny looked at her pleadingly.

"Bye, Sonny," Coco said. She lowered her voice. "And please don't come back."

Sonny looked back and forth between Mrs. Warren and Coco before tucking the ring back in his pocket. He looked like he wanted to kill one of them. Yet he didn't say anything else as he opened the Mercedes's door and climbed inside. When he sped off, Coco couldn't help the eerie feeling skittering in her stomach. Somehow, she knew that wasn't the last she'd seen of Sonny Fuqua.

24

"What's up, little man?"

Audra could not believe Chris had the nerve to be standing on her doorstep. She was so not in the mood to deal with him. She was worn out because she hadn't gotten home from Nita's party until three in the morning. Now here it was nine, and the man she despised most in the world was standing at her front door.

"You not gon' say hi to your daddy?" Chris asked Andrew, who was standing at his mother's side. Audra wished she hadn't opened the door, but she'd just assumed it was Bea. Why would she have thought it was Chris?

"Huh?" Andrew looked up at Audra in confusion. He hadn't seen Chris in three years. He hadn't even sent so much as a lollipop for Christmas two weeks ago. Audra had tried to emphasize that his dad loved him but just couldn't be with him right now. Part of her wanted to tell Andrew that Chris had died, but she didn't want to lie to him.

"Look here, little man. I brought this for you." Chris held out a small brown teddy bear.

Andrew slowly took it, then looked at his mom like, *What am I supposed to do with this?*

"He's too old for teddy bears," Audra said, snatching the bear away from him.

Chris laughed as he dug inside his jacket pocket. "But I bet he ain't too old for this." He whipped out a Nintendo DS.

Andrew's eyes lit up. "Wow!" he exclaimed. "Is that a DS?"

"It sure is." Chris handed the game to Andrew. "And it's complete with two games. All for you, little man, compliments of Daddy."

"Thank you!" Andrew said, taking the device and immediately flipping it open.

"Thank you what?" Chris said.

Andrew looked at his mother, unsure what he should say. Audra was grinding her teeth so hard, she felt like they would crack, but she didn't interfere.

"Thank you, sir?" Andrew said apprehensively.

"Thank you, Daddy," Chris had the nerve to say.

"Thank you . . . Daddy," Andrew said slowly.

"That's it," Chris responded.

"Baby, go over there and play with your game," Audra said, pointing across the room. Andrew raced over, sat on the floor, and began playing with the DS.

"What do you think you're doing?" she hissed.

"I just stopped by to see my kid."

"*What?* Since when do you care about your kid?" she snarled, just low enough that Andrew couldn't hear.

"I don't know what you're talking about. I love my little man," Chris said, loud enough for Andrew to hear. "I would come around more if you weren't trippin' all the time."

That caught Andrew's attention, and he glanced up in confusion at his mother. Audra wanted to haul off and slap Chris across the face, but Andrew had had enough trauma. "You need to go," she said sternly.

"Look, I just came by here to tell you I got a job. And when I get back on my feet, I'm going to give you some money. I need you to rescind that child support order you have out, though, or else they'll try to take it out of my paycheck."

She looked at him like he was crazy. She'd filed for child support four years ago, but since Chris never worked—at least anyplace legal—she'd yet to collect one dime. "You must be on drugs."

He finally lowered his voice. "Don't mess with me, Audra. It's not like I'm making a whole bunch of money, but I might as well not work if I have to pay my whole check to all my baby mamas."

Audra grimaced at his coarse insult. She'd never thought she would be someone's baby mama, let alone one of three. "You should've thought about that before you laid down with a bunch of different women." She was about to go off, but for the sake of her child she simply said, "Get the hell out of my house."

"You ain't said nothing but a word," he whispered. Then louder, "Hey, Andrew, Daddy will come back sometime and take you to the circus or something. Would you like that?"

Andrew jumped up. "Yay!" he sang.

Chris put on a puppy dog expression. "But if your mama makes me pay child support, I'm not goin' to be able to come see you. I'll have to work so much, I won't have time to do anything. So maybe you can talk to your mama about taking me off child support. Tell her you don't want me to pay child support, and I'll be around to see you. Maybe bring you more games, okay?"

Audra was so angry, her eyes were stinging. "Get. Out!"

Andrew jumped up and raced over to his mother.

"Mommy, please, please don't make Daddy pay. I want him to come back and see me."

As Audra looked down at her son's anxious face, she could no longer fight back the tears. If she'd thought she couldn't hate Chris any more, this proved she could.

Chris winked, handed Andrew a five-dollar bill, flashed a smirk at Audra, and walked out the front door.

"Mommy, please," Andrew said, tugging at her sleeve. "I want my daddy to come see me."

"Andrew, just go to your room," she said, her voice quavering.

"Why don't you want Daddy to see me?" he cried.

"Andrew!" Audra immediately caught herself and lowered her voice. "Baby, just give Mama a minute. Go play with your game, and we'll talk in a bit."

"Are you okay, Mama?" he said, noticing her tears.

Audra dabbed her eyes. "Mommy's fine. Just go play, okay?"

He looked unsure, but Audra flashed a fake smile. "For real. I'm fine. Now go play with your game."

The smile made him relax, and he immediately went to sit back down and continue playing his game.

Audra stumbled over to the phone, then went into her bedroom to call Lewis. He answered on the second ring, and she immediately began crying, only managing to stammer "C-Chris . . ."

"Okay, calm down and tell me what he did this time," Lewis said through clenched teeth.

Audra tried to compose herself, then told him what had just happened. "I'm sorry. I know tomorrow is your birthday. I don't want to be burdening you with this." She sniffed.

"You're never a burden. I wish I could get my hands on him," he growled.

Even through the phone, Audra felt protected. "I need to see you," she said softly.

"I need to see you, too. Especially today. I wish you were here," Lewis replied. "They're having a little reception for me at the church. But you know I'd much rather spend my birthday with you. Come to think of it, why don't you come?" He paused. "You know what, I wasn't even thinking. That last-minute ticket bought last time cost almost a thousand dollars."

She lay back across her bed. What she wouldn't give to be in Atlanta with Lewis right now.

"But, I mean, I guess I could pay it."

She sighed heavily. He hadn't complained about the cost the last time she'd gone to Atlanta, but that was a lot of money. "Lewis, I'm not going to let you spend a thousand dollars on a plane ticket just so you can make me feel better."

"That is so sweet. But you're right. That's a lot for a plane ticket," he said. "I'm gonna make plans to get there soon, though, okay?"

"Okay."

"I hate to let you go, but I have someone waiting in my office. Are you sure you're okay?" Lewis asked.

"I'm okay." Audra sniffed again. "I don't know why I still let him get to me."

Lewis paused, then said carefully, "Do you think it's because you still have feelings for him?"

"Hel——." Audra caught herself. "Ooooh, you almost made me say something ugly." She managed a choked laugh.

"That's okay. I've been known to utter a curse word or two myself from time to time."

"Well, that's the last thing you ever have to worry about, me wanting Chris, me being with Chris, me having anything but utter disdain for him." Just the thought that she'd ever loved him made her sick to her stomach.

"All right, baby. I'm just checking. I'll talk to you tomorrow."

"Okay."

"Audra?"

"Yes?"

"I love you." That wasn't the first time he'd told her that. He'd said those words one night shortly after they met. But she needed to hear them right about now.

"I love you, too, Lewis."

Audra hung up the phone, thankful that her hateful thoughts of Chris had been quelled. As she rose to her feet, a bright idea suddenly came to her. A plan started to form in her mind. She knew how she could lift both their spirits. All she needed was for her girl Nita to get on board.

25

The little voice in her head kept telling her this wasn't a good idea. But Audra pushed it aside. That was just her nerves talking. Lewis was going to be thrilled that she was surprising him. She knew she was taking a huge risk flying all the way to Atlanta without him knowing, but their relationship had been going so well that she knew everything would work out. Besides, she desperately needed to get her mind off Chris. Miss Bea had been happy to keep Andrew for a couple of days—well, until she found out where Audra was going. But Audra knew Andrew would be safe regardless, so she was looking forward to a relaxing weekend with her man.

Right after she collected her luggage from baggage claim, Audra felt her phone vibrating. She dug around and pulled it out. "Hello."

"Hey, girl. It's Nita and Coco. Are you in Atlanta yet?" Nita asked.

"I just landed," Audra said. Nita had reluctantly let Audra use her frequent-flier miles to make the trip. She hadn't wanted to, but Audra was able to convince Nita that she needed this trip.

"It's not too late to turn around," Nita said.

"I did not come all this way to turn around," Audra replied, pulling her suitcase over to the taxi area.

"Audra, Nita's right," Coco agreed. "This doesn't feel right. You don't fly halfway across the country to surprise someone. At least call and tell him you're there."

Audra flagged down a cab. "Look, Lewis told me I was welcome in Atlanta anytime and he wished I was here."

"Yeah, but I don't think he meant make a popcorn visit," Nita said. "I'm sure he didn't mean that literally, or else he would've flat-out asked you to come."

"He was the one trying to figure out how to get me here this weekend," Audra huffed. "Nita, when are you going to get it through your thick skull that Lewis and I are a couple? You don't hear me knocking your relationship with Marshall. You've gotten engaged in less than six months."

"Look, don't be getting funky with me," Nita barked. "I was just saying, men don't like their women popping up out of nowhere."

"I'm surprising him, not popping up out of nowhere," Audra protested as she climbed into a cab. "Hold on," she said as she gave the driver Lewis's address. "The last time I was here, I forgot to give him his extra house key back and he told me to keep it," she continued after she was settled in the taxi.

"Oh, you *forgot* to give it back." Coco laughed.

"Yes, I forgot. But I was going to mail it to him, and he told me to just keep it."

"Case in point," Nita stressed. "No man is going to give you a key to his place after just meeting you—unless you live a thousand miles away and can't use it."

Audra was starting to feel real doubts, and her reply wasn't as strong this time. "Nita, Lewis invited me to come back."

"No. What he said was 'you need to come to Atlanta again,' and I'm pretty sure that meant *let me know* when you come to Atlanta again."

"I agree, Audra," Coco said. "I'm sure that's what he meant. Besides, do you even remember how to get to his house?"

"I have his address," Audra said. "Look, stop worrying. I told you I wanted to surprise him for his birthday. What better way to do that than to show up at a reception he doesn't really want to go to?"

"I just hope you're not the one who ends up surprised," Nita tsked.

"Whatever. I'll call you after my blissful weekend." Audra hung up the phone, determined not to let their negativity ruin her good time. She called to check on Andrew, then quickly dismissed the part of her that wanted to let Lewis know she was coming. She really wanted to surprise him for his birthday.

Audra fingered his house key. Its solidity gave her comfort. Her girls just didn't understand. Lewis had made it clear that he wasn't seeing anybody, and she trusted him. And besides, why would he have given her a key to his place if he wasn't being truthful? Plus, he was available whenever she called, no matter what time. She'd glimpsed the code to his cell phone voice mail during her first visit, and she never found anything incriminating when she checked it. Plus, he was a man of God, and he had never given her any reason to doubt him.

No, she decided. She was not going to let Nita and Coco ruin this for her.

It took about thirty minutes to get to Lewis's apartment. She knocked first, just in case. When no one answered, she let herself in. Her heart warmed at the sight of the place, just as it was the last time she was there. She eased into the back bedroom and went straight to the medicine cabinet, looking for any signs that a female had been there. With the exception of an extra toothbrush, nothing looked out of the ordinary.

Audra picked up her bag and unzipped it, feeling better about her decision. Lewis had told her that his reception was at six. She knew he had a board meeting until five and would be going straight to the reception. She glanced at the digital clock on his nightstand. It was three-thirty, so she had more than enough time to shower and get ready. Audra decided to go ahead and shower now, though, in case Lewis decided to come home early.

She went into the bathroom, turned the water on, and had just taken out her overnight kit when her eyes glimpsed a pearl-colored invitation lying on the counter. She picked it up and read the fancy writing:

"Mr. and Mrs. Charles Woodruff request the honor of your presence at the marriage of their daughter Michelle Elaine Woodruff to Mr. Lewis . . ." Audra's heart dropped as she read the rest of the invitation. "To Mr. Lewis Jackson. Six P.M., Saturday, January 9, 2010."

Audra fell back against the wall to steady herself.

Stunned didn't even begin to describe what she was feeling. *Lewis was getting married. Today?* This had to be some kind of mistake, but when she saw the two tickets to Aruba next to the invitation, leaving tomorrow, in the name of Mr. and Mrs. Lewis Jackson, she knew this wasn't a joke.

She quickly grabbed her cell phone and dialed his number. The call went straight to voice mail, and she punched in the code to check his messages. The first four were pretty standard, but the last one was like a knife through her heart.

"Baby, it's your auntie Viv. We need the directions to the church. Your uncle Mason has no idea what he did with the invitation, and I don't want to be late to my only nephew's wedding."

Audra didn't bother saving the message as she hung up the phone. She couldn't fight back the tears, but they were tears of fury. How could he do this to her? She went on a rampage through his apartment. There wasn't much to destroy, but what she could, she did. She sobbed uncontrollably as she kicked over his coffee table, shattered two vases, and knocked everything off his bar.

After she'd gone crazy and the apartment was in a shamble, she stopped, then picked up her cell phone and punched in Nita's phone number.

"Nita," Audra sobbed, finally letting the pain overtake her anger.

"Audra? What's wrong?" Nita said, her voice panicked.

Audra was crying so hard she couldn't get her words out.

"Audra, where are you?" Nita asked.

"I'm . . . at Lewis's."

"What is wrong? Something happened, didn't it? I told you this was a bad idea. What is going on?" Nita frantically asked.

"It's Lewis."

"Sweetie, calm down and tell me what happened."

"He . . . he's getting married." Audra let out a loud sob again.

"Married?" Nita exclaimed. "Since when?"

"I have no idea. I just saw the invitation. They're getting married today. In two hours."

"Oh, my God. Okay, sweetie, listen. I want you to get your stuff, go back to the airport. Give me your ticket information. I will call and get your flight changed, and you come back to Houston right now."

Audra continued letting out loud, pain-filled sobs.

"Audra, I need you to calm down." Nita tried to speak sternly. "Listen to me, this is not the end of the world."

Nita continued rambling, but Audra had tuned her out. She'd put everything she had into Lewis. She had fallen for his lies. And she honestly believed he loved her. She'd believed him when he talked about their future. Everything he'd said had been a lie. There was no way this was over. She couldn't just get her bag and go back home.

"Nita, I have to go," Audra said, trying to compose herself.

"Audra, wait. Don't do anything crazy."

Audra didn't listen as she punched the End button on the phone. She turned the phone off because she knew Nita would be calling her right back. And then, Coco would start calling as well. And Audra didn't need anyone trying to talk her out of what she was about to do next.

26

Rage continued to consume her. As Audra sat in the back of the cab, she replayed how she had let herself be placed in this position—again. How she'd let a no-good man into her life—again.

"Is this it?" the cabdriver asked.

Audra looked up at the large brick church, then glanced back down at the invitation. "Yes." She handed the driver two twenties and didn't bother with her change. She was about to let Lewis know he'd screwed over the wrong woman.

Audra knew she looked a hot mess, with red, puffy, and swollen eyes, her mascara running down her cheeks. But she couldn't care less as she stomped up the stairs of the church. Pain takes precedence over pride. Several people stopped and stared as she made her way inside.

"Hi, may I help you?" one of the hostesses asked, rushing over as Audra burst through the doors.

"No, you may not," Audra snapped as she glanced inside the sanctuary. There were a few people putting up last-minute decorations. She spun around and started walking down the hallway.

The hostess was right behind her. "Excuse me, excuse me, where are you going? This is a private event."

"Lewis!" Audra screamed, walking up and down the corridor. "Lewis! Lewis Jackson, get out here right now."

Before long Lewis came running down the hall. "Oh, my God," he said as soon as he laid eyes on her.

"Oh, now you wanna call God?"

Lewis looked nervously around as he eased toward her hesitantly. "Audra, don't do this," he pleaded.

"Don't do what?" she said loudly. "Let all your little friends here know you're a lying piece of sh——."

"Audra!" Lewis snapped. "Please go." He looked desperate.

Several people were staring, but she could care less. Her heart was broken, and she wanted the man responsible to know how much he had hurt her.

Audra took in his appearance. He was immaculately dressed in a black tuxedo with a hunter green bow tie and cummerbund. "You sure look nice today,

Lewis. A little overdressed for a birthday party, don't you think?"

Lewis buried his face in his hands.

"Congratulations on your marriage." Audra fought back the tears that were threatening to overtake her. "Tell me something. When were you going to let me know about this little marriage? After you got back from Aruba? Never? When, Lewis? When was I going to be told the man who claimed to love me was married to someone else?"

"Audra, you need to chill." He sighed heavily. "Don't do this."

"Don't do what? Let everybody know the truth? Where's the future Mrs. Jackson?" Audra started looking around the church. She pointed at the hostess who had chased her in. "Do you know where she is? Does she know what a lying dog she's about to marry?"

"Audra, stop it," Lewis said, grabbing her arm.

She jerked away from his touch. "Let go of me." She stared at him for a moment, then said, "How could you do this to me?"

Suddenly a beautiful Cajun-looking woman appeared. She had ringlets framing her face and was wearing a long, gorgeous white gown. Her makeup was flawless on her sandpaper-colored skin. If not for the look of horror etched across her face, she could've been gracing the cover of a bridal magazine.

"Lewis, what's going on?" the woman said, her voice soft.

"Baby, it's nothing. Go back to your dressing room."

"Oh, so now I'm nothing?" Audra cried. She knew she was going way overboard, but she couldn't believe this was happening to her. She'd never felt a pain like what was shooting through her body right now. "Now I'm nothing? You've been screwing me for six months, talking about our future and how much you love me and want to be a father to my son. All that and I'm nothing?" she asked incredulously.

Lewis's eyes grew wide again.

"Lewis, you'd better tell me right now what is going on." The bride had moved closer to him. Now, with her train swept up in her arm, she looked anything but sweet.

"Michelle, let me handle this." He tried to pull Audra's arm. "Let's go."

She jerked it away again. "How could you do this to me? How could you do this?"

"Look," he said, exasperated. "I never meant to hurt you. I was just having a good time, sowing some wild oats before I got married." He was talking to Audra, but his eyes were fixed on Michelle.

Audra felt like someone was digging her heart out with a sharp fork. "*Wild oats?* All that about loving me was a lie?"

He ran his hand over his head, finally looking at her. "It's not a lie. I mean, you're cool, you really are. I loved kickin' it with you."

"*Kickin' it?* We were *kickin' it?*" Audra was dumbfounded.

Michelle came and stood by Lewis's side as the crowd continued to grow.

Audra took a deep breath and turned to Michelle. "You know, sister, I don't mean any disrespect to you. I had no idea he was getting married."

Michelle glared at her as she stepped in Audra's face. "I'm not your sister. And you show up at my church on my wedding day, crying to my soon-to-be-husband and you don't want to *disrespect me?*"

Audra bit down on her lip, trying to keep herself in check. She knew this woman was hurting just as much as she was, but if the broad didn't back up off her, there was no telling what she might do.

"Michelle, please," Lewis said.

"Don't please me," she said, snatching away from him. "This is my wedding day, for Christ's sake." She motioned around to the crowd peering at them like this was a juicy episode of *Cheaters*. "You got my family and friends up here witnessing your jump-off try to destroy our wedding."

"I know, baby." He gently rubbed her face. "I am so sorry, and I will spend my life making this up to you. Remember the ministry we're trying to build. Don't let Satan destroy that. I was weak in the flesh, but baby, I'm about to handle this. I'm rebuking this devil!"

If Audra wasn't so furious, she would've broken into a fit of laughter. Lewis seemed like he really believed that nonsense. Even worse, the way Michelle's face began to soften, she seemed to believe it, too.

Lewis turned to Audra. "Look, I don't know why you decided to show up here in Atlanta, but you need to get on that plane and go back to Houston." He took Michelle's hand as if he was trying desperately to reassure his wife-to-be. "This is my home. This is about to be my wife, and that's the end of the story."

Audra couldn't help it. She reached back with all of her might and slapped him across the face. "You bastard."

"Get out before I have you thrown out," Michelle hissed as two burly guys dressed in tuxedos stepped on both sides of Audra. "My brothers will not hesitate to throw you out on the street."

Audra looked at both of the men. They definitely meant business.

"I hate you," she mumbled through her tears. She pulled herself together. She'd acted a fool enough. She'd lost all semblance of dignity. She brushed her shirt down and turned around and walked out of the church with her head held high, even though her heart was crushed and she barely knew where she was going.

27

Nita tossed her phone across the room. "Uuughhh! It's a doggone shame when even a so-called man of God is a dog," she snapped. Coco had just finished filling her in on the disastrous time Audra had. Audra had called Coco on her way from the wedding. She knew who to call, because Nita would still have been going off at her.

"He gets up in the pulpit talking about living a righteous life, and he's just the devil in disguise," Nita ranted.

"What are you talking about?" Marshall asked, looking up from the sermon he was working on. He was sitting on one end of the sofa, writing on a legal pad.

Nita rolled her eyes as she recounted the story. Marshall shook his head while she talked, and when she finished, he said, "Well, don't judge all of us men of God by one man's actions."

"Umph, I just can't believe he did that to her. He was getting married. Boy, he ran some major game." She tried to think back, looking for some kind of signal that this was coming. Shoot, she couldn't be mad at Audra. Lewis had had her fooled, too. Even though she knew no good could come from Audra's popcorn visit, she'd never thought her friend would discover something like this.

"Unfortunately, there are a lot of men masquerading as men of God. I didn't have a good feeling about him from the beginning," Marshall said.

"Then why didn't you say something?"

Marshall narrowed his eyes at her accusatory tone. "That wasn't my place or my business. Besides, I didn't know him well enough to be giving Audra advice on what kind of man he was. But I had issues with the fact that you told me they slept together on the first night."

Nita grimaced at that piece of business thrown back at her. That was one thing she didn't like about herself around Marshall. She got extremely relaxed and comfortable, and she shared details—like her girls' business—with him that, in her right mind, she probably wouldn't have.

Nita could tell Marshall was a little bothered when she'd first told him that Audra and Lewis had been intimate. She didn't know why she'd shared that detail with him. They'd just been talking one day and it came out. "Why didn't you say something, then?"

"Like I said, it's not my business, and I don't stand in judgment of anybody. I leave judgment up to God," Marshall said.

"Well, I'm judging him, and he's a dog."

"Yep, it's very unfortunate. I hope she'll be all right." Marshall went back to his writing.

Nita continued haplessly flipping through the bridal magazine. She had been excited about looking for a wedding dress, but right now she couldn't focus on anything except what Audra was going through. Coco was picking her up from the airport in a couple of hours, so they were slated to hang out later. In the meantime, Nita told herself to just let it go. But as she watched Marshall, she couldn't help but wonder if he would be capable of dogging her.

As if he were reading her mind, he looked up. "Don't stare at me. I would never do anyone like that, let alone someone I cared about." He smiled, then went back to work.

Nita gazed at the man that was going to be her husband. He was a far cry from the many athletes she had pursued. But despite the ones she had been with, most of them had regarded her as nothing more than a good time. Yeah, sure, some of them, especially Neil, kept coming back for more, and she reaped the benefits. But nobody had delved beneath the surface like Marshall. Nobody made her feel like they truly loved her. And while she cared for Marshall deeply, Nita actually was looking forward to reaching the point where she loved him as much as he loved her.

The longer Nita watched Marshall at work, the more she questioned what he saw in her. It was strange to have a man really like her, let alone love her, without ever having had sex with her. She was used to them falling for her after the fact. But to be in love with her, and give so much, without ever having had sex, that was unprecedented.

The thought of his abstinence made her groan inside. While it was a great feeling to know that Marshall wanted her for more than just her body, Nita couldn't deny it, she wanted him, bad. She hadn't had sex since she'd met him, and that was a record.

"You know what," she finally said, closing the magazine. "I'm going to try not to worry about Audra and just wait until she gets back. For now, I want to focus my attention on my future husband." She sashayed over and straddled Marshall's lap. He smiled as he set his pen down and looked up at her. No matter what he was doing, he would always stop and give her some time and attention. That was one area she definitely couldn't complain about.

"Ummmm, you sure do know how to get my attention," he joked.

"Have I told you today that you are the most fabulous"—she kissed him on the left cheek—"wonderful"—she continued, moving to the right cheek—"magnificent man I've ever met?" Her lips met his, and they kissed passionately. Nita could feel the love coming from his body. It made her own feelings intensify. She moved down and kissed his neck as she began trying to unbutton his shirt. Yes, he'd already voiced his concerns about temptation, but that was before they were engaged. Plus, they were alone in his place now. No way could he deny her.

"Whoa, whoa," he said, pulling away and sitting her up on his lap. "Don't you think we need to stop before we cross a bridge that we don't want to cross?"

She leaned back in. "Oh, I want to cross, all right."

He pushed her up again. "Nita, sweetheart, stop."

"No." She began removing her blouse and letting it seductively drop to the floor. "I don't want to stop. I want you." Her breathing was labored, and she couldn't believe the way she was acting. But she was worked up now and ready to go all the way.

"I want you, too, Nita," he said.

"Then what's the problem?" she asked, getting frustrated.

"Nita"—he took her hands and looked at her solemnly—"baby, you know how I feel about this, and you said you could deal with that."

"We're about to be married," Nita protested.

"And when we are *officially* married, and say our vows before God, I promise you, I'll make love to you all night long."

Nita could not believe this. She'd never in her life been turned down by a man, let alone a man she was throwing herself at.

"Baby, I know it disappoints you, but this is a conviction I feel strongly about. I don't want to have sex with anyone other than my wife."

Yeah, he'd said that from the beginning. But he was still a man, and that was reason enough for Nita to think he'd give in at some point. Her mind flashed to Neil. If she had tried to seduce him, they'd both be naked on the floor now.

Nita quickly shook off thoughts of Neil. She hated when he popped into her mind, especially at the most inopportune times. "You said it yourself, Marshall, we're human. God knows, no matter how hard we try, we're going to fail from time to time. Nobody's perfect but God."

"I know that. I'm not trying to be perfect. But I do try to live a righteous life."

"Come on, baby," she said, running her hands up his shirt. "Make love to me. He forgives, remember? He forgives." She grinned widely. Marshall definitely wasn't amused.

"Juanita!" he said, grabbing her a little more forcibly. "Don't play around with God."

Nita sat back, her mouth falling open. "So, I'm sitting here in my Victoria's Secret pink lace bra and you're going to tell me no?"

He looked at her, the love still dominant in his eyes. "I love you, honey, but yes, I'm still going to tell you no. And I hope that you can respect my decision enough to understand that."

Nita blew an exasperated breath as she pulled herself up. "Well, we might need to just go to Vegas and get married soon, because I don't know how much longer I can take being denied," she said, slipping her blouse back on.

"Nita, don't be mad."

"I'm not mad, Marshall," she lied. She sighed as she

ran her fingers through her hair. "I'm gonna go check on Audra. I'll talk to you later." She didn't mean to be so harsh, but she couldn't help it. She was worked up and, at this rate, relief wouldn't come for months since their wedding date was six months away. The bad part was, Nita truly didn't know if she could wait that long.

28

"You're better than me," Nita declared, "because I wouldn't have walked up out of that church. It would've been a service goin' on, all right, somebody's funeral."

Audra rolled her eyes. Nita could be loud and obnoxious sometimes, but her bark was worse than her bite.

"So, tell me again, what did he have to say?" Coco asked.

"He said he was sorry," Audra replied as she curled her bang. The three of them were in her bathroom getting ready to go to their friend Jodi's birthday dinner. "I just don't understand why he would do this."

"Because you let him," Miss Bea said. She'd been in the living room with Andrew, and neither of them heard her come into the back, where they were getting ready.

"Ummm, Miss Bea, no offense, but this is an A, B, and C conversation," Nita said, motioning between herself, Audra, and Coco.

"Here's some alphabet soup for you. I'm seeing my way in this conversation because you girls are always blowing me off. But you need to listen to me. I'm trying to tell you. I told you from the git-go, the way you two started was wrong."

Nita flashed Audra a look and mouthed, "You let her know y'all slept together?"

"She didn't have to let me know," Miss Bea said. "I've been around the block enough to know. Audra, baby, you know I love you, but you reek of desperation, and you open yourself up for a man to stomp on your heart. You need to guard it. Y'all women so busy running around trying to snag you a man, make him fall in love with you. You need to be falling in love with yourselves. You're trying to drive your life into the direction you want it to go. But sometimes, you got to take your hands off the steering wheel and let Jesus take the wheel."

Nita rolled her eyes, but Miss Bea ignored her. "All I'm saying is get yourself together and the rest will come."

"I beg your pardon," Nita said, her hands posted on her hips. "I am together."

"Are you really?" Miss Bea responded. "Are you happy with yourself?"

"I sure am," Nita quickly replied.

"And what is your definition of happiness? Finding the man that's gon' take care of you? Give you the life that you *think* you deserve. You need to be careful, because the Bible said do not mate an ass and an ox."

"What is that supposed to mean? You trying to say I'm an ass or an ox?" Nita was getting an attitude.

"See, you're always on the defensive. I'm trying to say you're unequally yoked." Miss Bea wagged her finger at Nita. "Reverend Wiley is spiritually right with God. You're playing with God. The man is committed to his celibacy. You committed to sell a bit to the highest bidder. He loves you. You love what he can do for you. *Unequally yoked.* And you can pretend all you want, but sooner or later that will come to the surface."

"Okay, Miss Bea," Audra said, stepping in. She'd been in tears all night and needed to get out and have fun at this birthday dinner. The last thing she wanted was for their evening to be ruined by Nita and Miss Bea going at it.

"Are you eavesdropping now?" Nita asked. "And how do you know all my business?"

"I don't eavesdrop. I hear things and I don't hold my tongue," Miss Bea proclaimed.

For the most part Nita tried to remain respectful, but at the rate Miss Bea was going, Nita would soon be on the verge of completely losing it. Audra was more forceful this time. "Miss Bea, that's enough." She turned to Nita. "Just leave it be. You know how she is."

"I'll have you know I am the woman for Marshall, and I don't care what you or anybody else thinks," she said, ignoring Audra. "I can make him happy. I *will* make him happy. And I can be a good woman to him."

Miss Bea looked at her in pity. "Who are you trying to convince, me or yourself?" She shook her head as she walked back into the living room. "I'm going to pray for y'all."

After she left, Nita spun toward her friend. "Ooooh, Audra, you're lucky you need her help, because I was two seconds from going off on her."

"I know," Audra said, "and I appreciate you holding your tongue."

"Well, if she gets up in my face talking crazy again, I can't make any promises."

"I'll talk to her, Nita, okay?"

Nita must have noticed the forlorn look on Audra's face, because she said, "I'm sorry. The last thing you need to be dealing with is me and Miss Bea going at it. But the one thing she was right about is screw that fool Lewis. You deserve better than him, and God's gonna send you someone better than him."

Audra forced a wan smile. "Look at you. Marshall is rubbing off on you."

"Girl, whatever." Nita waved her friend off. "So are you okay?" Nita asked.

Audra was still reeling in shock, but she knew she had to move on. "I'm okay. I guess I'm just starting all over. I sure don't want to go back into the dating game." That was really the only reason she was going to this dinner, because she had to get her mind off Lewis. Otherwise, she would've bowed out.

"Well, look. I might not be able to be on the hunt with you, but I can definitely help you find a man," Nita said.

"Me, too," added Coco.

Audra looked at her friends as Miss Bea's words rang in her head. *Stop looking for love and let love find you.* "You know what, guys? I'm gonna take a pass. Lewis broke my heart, and I'm not in a place where I want to even think about giving it to someone else. I'm just going to enjoy myself and show Jodi my support."

Nita was about to say something hopeful when her cell phone rang. Her eyes lit up when she looked at the caller ID. "Hello?" she said, answering the phone.

A wide smile crossed her face. "Ummm, I hear you," she said flirtatiously. "But I told you, I'm from Missouri. You got to show me, baby." She giggled, paused, then said, "Okay, I'll do that. I'll call you later."

As Nita hung up the phone, Audra stood with her arms folded. "And who was that? I know it wasn't Marshall. That sounded like a freaky conversation."

"Oh, you know it wasn't Marshall. Not if it had anything to do with being freaky." Nita smiled mischievously. "That was Neil. And before you start going off"—she turned and glared at Coco—"it's just some harmless flirting. Shoot, I can't have sex, but at least I can talk about it, can't I?"

Coco just waved her hand in disbelief. Audra looked like she wanted to say something but then stopped herself. "You know, after what I've been through, I'm not in a position to judge or offer advice. The only thing I can tell you is be careful. Don't mess things up with Marshall."

"Would you chill? I got this. Like I said, men do it all the time. It's harmless as long as I don't cross that line, right?" She winked as she walked out the door.

Audra had a sickening thought. Had Lewis considered flirting with her harmless in the beginning? She quickly turned her attention back to Nita. That smile on her face was worrisome. It was only a matter of time before that line was indeed crossed.

29

Audra massaged her temples. She had a throbbing headache, and the stack of papers spread out across the kitchen table was only making it worse. She'd had trouble focusing on anything lately. Three weeks had passed since Lewis's wedding, and she still hadn't heard from him. She couldn't get his betrayal off her mind. The fact that he hadn't called to apologize only deepened her pain. She still wanted to pay him back, but she figured she'd done enough damage by showing up at his wedding. Right now, though, she had to let that go. She had to deal with the newest crisis in her life.

"Tell us why you think you're deserving of a financial scholarship," she said, reading the paper.

As Audra tossed it down on the table, the doorbell rang. "Because all my son talks about is going to this stupid soccer camp that I don't have the money for. So I'm supposed to crush his dream because I'm broke and his daddy is trifling?" she mumbled as she stomped toward the door.

"Who are you in here talking to?" Miss Bea said after Audra opened the door.

"Nobody."

Miss Bea walked in and surveyed the room. "So, you just havin' a conversation with yourself?"

"I'm trying to work out a problem. Things are just rough." Just verbalizing her struggles made her heart heavy.

"Money or man troubles?"

"Both. But right now all I really care about is the money trouble." Audra sighed as her voice cracked. "I don't know how I'm even making it from day to day. It's been over a month since I was laid off, and I'm not having any luck finding a job."

"Well, baby, I wish I could help you, but you know I barely get by on my Social Security check." Miss Bea gently rubbed her shoulder. As much of a nag as she could be, Miss Bea had a compassionate side that Audra loved.

"I know." Audra patted her hand. "You help me enough. I'm the one who wishes she could help you."

Miss Bea smiled reassuringly. "Well, God is gonna

help us both. I know you're a little down, so I made a pecan pie and it's in the oven now. I'll bring it over later."

Audra smiled faintly. She absolutely loved Miss Bea's pecan pies. "Thank you so much."

"Okay, well, are you gon' be here when Andrew gets out of school, or do you need me to come over?"

"I'll be here. I'm filling out this paperwork for his soccer camp." She motioned toward the papers.

"Oh, chile, I'll be glad when that camp comes," Miss Bea said dourly. "That's all he's been talking about." She made a face. "He wants to go somewhere to learn how to kick a ball. Don't make no sense to me."

"I know, but he really wants to go. I have to become one of the two people they give a scholarship to, because it's the only way he can get there. So I have to get this application in the mail, then run a few errands so I'll be back before Andrew gets home."

"Okay, sugar. You call me if there are any problems." Miss Bea looked like she was about to leave, then added, "Have you prayed on it?"

Audra chuckled as she got up to walk her neighbor to the door. "Yeah, right," she muttered. Shoot, if she had a hard time turning to God *before* Lewis dogged her out, she sure didn't see herself doing it now.

"Yeah. Right," Miss Bea reiterated.

"God doesn't stop by this apartment," Audra informed her.

"Maybe it's because He knows He's not welcome." Miss Bea gave her a knowing look before turning and walking off. Audra was about to close her door when she heard someone calling, "Miss Bowen, Miss Bowen!"

Audra silently cursed when she saw the office manager hurrying toward her. It was going on a month and a half since she'd paid her rent, so she considered slamming the door. But the woman had already spotted her.

"Miss Bowen, how are you?" the woman said, trying to catch her breath.

"Mrs. Anderson, I'm making it. It's hard, but I'm trying."

"Well, that's wonderful." She shifted nervously. "I've been sending you letters."

"What letters?" Audra feigned an innocent expression.

"The same letter I gave you last month and the month before that. The one about your rent being late," the woman said timidly.

"Hmmm, someone must have taken it off my door, because I haven't seen that."

Mrs. Anderson handed a piece of paper to Audra. "Well, see this one. If I don't have the rent by Friday, I'm going to be forced to evict you."

Audra reluctantly took the letter. "Sorry, have a nice day," the woman said as she walked off.

Audra closed the door and softly banged her head against the wall. She was grateful that her home phone was disconnected, because otherwise she'd be dealing with this kind of stuff all day from bill collectors. The landlord would have to get in line like everyone else. There was just one problem. She couldn't take a chance on getting kicked out with Andrew. So what in the world was she going to do? Audra was pondering that thought when her cell phone rang. When she saw the number, she immediately froze. It rang again. She gritted her teeth and pressed the Talk button.

"I can't believe you had the nerve to call me," she hissed.

"Hello, Audra. How are you doing?" His words were slow and deliberate . . . and still made her knees weak.

"I'll ask you again, what do you want?"

He paused, then said, "I just want to say I'm really and truly sorry."

"About what? Playing me? Lying? Pretending to

be a man of God? What?" Audra had a laundry list of questions she wanted to ask him. She desperately needed answers.

"Sorry about everything," Lewis said. "I know I said some hateful things in the church, but I freaked out. I didn't mean that stuff."

"You said what you meant," Audra replied. "Lewis, sell that bs to your wife, because I'm not trying to hear it."

"You have to believe me," he pleaded. "You know I love you."

She closed her eyes, not believing he would dare go there.

"Just hear me out," he continued. "I've never met a woman like you. And honestly, I was just looking for a little fun when I met you, but from our first day together, I knew you were special." He talked fast, like he wanted to get the words out before she hung up on him. "Everything I said to you before that day was true. Well, everything about me loving you and wanting to be with you. And in an ideal world, you are the woman I would be with. But it was already arranged that I would marry Michelle."

"Arranged? Oh, so now we live in India?" She wondered how long Lewis had taken to dream up this cockamamie story. Did he really think she'd believe it?

"If I was going to lead this church, Michelle was part of the deal," he explained. "Her father is the retiring pastor, and our wedding has all but been planned since we were sixteen."

The pain she felt was still raw, and nothing he could say would change that. "And again, your purpose in telling me this would be?"

"I need to see you," he blurted out.

"You need to go to hell."

"No, I think I can explain so much better in person. I need you to understand why I did what I did. I could come this weekend, but we need to sit down and talk."

She was dumbfounded. What did he expect from her? Did he really think he could break her heart like he did, then waltz back in with a simple apology?

"Look, Lewis, I have bills coming out the wazoo. I'm about to get kicked out of my apartment. I still haven't found a job, and the last thing I feel like dealing with is more of your lies. Please don't call me again." She slammed her cell phone closed, steaming. As if she didn't have enough to worry about. Now she had to rid her mind of all thoughts, ever, of Lewis.

30

Nita was glad she was in a church, because she was going to need some divine intervention to keep her from going off.

". . . so, all I'm saying is, this meeting is about church business, and it seems like to me you should be a member before you come up here all in our business," Vera said.

Nita folded her arms across her chest as she struggled to remain calm. Marshall had been after her to make her membership official, but she wanted her feelings about churchgoing to come naturally, so she'd yet to join. But she had promised Marshall that she would try to get along with these women, and she meant that. Or at least she'd meant it before Vera and her crew had formed a line blocking Nita's path down the hallway to the conference room.

"I will tell you again. Marshall asked me to meet him here, and he said I was more than welcome to sit in on the meeting," Nita said with as much politeness as she could muster. Oddly enough, she had planned to join church last Sunday, but when the time came, she just couldn't pull herself up off the pew bench. Even still, that didn't give these biddies the right to deny her access to the meeting.

"Well"—Addie threw up her hands in disgust—"Reverend Wiley obviously isn't thinking with the right head."

The other three women turned and looked at her in horror.

"Well, he ain't," Addie said, scrunching up her nose.

Vera cut her eyes before turning back to Nita. "Why don't you just go wait in the sanctuary foyer?"

"Or better yet, go wait in your car," Lucy threw in.

Okay, enough is enough. Nita stepped in Vera's face and wiggled her finger. "Let me tell you something! I don't know who—" Before she could finish her sentence, Vera had reached into her purse, taken out a small bottle, and flung the contents at Nita. Nita jumped as she wiped the liquid off her face.

"Oh, my God, what did you throw on me?" she asked, dabbing at her eyes.

"Holy water," Vera said triumphantly.

Nita knew holy water was harmless, but she didn't like anything being thrown in her face. She reached out and shoved Vera with all her might. The woman screamed as she went careening to the floor.

"Juanita!" Marshall yelled. She turned around to see her fiancé standing in the hallway with two of the deacons.

"Oh, Lord Jesus, I think she broke my hip," Vera said. "I'm just a little old lady, and she attacked me. Help me! Help me! I think I'm having a stroke."

"You attacked an old woman!" Lucy yelled at Nita as she knelt down next to Vera.

Vera dramatically grabbed Lucy's blouse. "Lucy, don't let me die. Please don't let me die."

Nita's mouth dropped open. She couldn't believe the performance this woman was putting on.

"Sister Vera, are you all right?" Marshall said, concerned, leaning down beside her.

"No. That Jezebel attacked me without cause!" Vera clutched her chest. "I was just trying to spread the word of God, and she attacked me."

"She threw something in my face!" Nita yelled.

"Are you okay?" he asked Vera.

"I just dashed a little holy water, trying to bless her. Lord Jesus, that's all I was trying to do," Vera said in a pathetic voice.

Nita could not believe her eyes. *Were those tears coming down Vera's cheeks?*

Marshall stood, his glare fixed on Nita. "Juanita, I need to speak with you in my office right now," he demanded. "Deacon, can you see after Sister Vera?"

"Pastor . . ." Vera clutched Marshall's leg.

"Deacon Barrett will help you out," Marshall said, removing Vera's hand.

"Get up, Vera, because you know you're faking," Deacon Barrett muttered as he knelt to help her.

"Juanita, please. Come on," Marshall said firmly.

Nita stared at the debacle unfolding before her eyes. "Coco, I'll be back," she said before stomping off toward Marshall's office.

"Have you lost your mind?" he asked, slamming his office door, barely giving her time to get in.

"Me? What about them? They were the ones attacking me," she said defensively.

"On the contrary, it looked to me like you were the one doing the attacking. Do you remember? Vera was on the floor and you were standing over her."

Nita threw up her hands. "Okay, so I pushed her. I didn't know she was going to fall over."

"Okay, so she's seventy-five years old!" Marshall roared.

Nita had never seen Marshall this mad. Maybe

she had gone too far. The woman was old. Normally, Nita would've backed down to someone that old just out of respect.

Marshall took a deep breath, trying to calm himself. "Juanita, I know they give you a hard time. We talked about that. But you said you could handle them. Is this how you handle them?"

"Of course it's not," Nita said, discouraged. She knew she should've just walked away. It wasn't like she even needed to be at the meeting. She had come to wait on Marshall because they had dinner plans. He'd asked her to come back so she could meet all the deacons.

"If this isn't the right way to handle it, why'd you push Vera down?" Marshall asked.

"I guess I snapped."

"You can't snap on a seventy-five-year-old woman."

"Okay, fine. I shouldn't have pushed her. But she shouldn't have thrown that water in my face."

He sighed, then looked at her sternly, like he knew she was going to be upset at what he was about to say. "I need you to apologize to Sister Vera."

She raised an eyebrow. "You've got to be kidding."

"Juanita, for me, please apologize."

She stood silent, fuming for a minute. "Uuugh," she finally huffed. "Fine."

Marshall was grateful she hadn't continued to fight him on it. "Thank you."

Nita cut her eyes. If this didn't prove she was into Marshall, she didn't know what would.

"Come on," he said, heading toward the door.

"Where are we going?" Nita asked.

"To go apologize."

"*Now?*"

"Now is as good a time as any."

Nita rolled her eyes but then caught herself as Marshall shot her a stern look.

"Fine," she snapped again, nearly knocking him over as she stomped into the hall.

Vera was sitting in the kitchen area, a wet towel across her forehead. Her friends were hovering around her like crows tending to their wounded. As soon as they noticed her, each of them shot her the evil eye.

"What, you came to finish her off?" Lucy snapped.

Nita looked at Marshall, who nodded reassuringly. "Well," she said, turning back to face Vera, "I just came to a——." She stopped as a cough got caught in her throat. She coughed for a few seconds before continuing. "I just wanted to apologize if I hurt you, Vera."

"*If* you hurt her," Lucy said.

"Ooooow," Vera groaned as she dabbed the towel over her face. "I think I have a concussion."

"Vera, you don't have a concussion," Deacon Barrett said disgustedly from the back of the room. Nita hadn't even noticed him standing there, sipping on something in a foam cup.

"How do you know she doesn't have a concussion?" Lucy asked.

"'Cause she wouldn't have been sitting up here cackling with you all just a minute ago if she did," Deacon Barrett said.

"Well, my head still hurts," Vera groaned.

"Well, I'm sorry. I was out of line pushing you," Nita said, without much feeling.

Vera sat up and pointed her finger at Nita. "You sure were. And this is exactly why Pastor doesn't need—" She stopped when Lucy sharply squeezed her shoulder. She must've realized how quickly she'd forgotten what pain she was in, because she leaned back against the chair, put the towel back over her eyes, and moaned. "Oooow, I need to go to the emergency room."

Nita exhaled in frustration as she shot Marshall a see-what-I'm-dealing-with look.

"Sister Vera," Marshall said, taking a seat next to her, "you do know we're in the House of the Lord.

He wouldn't like you sitting up here being untruthful about the extent of your injuries."

Vera removed the towel, her expression saying she hadn't thought about that. "I am hurt," she said meekly.

"Then I will call an ambulance," he responded, easing out of the chair.

She grabbed his arm. "But I guess I'll be all right." She cut her eyes at Nita. "Just keep your woman away from me."

Nita walked to the other side of the room, to remain out of temptation. These women made her sick.

"Sister Vera, I know you and the others only have my best interest at heart," Marshall said. "But I need you to show Juanita some respect."

Vera scoffed. "Please."

"Yes, please," Marshall replied. "Whether you like it or not, she is going to be my wife. And your first lady."

"But, Pastor, you deserve someone so much better . . ."

"Better by whose standards?" he gently said. "Do you remember Bible study a few weeks ago when I talked about Second Corinthians, five:ten? For we must all appear before the judgment seat of Christ?"

"I'm ready," Vera said defensively. "I have no

doubt God is gonna open those pearly gates for me. But I can't say the same about that woman you want to marry."

It was taking everything in Nita's power to remain quiet, but she wanted to let Marshall handle this. She was just grateful that he was finally putting these women in their place.

"That's great that you're ready," he said. "But you don't know Juanita's relationship with God. You don't know where she's come from, or where she's going."

"I know where she's going," Lucy chimed in. "Straight to hel———."

"Sister Lucy, please!" Marshall said, cutting her off. "My point is, that judgment they talk about in Second Corinthians is one that realizes that until the *last day,* there is always room for repentance and forgiveness and that *only* God knows the heart and what stage of work He is at in a man's heart. It is a judgment of things temporal and not eternal, for *only God* can judge the eternal salvation of man."

Vera was at a loss for words. For the first time in as long as she could remember, Nita was moved by a spiritual insight.

"Fine," Vera said, standing up and motioning for the others to come on.

"So, you'll try to be nicer?" Marshall asked.

Vera rolled her eyes. "I'll try. But I can't make any promises." She stomped out of the room, her friends in tow, none of them bothering to look at Nita as they exited.

"Oooh, Pastor, you have your hands full," Deacon Barrett said as he followed them out.

Marshall looked gravely at Nita, who was still standing in the corner. "Sorry I couldn't get her to commit to being nicer."

Nita smiled to show her appreciation. "No, what you did was more than enough." She reached out to hug him.

"Just trust in me, okay?" he asked, walking into her arms.

"I'm trying," she said, squeezing him tightly. She'd never known a man like Marshall. Between the celibacy, the ability to take a Bible verse and relate it to everyday life—something her childhood pastor used to do—and his standing up for her, something no man had ever done, Nita felt herself drawing closer and closer to him. She shivered as she thought of the fact that every good thing in her life she'd messed up. Marshall was the real thing.

31

Audra counted out the stack of money one more time. ". . . eight hundred, nine hundred, one thousand. And here's the promissory note." She slid the paper toward Coco.

"Audra, is all of this really necessary?" Coco said, groaning.

"Yes, it is," Audra said, "because you know how I feel about borrowing money from friends."

Audra had turned to Coco in a last-ditch effort to scrounge up the money for her rent. The office manager had given her until today to pay or she'd be evicted. Since Audra already owed Nita three hundred dollars, Coco was the only person left to turn to.

Audra had felt sick driving over to Coco's job to pick up the money. As broke as she always was, she knew things were tight for everyone. But Coco had graciously agreed to loan Audra a thousand of the three thousand dollars she had in her savings account.

"You know I would not be doing this if I wasn't desperate," Audra said.

"I know that, girl," Coco replied softly. "Just take the money. I'm blessed to be able to help other people out. I mean, you'd do the same thing for me, so I don't know what the big deal is."

Audra tucked the wad of money into her purse. "I feel better if we have something in writing, that's all. That way you can be sure I'm going to pay you back."

"Okay," Coco said, folding the note up and putting it in her pocket. "Whatever makes you happy."

Audra reached over and hugged her friend. "You're a lifesaver. Thank you so much. I know you need to get back in there to your class, and I need to get over and pay this rent before they put me out."

Audra said good-bye, raced to her car, and then headed back to her apartment complex.

"Hi, Shawnda, how are you," Audra said, making her way into the leasing office. She was grateful that the manager wasn't at her desk. She preferred dealing with the assistant, who at least would try to be nice to her.

Shawnda, a honey brown girl with a head full of burgundy braids, was standing over her desk, sifting through papers. "Hey, how are you?" she said, smiling pleasantly.

"I'm good. I just wanted to drop off my rent," Audra said, digging in her purse for the money.

Shawnda frowned, then shuffled some papers on her desk. "You're in Unit Twenty-three, right?"

"I am," Audra said, laying the cash on Shawnda's desk. "Here's the rent plus the late charges. I want to apologize for being late. It's just that I was laid off and things have been really hard."

Shawnda looked confused. "I'm sorry. There must be some mistake."

"What do you mean?" Audra asked.

"Your rent is paid."

"Excuse me?"

"Your rent is paid. For the past due amount, plus the next two months."

"What? Paid by who?"

Shawnda sifted through some more papers and pulled out a manila folder. "A Mr. Lewis Jackson called in and paid it."

Audra was floored. Lewis knew about her financial problems, but she never would've expected this. "When? I mean, Mrs. Anderson was just at my place Tuesday. She gave me until today to pay."

"He called in the day before yesterday. That's why

I remembered," Shawnda said. "He overnighted a cashier's check." She held up the check, which was attached to the piece of paper she'd been reading from.

"Wow" was all Audra could say.

"So you didn't know anything about it?"

"No, I didn't."

Shawnda put the check in the drawer, picked up the cash, and handed it back to Audra. "Well, I don't want to get all up in your business, but is that your boyfriend?"

"Ummm, he was," Audra said, taking the money. "We broke up."

Shawnda looked very curious to hear the story. "Umph, sounds like to me somebody is trying to get back in good graces. Girl, I wish I had a man like that." She fanned herself a little. "I don't know what he did, but paying three months' rent should be enough to make you forgive him. I'm trying to get my man to give me twenty dollars on this month's rent, and he lives with me."

Audra mumbled a halfhearted thank-you as she backed toward the door.

"Girl, forgive him," Shawnda called out after her. "Men don't just come up with that kind of money if they're not serious about you."

Audra tuned her out as she walked back to her apartment. So, Lewis was trying to buy his way back into her good graces. The more she thought about the nerve of him to think she'd be that easy, the angrier she became. Yes, she'd vowed not to call him, but this was a plausible exception.

Audra stomped into her apartment, grateful that neither Miss Bea nor Andrew was home. She snatched up her phone and punched in Lewis's cell phone number.

"Hello." Lewis answered like he was expecting her call.

"So you think you can just pay my rent and that'll make everything okay?" Audra snapped, skipping the formalities.

"Wow, what happened to 'Thanks, Lewis, I really appreciated that because I didn't know how I was going to pay my rent and me and my son would've been out on the street'?"

"I would've found a way to pay my rent. I did find a way to pay it," she spat, even though in the back of her mind she was already thinking she could take the money she'd borrowed from Coco and pay for Andrew's soccer camp. "So you don't have to worry about me or my son!"

"Okay." He chuckled defensively. "I believe you.

All I was trying to do was make things a little easier. I know times are tough."

"Don't worry about how tough times are." She took small, deep breaths. Just talking to him was getting her worked up. "You need to be worrying about your wife."

"Look, Audra. I don't know what to say. I'm sorry again. A hundred times I'm sorry."

Audra wanted to continue going off. She had so much pent-up anger that she didn't know what to do. But another part of her longed for answers. Just some rational reason why he would hurt her the way he did. She was quiet a minute before saying, "Did you ever have any feelings for me, or was this all just a big game?"

"Audra, you have to understand, I wasn't lying about my feelings for you." The cockiness in his voice was gone, and he now sounded genuine. "When I met you, you made me feel alive. I was serious when I said my marriage to Michelle has all but been arranged since we were teenagers. We were members of the same church. We went to the same college. We were destined to be together." He sounded like all this planning was tedious to him. "But Michelle is the consummate first lady. We can't do anything that might embarrass us. There's no spontaneity, no excitement whatsoever. You brought that to me, made me realize what I was missing."

"Why weren't you just honest?" she asked, her rage subsiding.

"Would you have given me half a chance if I had been honest?"

Audra remained silent, and he answered for her. "Of course not."

"Well, how long did you think you could carry this on?" she finally said.

He sounded contrite, like he knew he hadn't been thinking. "I don't know. When I first started talking to you, I was just living in the moment. I knew my life was about to change drastically, and I just wanted to have some fun."

"Yeah, at my expense."

"I never meant for it to be that way. I came to Houston to have a good time, and that was supposed to be it. Then I started enjoying spending time with you so much that I didn't want to let you go."

None of this explanation was making her feel better. "So, you were going to marry her, then what?"

"I don't know," he exclaimed. "I played it out in my head so many times and still couldn't come up with an answer. You mean a lot to me. But leading this church means a lot to me as well. It's my calling."

Audra couldn't believe he was talking about leading a church. He was a lying dog and still talking like he was ordained from God.

"I'll be honest with you," Lewis continued. "I'm not in love with Michelle, not like a husband should be in love with his wife. I knew that when I married her. But I told myself maybe one day I'll get there. For now, we'll just build this church up. She's good at that. She's what I need in my life professionally. But you're what I need in my life personally. Audra, I love you and I don't want to lose you."

Audra felt sick in the pit of her stomach. This entire mess was too much for her. Why was her luck with men so bad? She finally finds a man that's really into her, and he belongs to someone else.

"All I know is, since I've met you, I've been happier than I've been in a long time." Her silence must have empowered him, as if he knew he was getting to her, because his words became more passionate. "I've been absolutely miserable without you. And then you wouldn't take my calls or answer my e-mails. So if paying your rent was the only way I could get you to call me, then it's worth every cent. Even if you hang up and never talk to me again, I'm just happy I got a chance to tell you how I really feel."

Audra was so confused. Was this more of his game? And if so, why did he sound so sincere?

"Audra, I know this is asking a lot, but don't give up on me." His voice cracked with desperation.

She started pacing back and forth. "Lewis, do you hear yourself? *Don't give up on you?* You're married! You just got married."

"I know," he said quietly. "Just give me some time to figure all of this out."

"And what am I supposed to do while you're figuring all of this out?" Her heart was aching so bad, and she hated the fact that his words were making it hurt even more.

"Just be there for me," Lewis said. "Let me be there for you."

"How? How are you going to be there for me when you're in Atlanta? With your wife."

"I don't know," he cried. "I just can't lose you."

"So you want me to be your mistress? You think that's all I want out of life, to be somebody's mistress?" Audra didn't give him time to respond. She was tired of talking to him, and she felt like the more she did talk to him, the more he was digging his clutches into her, and that was something she definitely didn't want.

"Lewis, I'm going to say this to you again,"

she said as calmly as she could. "I started with you thinking that we had a future, and you knew the whole time that we didn't. I'm sorry, but I'm all out of chances. So thank you for paying my rent. I don't know how or when, but I will pay you back. Until then, please don't call me again." She slammed the phone down before she changed her mind.

32

As Coco stepped out of the shower, her cell phone rang. She picked it up, not recognizing the 903 number. She answered anyway because she did know the call was from Tyler. Maybe her mom had gotten a new number.

"Hello," Coco said.

"Cosandra?" the voice said hesitantly. "Hi, um, my name is Laura. You don't know me, but I'm a friend of your mom's."

Coco's heart began racing. "What's going on?"

"I don't know quite how to tell you this . . . but there's been an accident. Your mother has been hurt."

"What? Is she—"

"No, she's okay, although it's pretty bad."

"What happened?" Coco asked, becoming more frantic.

"We don't know," the woman responded. "They think she might have been attacked. Robbery maybe."

"A robbery? In Tyler?" Coco knew it sounded crazy. As if there were no criminals in Tyler, Texas.

"Is there any way you can come?" the woman asked.

"I'm on my way. Where is she?"

"The East Texas Medical Center."

"Okay, I'm on my way."

Coco could barely keep her hands steady as she closed the phone. She grabbed a dress, slid it over her head, and raced into Nita's room. She swung the door open without even knocking.

"Hey, girl, what's up?" Nita asked. She was lying across her bed watching the *I Love New York* marathon. The distressed expression on Coco's face caused her to immediately sit up. "What's wrong?"

"Mama's been hurt. They said it's bad. I have to go to Tyler."

"Then I'm going with you." Nita tossed back the covers and jumped out of bed. "You just try to relax," she said as she threw on some clothes. "Go grab a bag, and we'll be on the road in ten minutes."

"Okay." Coco was relieved that Nita had offered

to drive her, because, to tell the truth, she didn't know how she would've been able to drive all that way herself.

Four hours later, Nita and Coco pulled into the parking lot at East Texas Medical Center. Coco had tried to find out more details on the drive up. But she hadn't been able to get in touch with her father or Laura, and the hospital wouldn't tell her anything over the phone.

Nita let Coco out while she went to park. Coco raced inside and was directed to her mother's room.

Coco eased the door open, expecting to see her father sitting at her mother's bedside. When she didn't see him, her antennae immediately went up. With slow steps, Coco made her way into the room. She had to struggle to fight back tears. Her mother's right eye was swollen, her left arm was in a cast, and her lips were a deep shade of blue.

"Hey, baby girl," she said, her eyes fluttering open.

"Mama . . ."

"You shouldn't have come," her mother struggled to say.

"Ssssh, you know I was going to come, so don't even waste your energy talking that foolishness," Coco said, gently kissing her mother on the forehead.

"I don't want you to see me like this," her mother said, ashamed.

"Mama, what happened?" The more Coco thought about it, the more a robbery story didn't add up. No way would her mother have gone to a store at night by herself. The way her mother's eyes closed, Coco knew her hunch was right. "Mama, the lady that called me said there had been a robbery. That isn't true, is it? Be honest. Did Daddy do this to you?"

She could tell her mother was torn. "He's been under a lot of stress lately," she finally said.

Coco grimaced as she squeezed the tissue tightly in her hands.

"I was leaving him," her mother blurted out, like she'd just decided to go ahead and be honest. "I mean, for real leaving him."

"What?" In all the years that her mother had been suffering abuse at the hands of her father, Coco had no idea she was contemplating leaving.

"I told him I was leaving," her mother repeated. Her voice was raspy, and her face was weary. "I was just tired. It's been a lifetime." Her mother almost seemed to be talking to herself. She swallowed hard, then turned to Coco. "You know, you gave me the strength."

"What did I do?"

"What I couldn't," she said matter-of-factly. "You walked away from Sonny. You had the strength I never did. Watching you going on with your life, picking up the pieces after Sonny, I don't know, it was just empowering for me. I was proud of the woman you'd become and"—she paused and swallowed hard—"it inspired me to change myself."

At this point Coco could no longer contain her tears. The ironic part was she'd finally found the strength to leave Sonny because she didn't want to end up like her mother.

"For years I've been judged," her mother continued. "People have looked at me crazy for staying with your father, but I knew the good side of him and I kept trying to recapture that. Then I realized that I had lost my way with your father. From the beginning, I let him think it was okay to abuse me. I wanted to leave many times, but I always had an excuse. You, our life." Her lips pursed in hopelessness. "I felt like I could change him. I knew it would be hard trying to be a single mother. I always had an excuse."

"I hate him," Coco heard herself saying. She'd never been close to her father, and this latest attack was only going to deepen the divide.

"Don't hate him, baby," her mother pleaded. "It's

the only thing he knew. It's how he was raised and he just continued the cycle." She coughed, then took a sip from the cup on the nightstand. After she'd rested for a minute, she continued. "It broke my heart the first time I learned Sonny put his hands on you. I prayed that it was a onetime outburst, and the fact that you never mentioned it again made me think that it was." Coco stared at her mother as she bared her soul. Yeah, she'd stopped telling her mother about Sonny's abuse, but only because she was too embarrassed to let her mother know, especially because as a teen she had so fervently wished her mother would leave her father.

"Then to find out you were putting up with that." Her mother sighed wearily. "Well, I knew you were only putting up with it because it was what you knew. I wasn't a good example. I knew I couldn't change what I had done to you, but I could change my future. What was left of it, anyway. So I told him I was leaving. He laughed at first and told me to go sit down and shut up, which is what I did." She met Coco's eye. "I tried to leave today when he went to work. But he came home early just as I was leaving and flew into a rage."

"Mama, where is Daddy now? Did you report it?"

A tear trickled down her mother's cheek. "Baby,

that's your father. I don't want him to go to jail or lose his job. I just want him to get some help. He used to be such a good man, but his demons finally took over."

Coco felt like she was looking into a mirror. Those were her same reasons for not reporting Sonny.

Coco could tell the conversation had drained her mother; her eyes were heavy. "Mama, just be quiet. Get you some rest. You don't have to deal with all of this right now. You get better, then you can come stay with me."

Her mother vehemently shook her head. "No, baby, I got a good feeling about you and Davis, and I want you to build a beautiful life together without any interference from your mother. And besides, I don't know how your dad is gonna take me really leaving. I'm not going to bring that drama into your life."

Coco was grateful to hear that her mother was still planning to leave, but she couldn't just let her fend for herself.

"But, Mama . . ."

"But Mama nothing. I've already talked to Shirley," her mother said, referring to her sister in Georgia. "As soon as I get better, I'm going to leave here. He doesn't know where Shirley lives, you see. I never told him that she moved from Orlando."

Her mother must've read her expression because she repeated, "Coco, I'm going to be all right. Don't hate your father, okay?"

Coco felt her blood boiling. At sixty years old, her mother was having to virtually go underground to escape her husband. She wiped away her tears. Not hating her father was going to be mighty hard, because when she looked at her mother lying in that bed, beaten and bruised, all she felt was a desire to strangle him.

33

This woman was definitely about to make her change her mind.

". . . so, I don't know what little plan you have up your sleeve, but Lewis is off-limits," Michelle said.

Audra had been shocked beyond belief when she'd answered the "private" number on her cell phone and heard Lewis's wife on the other end. She'd debated hanging up instantly, but the fact that this woman was calling her made Audra want to hear her out.

"Now, I know you've done something and got Lewis's nose all wide open, but nobody is going to mess up what I have going," the woman said.

Audra was still stunned. Michelle seemed more concerned with the fact that Audra might be jeopardizing "her plan" than that she was sleeping with her husband.

"I will say this again, Michelle, you need to be talking to your husband and not me," Audra finally said.

"No, I'm talking to who I need to be talking to," she retorted. Lewis's wife was trying her best to sound tough, but Audra could tell from the shakiness in her voice, she was full of hot air.

"See, I know your type," Michelle continued. "You prey on lonely men like Lewis."

"You need to be asking yourself why your man is lonely. If he loves you so much, why was he cheating with me?" Audra hadn't planned to go there, but Michelle had a lot of nerve, calling her and charging her up.

"What's love got to do with it?" Michelle laughed. "Lewis doesn't need to love me. Just like I don't need to love him. Love is irrelevant. The only thing we need to love is the life we're going to build."

Was she for real? Did she just admit that she didn't love Lewis? And she knew Lewis didn't love her? What kind of woman was okay with that?

"So, I'm telling you for the last time, back off," Michelle said.

"And I'm telling you for the last time, I haven't been calling your husband. Your husband has been calling me."

"I know that," Michelle said. "And I'm telling you, the next time he calls, you need to make it clear that it's over."

"I've already done that. It's not my fault he won't listen." Lewis had been calling nonstop. "Look, I told you, I didn't know Lewis was involved with someone, let alone getting married. So if you have issues with anyone, it needs to be your husband."

Michelle sighed heavily, like she couldn't believe she was wasting her time. "Look, I know you are a struggling welfare mother—"

"Excuse me," Audra said hotly. "I don't know where you get your information, but I am not on welfare."

"Whatever," Michelle said. "I know you are a struggling single mother, and I could make it worth your while to disappear from our lives."

Audra had to lean back in her chair. Was Michelle so threatened by her that she would pay her to disappear? As much as she needed money, Audra wasn't about to sell her soul to the wife of the man she loved.

"Ten thousand dollars. Delivered in your account tomorrow," the woman said. The way she said it made Audra feel cheap, like she had no doubt Audra would jump at the money.

"Michelle, let me tell you what you can do with your money—" Audra growled.

"Okay." Michelle cut her off. "I'm sorry. I wasn't trying to offend you." Her voice had taken a softer tone. "Lewis and I just don't need this drama. Our plan—"

It was Audra's turn to cut her off. "*Your plan.* That's all you seem to be concerned with."

"That's all that matters," Michelle retorted. "What, I'm supposed to pretend that love can help us accomplish our dreams?"

"Do you even love your husband?" Audra couldn't help but ask.

Michelle laughed. "I told you, what does love have to do with it?"

"I'll take that for a no." Audra was so disgusted. She'd finally found some happiness in her life and it was destroyed by a woman who didn't even want Lewis's love. "Look, if you have an issue with me, you need to talk to your husband. I'm not contacting him. I don't want to contact him, and we are over." The words stung even as they left her mouth. "So please do not call me again." Audra slammed her phone shut. She closed her eyes and took a deep breath, trying to ward off the tears and the thoughts of how, given the chance, she could've loved Lewis like he deserved to be loved.

34

Coco sipped on the chamomile tea as Davis gently massaged her feet.

"Thank you so much for being here with me," she said.

He smiled. "I wouldn't be anywhere else. I just hate that you didn't call me to go to Tyler with you."

It had been a full twenty-four hours since Coco and Nita had returned from Tyler. She'd called Davis on the way there, and he'd tried to get off from work and come meet them. She'd convinced him to wait, but he wasn't happy about it. They'd stayed in Tyler for three days, and she had to literally beg him to stay at home.

"You know, if I'm going to be in your life, you need to let me be there for you," Davis said.

Coco could only stare at him. She wasn't used to such compassion. Sonny would've only been worried about how soon she was coming back.

"I guess I have to get used to that," she said.

"Used to what?"

She shrugged. "I don't know, the whole 'being there for me.'"

He moved her legs out of his lap, took her cup, and set it down on the coffee table. He then took both of her hands in his. "Coco, I need you to understand, I don't play games. I'm old school, and that means I believe in my woman turning to me in times of need. I understand your girls have your back, and I'm appreciative of that. But promise me that, from now on, you'll turn to me in a crisis."

A faint smile crossed her face. "I promise."

He put her feet back on his lap and resumed massaging.

"So how's your mom?" he asked.

"She's on her way to Georgia. They released her right before we left."

"I'm sure your dad was happy she was able to get out so soon," Davis added.

Coco cringed at the mention of her father. He'd been calling her all day trying to find out where her mother had gone. When she wouldn't tell him, he'd gone off, and Coco hadn't answered any of his calls since.

Before they'd left Tyler, Coco had wanted to go see her father, let him know how she felt, but Nita had talked her out of it, convincing her that they had no idea what frame of mind her father was in. They had staked out the house, and when he left, they went inside and collected some of her mother's important items. They knew he would be upset, but Coco also knew her father was scared of going to jail, so she wasn't worried about him showing up at the hospital.

Coco debated telling Davis the truth about her mother's situation. But she hadn't shared her own history with him, so she didn't know how to broach the subject. Finally, though, she decided to be honest.

"Ummm, Davis, my mom isn't going to Georgia to visit. She's going to stay. She's leaving my father. She's gonna file for divorce."

"What?" Davis exclaimed. "Didn't you tell me they'd been married for years?"

Coco sadly nodded. "They have, but truthfully, my mother should've left a long time ago."

Davis's expression was conflicted.

"What?" Coco said.

He shook his head. "Cosandra, have you tried to talk to your mom?"

"Yeah, I've been telling her she should leave."

He looked at her in amazement. "Are you serious? You've been pushing your mother to leave her marriage?"

Coco dropped her feet to the floor. "Yes." She stared at Davis intently. "My mother was being abused. My father has been abusing her for years."

Coco's hackles rose when Davis didn't flinch.

"Did you hear me?" Coco asked. "My father is physically abusive."

Davis was quiet for a moment, then said, "The Bible only allows for divorce under infidelity and abandonment."

"So you think a woman should stay married even if she's being abused?" She was dumbfounded. Never in a million years would she have thought that Davis would have such a patriarchal view of wedlock.

"The Bible doesn't advocate divorce for abuse. That's the bottom line," he said matter-of-factly. "The couple should separate and try to work things out, but divorce shouldn't be an option."

Coco continued to stare in disbelief. Her grandmother used to have a saying that someone was "so heavenly that they were no earthly good." That was the image that was coming to her mind with Davis.

Davis must've known he pushed a wrong button,

because he said, "You know what, let's just agree to disagree for now. I wasn't trying to upset you. You've had a rough couple of days."

Coco was all too happy to let that issue drop, because she was now wondering if Davis had other old-style views.

"Matter of fact," he continued, "I need to call my job and tell them I'm not coming in today."

"No, Davis," Coco said. "A supervisor shouldn't be calling in." Part of her was thinking maybe he should go ahead and go to work so she could process everything he'd said.

He looked like he knew she was right but didn't want to admit it.

"Seriously, Davis," she said. "You worked hard to get that supervisor spot, and you don't need to be taking off to babysit me. I'm just going to lay here and get some rest. I'll be fine." Coco was trying not to let her irritation show, but she must not have been succeeding, because Davis took her hand.

"Are you mad?"

Coco tried to shrug him off. "Like you said, we'll agree to disagree." She stood up and pushed him toward the door. "Now, go to work."

He kissed her gently. "You call me if you need anything."

"Bye, Davis," she said, opening the door.

Coco tried to push his comments out of her head. Maybe she was reading too much into them. Davis was dang near perfect. Surely he wouldn't condone a woman staying around to get beat up.

At last Coco got comfortable on the sofa and began grading papers. She'd been reading for ten minutes when her phone rang. She was almost positive that it was Davis calling to check on her already.

"Hello," she said into the phone.

"Hello, beautiful."

Sonny's voice stopped her cold. It was bad enough he had tracked down where she was staying. Now he had her new cell phone number, too? Coco silently cursed her father. He had to have given it to Sonny when he'd given him the address.

"Sonny, why are you bothering me? I told you it was over, and unless you want your mug shot all in the newspaper, leave me alone."

"What difference does it make now?" he said, dispirited. "I got the diagnosis back on my knee. I'll never play again."

That made her stop. She knew he had to be devastated by that news. That was part of what began his downward spiral. His devastation at being cut, then the revelation that his knee was injured so badly, his chances of getting picked up were slim. But he'd stayed hopeful that the latest surgery would repair his torn ligament.

"So when I'm down, you bounce out, huh?" he said.

"Sonny, let's not do this."

"I'm not understanding how everything was fine for so long, then all of a sudden, you want to start trippin'."

"Everything was not fine, Sonny!" She took a deep breath. "I stuck around hoping that you would turn around one day. But you didn't. And it took me losing my baby to realize that the man I once loved didn't exist anymore. The whole football injury thing has made you bitter and unbearable." Coco didn't know where this newfound strength was coming from, but regardless, she liked the new her, the one willing to stand up for herself. Maybe being with Davis had made her realize she deserved better. Maybe knowing her mother had been inspired by her made her feel like she couldn't let her mother down. Either way, Coco wasn't going to be Sonny's punching bag anymore.

"Sonny, look, part of it is my fault, because I let you do the things to me that you did."

"Coco, just give me another chance," he pleaded. "I need you."

"Sonny, no. I'm done. I've moved on."

"What does that mean?"

She sighed heavily. "It means what it means."

"Are you seeing somebody else?"

While she might have some renewed strength, she wasn't crazy. She was not about to tread down that road with Sonny. At the same time, she didn't want to deny what she and Davis had.

"Sonny, you know what? We're over, and I'm asking you for the last time, please stop calling me."

She slammed the phone shut before he could say another word. Just as she did, a small smile spread across her face. That was liberating. But as quickly as the smile came, it disappeared—because she knew Sonny. He didn't take rejection well. She could only imagine how he would react.

35

Nita stood off to the side and watched while Marshall greeted the members and guests as they left the church. She couldn't help but notice the number of women who lingered a little too long, let their hands fall a little too far down Marshall's back. Some did everything but take their panties off and write their phone numbers on them.

Marshall, as usual, seemed oblivious. "Sister Ellen, you're working that canary yellow."

Ellen put her hand to her chest. "You like, Pastor? Gotta look good for the Lord."

"Well, now, you know the Lord don't care how you look when you come to praise Him."

She giggled like a silly schoolgirl, and Nita couldn't help but roll her eyes.

"Still want to be first lady?" Coco walked up behind her friend and whispered in her ear.

Nita let out a heavy sigh. "Girl, I don't know anymore. Between these desperate hoochies feignin' over my fiancé and the Holy Rollers sitting in judgment, I don't know how much more I can take."

Coco nudged Nita with her hip. "I gotta go, Davis is waiting. But speaking of Holy Rollers . . ."

Coco darted off, and Nita turned her attention to Vera and Lucy making their way over to her. Vera and her crew didn't harass Nita anymore, but their looks spoke volumes. Nita wondered how they got anything out of the service since they spent so much time gawking at her.

"What?" Nita asked as they approached.

Vera waved a white handkerchief. "We come in peace," she said, like it pained her.

Nita eyed them skeptically.

"Look, you know how we feel, but Pastor made some good points. We don't want to judge anyone. And I sure don't want God to hold anything against me when I go meet Him. So, I'm sorry."

Nita waited for the punch line. When Vera didn't say anything either, she said, "Okay, I'm sorry, too."

"But," Vera added. Nita should've known there

was a but. "Well, there's some things we can't keep quiet on and"—she pointed to Nita's short paisley peasant dress—"if you're goin' to be our first lady—"

"You can't be wearing trampish outfits like that," Lucy interjected.

Vera shot her an exasperated look.

"What?" Lucy exclaimed. "All this hemming and hawing around. Just tell the girl already."

Vera turned back to Nita. "We're just saying, if you have to be our first lady, you have an image to uphold. Now, we know a good place where you can get some lace suits and some wonderful hats."

Nita looked at them like they were crazy. "I'm not wearing a lace suit, and I dang sure ain't wearing a hat."

Vera gasped. "What kind of first lady doesn't wear a hat?"

Nita held her hands up. She wasn't about to do this. "You know what . . . I'm leaving before I tell you what you can do with your hats."

Nita spun and stormed off. She'd parked in the back, so she had to pass Marshall as she headed down the corridor that led to the back parking lot. "Juanita!" he called out.

"What?" Nita said, spinning to face him.

"What is going on? Why are you racing out of here like that?"

"Because I'm sick and tired of these people!" She massaged her temples. Once again, they'd given her a headache.

"What now?" he asked.

"Now they have the nerve to complain about what I have on."

He eyed her outfit. "It's cute." He hesitated, then smiled. "But I'm gonna have to agree, it's a little inappropriate for church."

"Are you serious?" she asked incredulously.

"Don't be mad, sweetie. We just need to go shopping for some more appropriate church clothes. My treat."

She was fed up. "I can't believe you. So these people can disrespect me, judge me, tell me how to dress, how to worship. I have to deal with all of that *and* you won't screw me! How much am I expected to take?"

He looked horrified. "Can we not have this discussion in the church hallway?"

"What? Your loyal followers would be proud to know that their pastor is celibate." She hadn't intended on going there, but since she had, she was about to tell him how she really felt. "You don't want me to touch you, but you let those women out there feel you all up!"

"Juanita!" he huffed. "Do not do this!"

She motioned down the empty hallway. "You have got to be kidding me. There's no one around."

"That's not the point," he said. "You will not make me feel bad about my decision to honor God's wishes."

Nita was about to light into him when Deacon Barrett appeared at the other end of the hall.

"Pastor!" he said. "Come quick! Sister Ellen fell. She might've broken her leg. She's calling for you."

Nita rolled her eyes. "Oh, good grief."

Marshall quickly pecked her on the cheek. "We'll talk later today, okay? Love you." He darted off.

Nita couldn't remember the last time she'd been so livid. Not only did Marshall agree with those old women but then he had the nerve to blow her off for that hussy Ellen, who was probably faking anyway.

"I think your outfit looks great."

Nita's mouth dropped open and her eyes grew wide as Neil rounded the corner. "Neil, what are you doing here?" she said, her eyes darting up and down the hallway.

He shrugged, taking in his surroundings. "I know, it's been a minute since I've been in a church. But I had to come see this great Marshall Wiley that has the love of my life ready to give up on us."

In a panic, Nita grabbed Neil's arm and pulled him out the back door. "The great love of your life is your wife," she hissed once they were outside.

Neil was amused. "You know it's not."

"Why are you here?" she asked again.

"What do they say in the Bible? If Mohammed won't come to the mountain, the mountain goes to Mohammed."

"I don't think that's in the Bible."

"Whatever," he said, laughing. "I need to see you. I miss you so bad." He gave her a broad wink. "And did I hear you say he won't have sex with you?" He ran his eyes up and down her body as he licked his lips. "Has he lost his mind? You are the sexiest woman I've ever seen in my life, and he doesn't want you?"

That stung, and Neil knew it; he moved in closer. "Baby, I want you enough for us both."

"Neil, don't, please," she said. Her knees were starting to feel weak. "M-Marshall is just trying to live right."

"That's cool and all. But you and me, we're *right now* kind of people." He took her hand and eased her index finger into his mouth, sucking it gently. Nita quickly pulled her hand away. "If that didn't make you feel anything, then I guess I'm wrong." He bit his bottom lip like he knew he was right. "But if it did make you feel anything"—he took her hand again, eased something into her palm, then took a step back—"then you'll come and let me make you feel a whole lot more."

He blew her a kiss as he turned and walked away. Nita looked back at the church, then down at her hand. She opened her palm to the small key and piece of paper with an address written on it. She felt a familiar jolt of longing. It was almost like the key was summoning her to throw caution to the wind. She sighed as she debated what to do. Maybe just one time with Neil would get him out of her system for good. Maybe just one time would satisfy her itch that Marshall didn't want to scratch. Just one time, then she could truly focus on being the woman Marshall wanted her to be.

Nita noted the address, dropped the key in her purse, and didn't know whether to smile or cry as she climbed into her car.

36

Audra couldn't believe what she was doing.

Everything inside her was telling her not to do it, but just like she didn't listen to that voice when she went to Atlanta and discovered Lewis was getting married, she wasn't listening now.

Lewis's voice mails were finally crumbling her resolve. He'd apologized for Michelle calling her. He'd left six heartfelt messages, begging for another chance.

And here Audra was on the brink of giving him one. She knew she deserved better, but Lewis had a way with words. He had a way of reaching that part of her that wanted love so bad she'd settle. At least until he figured out a way they could be together.

"Audra, baby, you don't know how happy I am that you called," Lewis said. He sounded thrilled, like he'd really never expected it. "I've been so miserable. I've missed you so much."

His words made her heart heavy. She'd sat with the phone in her hand for nearly three hours before she finally called. A week had elapsed since his last message, the one when he said he wouldn't bother her again. She'd gotten to the point where she was waiting for him to call and leave a message just so she could listen to his voice over and over.

After three days of no calls, Audra found herself justifying what he'd done. She'd seen for herself that his relationship with Michelle was exactly what he'd said it was—a farce. Michelle didn't love him and he didn't love her. No matter what his relationship was with his wife, she knew without a doubt that his feelings for her were real. So, after going back and forth, she'd finally dialed his number.

"Lewis, I don't know why I'm calling you."

"I know," he answered. "You're calling because you love me. No, our situation isn't right now, but our feelings can't be helped."

"Lewis, you're married," she all but whispered.

"In name only. And for professional reasons only. I'm sorry again that Michelle called you."

"Yeah, she's lucky she caught me on a good day."

"Well, I can't believe she did that, but I told you,

she knows how much I love you, and she just wanted you out the picture."

"Lewis, why would you marry her if you don't love her?" Audra asked. She needed to understand.

"I told you, Audra. It's almost like a corporate merger. We could accomplish more if we were together."

"But what does that mean for us? You're asking me to be there for you. Do I just wait this out? Are you even moving in a direction that we could be together?"

"Honestly, I wasn't, because you made it clear you didn't want me. But if you tell me we still have a chance, I will figure something out. Just give me some time."

Audra didn't know what to say. She held the phone as Andrew came racing in the room. "Mommy, Mommy, I just saw on Nickelodeon where you can go to Disney World free on your birthday. Can you take me for my birthday next month, please, please, please," he begged.

Audra dabbed her eyes. "Baby, Mommy's on the phone. I'll talk to you about it in a minute."

"Say yes, Mommy, please!" He bounced up and down.

"Okay, Andrew, I'll think about it. Just go back to your room until Mommy gets off the phone."

"Yay!" he yelled as he took off.

"I'd love to take you and Andrew to Disney World next month," Lewis gently said. "I already bought him a puppy. It was supposed to be a surprise, but I figured I should at least warn you."

"A puppy?" Audra said. "Why would you do that?"

"Andrew needs someone to play with. It's a miniature Yorkie, already housebroken. And I paid the pet deposit at the apartment, so it's not a problem. It should be delivered tomorrow."

Audra loved dogs and Andrew was going to be ecstatic, but she didn't want Lewis to think they could be bought.

"Lewis, do you think buying us stuff will make everything all right?"

"Of course not, Audra," he said. "I messed up. I know the material things don't make up for that, but I want to give small tokens to show how sorry I am."

Audra wiped the tear that had begun slowly trickling down her cheek.

"Just give me some time and I promise you, I'll make you the happiest woman in the world," Lewis continued.

Audra didn't respond as silence filled the phone.

"Just say you'll give me another chance," he said. "Please. I can be good to you and to Andrew."

Audra fought back the feeling that was telling her to hang up. "One more chance. That's it," she softly said.

Audra could feel his joy through the phone as he shouted, "Thank you, baby. You won't regret it!"

She hoped not. But that nagging feeling in her gut told her she would.

37

The wave of guilt that was rippling through her body was unbelievable. Nita closed her eyes and asked herself for the hundredth time what she was doing.

"Let me see that ring," Neil said, interrupting her thoughts.

Nita pulled her hand away. "Why do you need to see my ring?"

"I'm just trippin' over the fact that you're getting married, and to a preacher at that." Neil propped himself up on the bed. Nita's eyes instinctively went to his bare chest.

"Shut up and hand me my bra," she said, looking away.

Neil laughed as he reached over the side of the bed and picked up her purple lace bra.

"Well, answer this, why are you getting married?" he asked, dangling the undergarment in front of her.

"What are you talking about? You're married." Nita snatched the bra.

"Yeah, but that's because it's cheaper to keep her," Neil said. "You, on the other hand, I thought you loved your single lifestyle."

Nita slipped her bra on, then climbed out of the bed, found her matching panties, and slipped them on as well. "In case you hadn't noticed, I'm not getting any younger, and you've been telling that lie about leaving your wife for years. So maybe I just want some stability," she said, slipping the dress over her head.

Neil burst out laughing, and Nita looked at him in disgust. "Sorry," he said, noticing her evil eye. "So you're marrying for stability?"

"Maybe I love him," she said unconvincingly. She knew she cared about Marshall. A lot. So much that she felt sick in the pit of her stomach over what she had just done with Neil. *What was I thinking?*

"If you love him, why are you here with me?" He smiled mischievously.

Nita turned and glared *Why was she here?* At what point in her life did love become more than just sex? "You love your wife, yet you've got me all up in your place."

"I told you, my wife doesn't know about this condo." That was pretty evident from the masculine décor.

Nita had suspected this place, with all of its chocolate leather, large plasma TVs, and surround sound, was Neil's private getaway. That was just like him to have a love nest. "So why are you keeping a secret apartment?" she asked with an attitude. The way she was acting toward him now, you'd never have known that just an hour ago she was loving him all over this secret pad.

"It's not a secret," he said with a smirk. "I just didn't tell her about it. Besides, I used to rent it out, and when the tenant moved out, I just moved in. Kind of my home away from home."

"Whatever, Neil." Nita just wanted to get out of there. All kinds of guilty feelings were unsettling her. She'd actually gone home Sunday after church, then she and Marshall had fought again. Nita stared at that key for two days—until she couldn't take it anymore. She'd phoned Neil and he'd met her here in a matter of minutes. Now she was sick with guilt. Marshall would be devastated if he ever found out what she'd done. And the thought of disappointing him was bothering her more than she would ever have thought possible. She couldn't believe she had risked it all for a man who couldn't give her anything more than a new bracelet and a few hours in the sack.

"I gotta go. This was a mistake," Nita said, walking out of the room.

Neil quickly jumped up and followed her. He stopped her right as she reached the kitchen, grabbing her arm and pulling her back toward him. "Aawww, baby, don't be like that. You can't say you didn't enjoy yourself."

"Neil, let me go," Nita said, trying to pull away.

He pushed her against the refrigerator and began kissing the inside of her lower arm. "I'm sorry, baby." He moved his kisses up her arm until he reached her neck. "Just one more for the road, okay? I've missed you so much," he mumbled as he covered her neck with kisses.

Nita closed her eyes and moaned. This man's kisses were magic.

"Look at what you're missing. When's the last time you felt this good?" he whispered.

Nita wanted to protest, but the truth was, she hadn't felt this good since the last time she'd been with Neil.

She squeezed her eyes shut tighter as she tried to fight the war waging between her head and her body. "Neil . . ."

He put his finger over her lips. "Ssssh, just let me love . . . AAAARRRGH!"

His scream made her eyes shoot wide open, and she watched in horror as Neil's body convulsed, then tumbled to the ground, shaking violently. Slowly, Nita's gaze made its way up to the source of his pain.

Standing two feet in front of him was a distraught woman. Tears were streaming down her face, and the stun gun she'd just used remained in her hand, her arm outstretched.

"Joann?" Nita said.

"Oh, so you know my name?" the woman spat. "Not as well as you know my husband, it appears."

Joann glared down at Neil, who was writhing in pain. She kicked him in the side. "Hello, honey," she sneered. She had a crazed look in her eyes. "Let me guess, you have a reasonable explanation."

"It's . . . it's not what it looks like," Nita stammered as she tried to slide toward the door.

Joann burst out laughing. "Shut up, tramp. It's exactly what it looks like. And don't even fix your dirty lips to lie. I've known about your skank ass for years."

Joann turned her attention back to Neil. Nita wanted to call for help because Neil looked like he was in excruciating pain, but she was too scared to move.

"But my dear husband swore to me that he was leaving you alone. And I tried to believe him. Even when he walked out yesterday, leaving his seven-month-pregnant wife at home while he laid up in a secret apartment with some tramp!"

Nita's eyes made their way down to Joann's swollen belly. This was the first time she'd noticed the woman was pregnant.

"I . . . I didn't know he was still married. He told me it was over," she stammered. She didn't know why she was lying. Well, yes, she did. She was lying because Joann looked crazed and Neil was in no position to dispute her.

"Shut up, you whore!" Joann said, waving the stun gun at her. "Before I send a thousand volts through you! You're a liar. I heard you say you knew."

Nita wondered how long the woman had been in the house. What had she heard?

"You got a good, decent man, but that's not enough. You still have to try and take mine," Joann cried. "Does the Reverend Wiley know you're here?"

Nita's eyes widened in surprise. How in the world did this woman know about Marshall? Joann noticed Nita's stunned look and wiped her tears.

"Didn't you hear me say I know all about you! You groupies wander in and out of his life so much that I make it my business to know everything. I'm not as dumb as I look!" she screamed.

"Look, I'm sorry," Nita said. She wanted to kick herself. Why hadn't she just left Neil alone?

"Not yet. But you will be. Now, get the hell out of my apartment." Joann looked down at Neil with smoldering anger. "And it will be my apartment, along with everything else your sorry ass owns," she told him.

That was all Nita needed to hear. She grabbed her purse and darted to the door, not even bothering to see if Neil was still convulsing.

38

Audra spun around to face her friend in the backseat. "She did what?"

"She stunned him," Nita replied. They were in the car, heading to the airport to drop Audra off for her trip to Atlanta. Lewis had sent her a ticket, saying he needed to see her and had a wonderful few days planned. Audra knew her friends were upset about her decision to visit Lewis, and she half expected them to use the drive to the airport to convince her not to go. But Nita had been so bummed out by her experience with Neil that that was all they'd been talking about.

"I would've loved to have seen that. I ain't mad at her. That's my kind of woman," Coco said as she pulled onto the freeway.

Both Audra and Nita looked at Coco. She would

be thrilled by someone having the courage to do what she only wished that she had done.

"Well, is Neil okay?" Audra asked, deciding not to go there with Coco.

"Girl, I don't know. I got the hell out of Dodge," Nita said, gazing out of the window.

"Okay, but tell me again why you were messing around with Neil in the first place," Coco said. "I mean, you are engaged to Marshall."

"And not to mention you know Neil is a dog," Audra added. Nita was wiping her eyes. Audra was stunned, because in all their years of friendship, she didn't think she'd ever seen Nita cry, except when her mother died.

"Look, I have beat myself up enough about this. I don't need you guys doing the same," Nita softly said.

"I'm sorry," Audra replied. Coco had been up when Nita came in last night. Nita had told her what happened, and Audra knew as soon as Nita left the room Coco had gone to the phone to call her. "Coco said she threatened you. What is that about?"

Nita sighed. "Neil's wife knows about Marshall, and I don't know whether she plans to tell him. All she said was I'll be sorry."

"Dang, that's messed up," Audra cried.

"Tell me about it. I just hope Neil talks some sense into her when he comes to," Nita said.

"*If* he comes to," Audra quipped.

"Whatever," Nita said. "Let's just talk about something else, like why you're still going to Atlanta to see this man after everything he did to you."

Audra knew Nita was just trying to get the attention off her, but the accusation still wiped the smile off Audra's face. They just didn't understand. No one did. Valentine's Day was in two days. She was lonely. And Lewis loved her, even if he couldn't be with her in the way she wanted. So she'd made up her mind that having a piece of the man was better than not having a man at all, especially considering that Michelle had confirmed they had a loveless marriage.

They didn't say much on the rest of the drive. Once at the airport, Audra unloaded her suitcases. "Nita," she said, closing the trunk. "I know you don't agree with my decision to go to Atlanta, but it's my decision, okay?"

"Fine." Nita threw up her hands. "You're grown. Besides, I have my own drama to worry about."

Audra leaned in and hugged her friends good-bye. She was happy they let the issue drop.

Checking in and going through security took almost forty-five minutes, but as frustrating as the whole process was, she couldn't help but smile. She would soon be in Lewis's arms. And that would make all the trouble worthwhile.

39

Agreeing to disagree was one thing. Getting over the fact that he felt that way in the first place was another problem entirely. That's why Coco found herself sitting on Nita's sofa, trying to get up the nerve to broach the subject with Davis again. If they were going to be together, they had to get on the same page with this whole divorce mentality.

She never expected Davis to harm her, but just the fact that he used religion to justify staying with an abusive spouse was a major turnoff. Religion could be used to justify all sorts of issues.

"So, are you going to tell me what's on your mind?" Davis asked again. It was his third time asking, and Coco knew she needed to get everything—her uneasiness with his opinion and her own troubled background with Sonny—out in the open.

"Actually, there is something," she began. She shifted to get comfortable on the sofa, but before she could continue, the doorbell rang.

"You expecting someone?" Davis asked, glancing toward the door.

Her heart dropped. What if it was Sonny? She couldn't do any drama, especially because she hadn't filled Davis in on everything.

"N-no, I'm not expecting anyone," Coco said. "Maybe it's someone for Nita."

Davis stood to answer the door, and Coco immediately grabbed his hand. "Just leave it."

He looked at her suspiciously, but both of their attention turned toward the door when the person on the other side started banging on it.

"Cosandra! Are you in there?" the voice on the other side shouted.

Coco furrowed her brow. "Daddy?"

Davis glanced at the door. "It's your father?" He didn't give her time to answer as he walked to the door.

The sight of Davis caught her father by surprise, and he hesitated. "Oh, hi," he said. "I'm looking for my daughter, Coco."

Davis extended his hand. "Hi, Mr. King. I'm Davis, Coco's boyfriend."

Mr. King shook Davis's hand, but he obviously wasn't in the mood for small talk. "Is Coco here?"

Coco had eased up behind Davis. Not that she expected her father to lash out at her, but she felt protected standing behind Davis.

"Hey, honey," Mr. King gently said when he noticed his daughter.

"Daddy," Coco said, devoid of any emotion.

"Ummm, can I talk to you?" he said nervously.

Davis stepped aside. "Come on in, Mr. King."

Coco stopped him. "You can talk from here."

Davis shot her a confused look, but she ignored it.

Mr. King sighed. "Look, baby, I know you're upset with me, but you know me and your mama love each other, and, well, we've had our issues, but we work through them. Always have, always will."

Davis nodded in satisfaction, and Coco didn't bother to hide her disgust. "You call putting Mama in the hospital working through things?"

"I'm real sorry about that," her father said quickly. "I need to tell your mama that. I need to convince her to give me another chance. To come home so we can work this out."

Coco couldn't help but note how much he sounded like Sonny.

"It sounds like you need to be having this conversation with Mama." Coco knew he couldn't be hoping that she would convince her mother to come back home.

"That's just it. I can't find her. I called your aunt Shirley, and they said she moved out of town." His voice reeked of desperation. "I know you know where she moved to. Your mom wouldn't go somewhere without telling you."

"Daddy, if Mama wants you to know where she is, she'll let you know."

"Don't play with me, Coco." Mr. King slammed his palm against the door so hard, both Coco and Davis jumped. Other than an occasional spanking growing up, her father had never hurt her. But she'd seen what he was capable of.

"Whoa, Mr. King," Davis said, instinctively stepping in front of Coco. "I understand you're upset, but—"

"But this is none of your business," Mr. King interjected harshly. "This is family business."

"Well . . ."

Coco had had enough. She was tired of living in fear—of her father, of Sonny. "No," she said, cutting Davis off. "He's not going to hurt me." She stared him in the eyes. "He only hits my mama."

That stung, and her father lowered his head. "Baby, I know I haven't been the best husband . . ."

"No, you haven't. And I will always respect you as my father, but I'll tell you right now, I am so happy Mama decided to leave you. You have made her life miserable. You made *our* lives miserable, and I'm glad she finally decided to do something about it."

Astonishment blanketed her father's face, but Coco was on a roll. "You don't have a clue how much you hurt her, how many tears we both shed behind you. You're the reason Carlos joined the army. He said he had to get away or else he would end up killing you. And Mama wanted him to go, because she knew he would do it. Do you know, as children me and Carlos used to pray that you would die in a car accident, or an explosion at the plant where you worked, anything?" Coco was crying now. "Do you know what that does to a child to grow up wishing your father would die? Feeling helpless as you watch your mother nurse her wounds? You never beat us, but you might as well have. Because emotionally, you beat us down. So if you came here looking for sympathy, forget it. If you came here hoping I would tell you where she is, forget that, too. The only thing I have for you is a prayer that you will get the help you need."

Coco felt a pang in her heart as her father's eyes welled with tears. At the same time, though, she felt a sense of relief, like she'd released years of pent-up frustration.

Her father took a step back. "I-I'm sorry," he said softly. His expression told her he had never expected this reaction. "Tell your mother that I love her so much." He quickly walked away.

Coco was still staring after him in shock when she felt Davis take her hand and pull her back inside. He didn't say anything as he took her in his arms, and Coco buried her head against his chest and cried.

40

It felt good being back in Atlanta. Audra's flight had landed just the way she liked it—uneventful. She had retrieved her luggage and was standing outside baggage claim.

She'd hoped to see Lewis there waiting on her, but he must've been running late because he was nowhere in sight. She took a seat on a bench and reflected on what she'd been through. Since high school, she'd had a stream of bad relationships. The one guy who really loved her, she'd wronged, cheating with his bad-boy friend. It had been one of her biggest regrets, and she'd yet to find someone who loved her as much as he did. That was until Lewis. Her heart told her that Lewis loved her. She didn't condone his ways, but she knew that much to be true.

Audra snapped out of her thoughts and glanced

down at her watch. Lewis was now more than thirty minutes late. She whipped out her cell phone and punched in his number, but it went straight to voice mail. Audra called to check in on Andrew, then waited another twenty minutes before calling Lewis's cell phone back. She blew an exasperated breath when his voice mail picked up again on the first ring. Audra paced as she watched the travelers coming and going. She was getting irritated now. The least he could have done was called and let her know what time to expect him.

No sooner had the thought crossed her mind than her phone rang. She didn't recognize the 770 number, but since she knew that was an Atlanta area code, she answered. Maybe something had happened and Lewis had gotten a new phone.

"Hello," Audra said.

"Yes, may I speak with Audra?" the female voice said.

"This is she."

"Yes, I'm calling on behalf of Reverend Lewis Jackson."

Audra frowned. The woman's voice sounded vaguely familiar, but she couldn't place it.

"Yes?" Audra said.

"I am so sorry to have to be the bearer of bad

news, but Pastor Jackson will be unable to pick you up from the airport."

"What? Why not? Should I take a cab?"

"No, unfortunately Pastor was called away at the last minute on business, so he's going to be unable to keep his appointment to see you at all."

"What do you mean, appointment? This isn't some business meeting. I flew here from Houston!"

"I'm well aware of your itinerary, and we tried to reach you before you left. However, the pastor's other commitment was not anticipated, nor could it be avoided."

Why did she know this voice? "Look," Audra said, "where is Lewis? I want to talk to him now."

"I've already arranged to get you on the next flight to Houston. It leaves in forty-five minutes, so you won't have to wait very long."

"This is crazy. Where is Lewis and why isn't he calling me?"

"He's not in a position to call."

"Where is he?" Audra demanded. "I don't want to talk to you. I want to talk to him."

"Look," the woman said, losing her professional demeanor, "it ain't going down like you thought it was goin' down. So just get on the plane, go back to Houston, and Lewis will call you when he calls you."

"Excuse you?"

"I'm sorry for any inconvenience," the woman said, returning to her proper voice. "Pastor will be in touch."

She hung up before Audra could respond. Audra immediately punched in the number the woman had called from, but all she got was a recording that said, "This phone is unable to receive calls."

"Arrrrgh," she screamed. Lewis had better be dang near death, she thought as she stomped back toward the Delta terminal.

As Audra reclined in her first-class seat, the woman's voice continued to nag her. She knew it from somewhere. So between that and the fact that Lewis had had her fly to Atlanta for nothing, there was a lot on her mind.

Audra felt her body relaxing, and she hoped sleep would overtake her. She was just about to doze off when her eyes popped open. She remembered when she'd heard the woman's voice.

Audra could barely contain herself the rest of the flight home. No sooner had the plane's wheels touched down than she was dialing information.

"Atlanta, Georgia," Audra told the operator. "Yes,

may I please have the number for a Lewis and Michelle Jackson."

"I have four Lewis and Michelle Jacksons in metropolitan Atlanta," the operator said.

Audra groaned. "Okay, how about Reverend Lewis Jackson?"

"Ah, yes. Here it is. Please hold for the number."

Audra held her breath as the recording connected her to the number.

"Hello," the woman who answered the phone said.

Audra paused, wondering if she should go through with it. She had to know. "Yes, may I speak with Michelle Jackson please?"

"This is she. Who may I ask is calling?"

Audra took a deep breath. "Ummm, it's Audra. Audra Bowen, the, um, from Houston."

Michelle was eerily quiet, and Audra could only imagine the look on her face.

"You have a lot of nerve," Michelle said. "How dare you call my house."

"Look, I'm sorry to call," Audra began, "but I need to ask you something." Before she even asked the question, Audra knew the answer. This was definitely not the woman who had called her. "I received a call from someone a couple of weeks ago," Audra began anyway. "The woman said she was you, and she proceeded to tell me that your marriage was a sham and in name only."

Michelle released a painful laugh. "Sweetheart, number one, I assure you, my marriage is not a sham. Number two, and most important, I did not, nor would I ever, fix my fingers to dial your number. I don't call my man's whores."

Audra bit down on her lip. She almost went off, but she could understand the woman's anger. She'd probably be using a lot worse language if some woman were calling her husband. "Well, the caller said she was Lewis's wife."

"Well, the caller lied," Michelle snapped. "And if I know my husband, the woman that called you is one of his blindly loyal followers." She let out a groan. "And from the sound of things, Lewis is back up to the doggish ways he had when he was just my boyfriend—ways he promised me he'd change once he became my husband." At this point Michelle seemed to be talking more to herself than to Audra. She must've caught herself, though, because her voice resumed its firmness. "I assure you, I did not call you. Yeah, my marriage is not ideal, but I actually believed him when he said he'd change." She let out another pained laugh. "And to think, we're about to head to

Vegas for a romantic Valentine's Day getaway. I called myself trying to surprise him. Hmph. I guess that makes me just as big a fool as you are. But at least I'll get something out the deal." Before Audra could reply, she heard the dial tone in her ear.

Audra sat with the phone clutched tightly in her hand. This was a low she never could have imagined.

"Excuse me, ma'am." Audra looked up to see the flight attendant standing over her. "We're going to have to ask you to deplane now." Audra glanced around. She was the last person in the cabin.

"I'm sorry. I . . . I was in another world."

The flight attendant flashed her a fake smile as she stood. "Are you okay?"

Audra nodded as she shakily grabbed her bag out of the overhead compartment. No, she wasn't okay. She didn't know if she'd ever be okay again.

41

Nita stared at the crowd gathered outside the church. "Why is everybody outside?" she asked. She and Marshall had met for breakfast before Sunday morning service. Nita had been on edge about Joann, and Marshall was starting to notice. He'd asked her to breakfast so they could talk. He thought her anxiety had come over his celibacy vow and everything that had been going on at church, and she'd just gone along with that, assuring him she was okay.

"Your guess is as good as mine," Marshall replied as he closed the car door and headed up the walkway.

One of the first people they spotted was Vera, off to the side, huddled up with the rest of her friends. Vera whispered something to the rest of her group, and they all turned their attention to Nita, scowls plastered across their faces.

"What is their problem?" Nita hissed.

Marshall didn't reply as he approached the women. "Good morning, sisters. What's going on?"

Neither of the women said anything as they looked at each other. Vera had an I-told-you-so smirk on her face.

Then Nita heard a man's voice in the crowd. "I can't believe y'all just gonna stand around lookin' at this. Take it down. Take it down!"

"Deacon Barrett?" Marshall strained to see over the crowd. "What's going on?" He began making his way through the small sea of people. Nita followed close behind. Was it just her, or was everyone looking at her with hatred and disdain?

"What in the world is going on?" Marshall asked once they reached the front of the crowd.

Nita's gaze was drawn down to a wad of papers in Deacon Barrett's hands.

"It's nothing, Reverend Wiley," the deacon said guiltily. "Just some folks being messy."

Marshall reached out for one of the pieces of paper. "Messy about what? Let me see that."

Deacon Barrett took a step back as his eyes darted over to Nita. "You don't wanna do that, Pastor."

"And why wouldn't I?"

"Yeah, why wouldn't he?" Vera snapped. Nita

didn't realize that Vera and the biddies had followed them through the crowd.

"Let him see it," Lucy ordered.

"Let me see what?"

Deacon Barrett sighed in defeat as he handed one of the pieces of paper to Marshall. "We arrived at church this morning, and these were pasted all over the doors."

Marshall's mouth fell open, and Nita gave the same reaction when she looked over his shoulder. It was a picture of her, butt naked, straddling Neil. Across the top were the words PRO HO. The date and time were stamped in the corner. 2-10-10, 10:13 P.M. Three days ago.

"Where did you get these?" Marshall demanded as he snatched the other pictures from Deacon Barrett.

"I told you they were taped all over the church, front and back. Even some of the kids from the youth ministry saw them."

"Jesus be my guide," Addie moaned.

"As if they don't see enough hoochiness in them videos, now they gotta see it in the House of the Lord," Lucy echoed.

"I warned you, I warned you, I warned you," Vera said.

"I got all the copies from the back," Deacon Barrett said. "They're in my office."

Nita was speechless. She knew she needed to say something in her defense, but she was frozen in place.

"So you got something to say for yourself?" Lucy asked.

"What could she possibly say?" Vera snapped. "I told y'all. You can't turn a ho into a housewife."

"Enough!" Marshall said. "It's bad enough someone would disrespect our church like this. But we are not going to add to it."

"It looks like it's your woman who is disrespectful, especially to you, a man of God," Vera said.

Marshall said in a strained voice, "Sister Vera, I'll ask you nicely. Please stop."

Vera folded her arms defiantly. "I'll let it go for now, out of respect for you, Pastor Wiley." She took a step forward. "But if you think for a minute that we'll allow this lady to be first lady, you got another think coming."

Lucy and Vera stomped into the sanctuary, followed closely by the other Holy Rollers.

"That's enough," Marshall called out to the assemblage. "You all go on inside and start Sunday school. We got some praising and praying to do."

"Shoot, somebody need to be praying for that harlot that's about to be your wife," someone mumbled as they passed by.

Nita ignored them, focusing all of her attention on Marshall, trying to gauge his reaction.

He glared at her, then spun off toward his office.

Nita didn't respond; she just hurried after him. Her mind raced as she tried to keep up. *Who could have done this to her?* No sooner had the thought come to her mind than Joann's scorn flashed in her head.

"Let me explain," Nita said once they were inside Marshall's office.

"I'm listening," he calmly said, closing the door and taking a seat at his desk.

Nita hadn't expected that. She was used to men who would've immediately gone off. Yelled, cursed, and screamed, even pulled a Sonny on her and slapped her across the room.

"I don't know where the photos came from," she began.

"Are they doctored?"

Nita was silent. She wanted to lie, but the words wouldn't form on her lips. Marshall glanced back down at the photo. "It doesn't look doctored, and judging from the date, this was just last week." He sat down. "I mean, I knew you weren't a virgin. I could look at you and tell that." He seemed to be talking more to himself than to her.

"What is that supposed to mean?" Nita asked.

He chuckled painfully, ignoring her question as he looked through the pictures. "But this, I would've never imagined this."

Marshall picked up his phone and pressed zero for his receptionist. "Kelly, can you go find Deacon Barrett and ask him to bring the rest of the papers he collected to me?"

"Marshall, don't do that," Nita said, struggling to fight back tears.

"Why not?" he asked coolly, hanging the phone up. "I just want to know what I'm dealing with. I need to see."

"No, you don't," Nita replied, sitting down in the chair in front of his desk.

"Yes. I do." He nodded slowly as he continued to stare at the picture. "Looks like I've been in the dark for too long."

Nita wanted to grab the photo and rip it up. But the pain that was etched across Marshall's face kept her frozen in her seat. And her misery didn't stem only from what he was feeling. She couldn't believe the pain she was feeling. She knew she cared about Marshall, but not until this very moment, watching him and realizing she could really lose him, did she realize how much she loved him.

Marshall was unlike any other man she'd ever met.

With the exception of the lack of sex, their relationship was near perfect. So what in the world had she been doing with Neil?

Dear God, please let me get out of this one and I promise you I'll live right, Nita prayed silently.

Her prayer was interrupted by a light tap on the door.

"Come in," Marshall called out.

Deacon Barrett eased into the office, the papers clutched tightly to his chest. "Are you sure you want to do this, Pastor?"

"Thank you, Deacon Barrett," Marshall said, extending his hand.

The deacon nodded, handed the pictures to Marshall, looked at Nita in pity, then walked out.

"Doesn't he play for the Rockets?" Marshall looked up at her. "Never mind."

Nita continued to sit in silence as Marshall studied photo after photo.

"Hmph, a wedding ring," he said. He turned the picture to face Nita. "And it's circled in a big red marker. Is the man you're in bed with here married?"

Nita didn't reply.

"I'll take that for a yes." Marshall set the picture down, then held up another one for Nita to see. "And I'm assuming this is his wife?" He showed her a wedding picture of Neil and Joann with a big red circle with a slash through it. Above their picture were the words A MARRIAGE DESTROYED BY A WHORE.

"So you're cheating on me with a married man?" Marshall said.

Nita knew she had to speak up or she was done. "Marshall—"

He held his hand up. "No, on second thought, don't say anything."

"No, I need to—"

"You don't need to do anything, because at this point I don't know, the stuff that comes out your mouth, I can no longer tell if it's a lie or the truth." He hesitated. "Why did you agree to marry me?"

"Because I love you." She had never meant those words before like she meant them now.

He laughed. "Either that's a bold-faced lie or you don't know what love is." He held up another photo. In that one Nita's eyes were slanted, a drink in her hand, an NBA player on either side of her. That was definitely an old picture, because she hadn't partied like that in over a year. How long had Joann been following her?

"Oh, wow," Marshall said, moving to another photo. "Faizon Martin, huh? That's one of my favorite players." He turned the picture to Nita. Faizon's hand was resting on her right breast. "Did you sleep with him, too?"

Again, Nita wanted to lie, but again, no lie would come. "Marshall, those pictures are old. My history is history." She was kicking herself. Why had she lied about her past? It would be so much easier to explain if she had been honest from jump. But she had played down her past.

"Who is this woman?" he asked, holding up one of the photos and pointing at her.

"I didn't tell you about the type of woman I used to be because I knew you wouldn't give me a chance."

"How would you know that? You don't know anything about me. Just like I obviously don't know anything about you."

He flung the last picture in the stack at her, the first sign of his true anger. "And to think . . . you were supposed to be my wife."

Nita refused to pick up the picture. All she could hear was Marshall's use of the past tense.

"You had sex with this man while I was out paying the caterer for our wedding?" he shouted, waving the photo dated February 10. "Oh, I understand now," he said as he pulled out another picture. She didn't want to look at that one either.

"Look at the picture!" he yelled. "Don't act shy now."

Nita finally glanced down at the paper. It was a picture of Marshall and Nita at the park, feeding each other ice cream, and at the top, the words THE WHORE'S NEW TARGET, THE RICH MINISTER.

"So I was all part of some elaborate plan?" He took a deep breath, composing himself as he leaned back. "Boy, you really made this woman mad." He laughed painfully.

Nita finally found her voice. "Marshall, yes, I did some things I'm not proud of. And I did lie, but one thing I'm not lying about is my feelings for you."

She got up and tried to move closer. "I mean it, I love you." The idea of losing Marshall was tearing her apart. She couldn't believe she'd sabotaged her chance at true happiness.

"Please don't give up on us," Nita softly said.

"Don't," he replied, shaking his head like he was trying to get her out of it. When he looked at her, he had tears in his eyes. "Do you know why it took so long for me to see another woman after my wife died? Because I didn't want to give my heart to anyone else. And the first woman I finally open up to breaks my heart and makes me look like a fool in front of my church."

"I'm sorry I embarrassed you."

"This is not about being embarrassed, Nita!" He pounded his desk. "This is about you cheating on me and me not knowing what type of woman you really are."

"I'm the same woman you were loving before you saw those pictures. Tell me you haven't stopped loving me."

He rubbed his temples and sighed heavily. "I still love you," he finally said.

Nita's heart flickered as he continued.

"And I know God teaches us about forgiveness." He paused. "And eventually I will forgive you." He exhaled sadly. "But this . . . I won't be able to forget this betrayal."

"Marshall, weren't you the one preaching about judging? Don't judge me. I can repent. I'll do whatever you want. Just don't throw us away." Her words were laced with desperation.

Marshall stood up abruptly and dropped the papers in the trash can. "I have to go get ready for service." He walked toward the door, then stopped and turned back to Nita. "The minister in me doesn't dare tell you not to come inside. But the man in me wants to let you know that if you have any shred of respect for me, you'll just go home."

From the pain written all over his face, Nita knew, without a shadow of a doubt, their relationship was over.

42

This was the way love should be. Coco leaned against the door and sighed. Davis had surprised her with breakfast from IHOP, her favorite. They'd eaten like two high school sweethearts, feeding each other as they giggled and played around. He didn't press her to talk about her father's visit and only said, "I'm sorry for being so judgmental," then left the issue alone.

Coco was supposed to meet Nita at church, but she couldn't tear herself away from Davis, who couldn't go to church because he had to work today. She was sad when it was time for him to leave, but he'd promised to return right after he got off. That left her with a smile on her face.

A knock on the door jolted her out of her euphoric thoughts. "You came back to see me?" she asked, swinging the door open.

"I sure did."

Coco froze at the sight of Sonny standing on her doorstep. He had on a black Nike warm-up suit and his signature Nike high-tops. He was smiling, but his eyes bore the look of someone on the verge of insanity.

"Well, you sure don't look happy to see me," he said.

Coco immediately tried to slam her door shut, but Sonny stuck out his large foot, blocking it. "Now, isn't that rude of you?" He pushed her aside, then walked in, leaving the door wide open. "It's bad enough you keep blowing me off, but then I get over here to find it's because you're entertaining some other dude."

"Sonny . . . ," Coco said, backing up against the wall.

Sonny stopped and looked around the room. "This is why you think you're all big and bad now, cuz you up here living with your girl. She probably filling your head with a whole bunch of nonsense and that women's empowerment crap."

"Sonny, Nita doesn't have anything to do with why I left you. You know why I left." Her hand instinctively went to her stomach.

Sonny groaned as he ran his hand up and down the back of his bald head. "All you're worried about is that baby. I told you, I'm sorry you lost it, but we need to be focusing on us."

Coco did not want to go there with him. There was no amount of apologizing he could do. While the doctors confirmed that stress could've made her lose her baby, Sonny was the one who made her world stressful. "Sonny, it's over."

"Is he your boyfriend?" Sonny asked.

"Sonny, leave."

"Is. He. Your. Boyfriend?" Sonny screamed.

"I told you if you came over here, I was going to call the cops." Coco moved toward the phone.

Sonny blocked her from picking up the receiver. "You would actually call the cops on me?"

"Sonny, move," Coco said with a conviction she'd never displayed before.

"No."

She kept her gaze on him as she reached down for the phone. Before she could pick it up, Sonny grabbed her hair in the back and flung her to the floor.

Coco screamed as she fell.

"You've lost your mind!" he snapped as he raised his foot and leveled a kick in her side.

She screamed in agony.

"Do you think for a minute that I'm going to let

you call the cops on me? First, you're gon' just leave me and I'm supposed to just accept it, after everything I did for you?"

He picked her up, his hands gripping her neck.

"No, Sonny, no!"

Sonny slammed her against the wall. A flash of pain shot through her head as she slumped to the floor. She frantically began crawling toward the kitchen.

"Oooh, don't run now. A minute ago you were big and bad," he said, following her.

Her head was throbbing in agony, but she reached the kitchen counter and pulled herself up just as Sonny staggered in. "Don't you know who I am? I'm Sonny Fuqua. You think you can just discard me like the NFL did? Naw, ma, it don't even work like that."

Coco managed to fling open one of the drawers, where she grabbed a twelve-inch butcher knife.

"Whatchu gonna do with that?" He laughed. "You about to cook me something to eat?"

"Get out!" Coco screamed.

"Or what?" he screamed back.

Tears were streaming down her cheeks as images of every time he'd laid his hands on her swam through her head. Every bruise she'd suffered, every tear she'd shed at the hands of the man she once loved. Then she relived seeing her parents, hearing her mother's screams as her father beat her. Coco felt her vision getting blurry. But she could see well enough to see Sonny coming toward her.

"Didn't I tell you if I couldn't have you, nobody could?" he threatened. "Now, put the knife down before I slap the taste out of your mouth."

She jabbed the knife in the air. "Get away from me."

He walked closer, until the tip of the knife was right in the center of his chest. "Do it," he hissed.

"Get out," she cried, her voice shaking.

"Or what?"

Her hands were trembling but she kept them firmly locked around the knife's handle.

Sonny raised his shirt in scorn. "Here, let me let you get a good aim." He leaned in, and she could see the tip of the knife piercing his skin.

Before she knew it, Sonny had grabbed her hair again and flung her head back. "I told you, it ain't over until I say it's over!"

She was screaming when she saw Sonny's eyes bulge out in horror. Then Coco felt the warm blood trickling over her hands. She looked down just as Sonny's grip loosened. His hands went to his chest, where the knife had plunged deep inside.

"You bit——." He collapsed before he could finish his sentence.

Coco stepped back in horror. "Oh, my God," she cried. She didn't know how long she stood there, stunned. Finally, a voice brought her out of her daze.

"Nita? It's Mrs. Warren from next door," the woman called out from the living room. "Your door was wide open and I heard a lot of ruckus so I was just checking to see . . . Lord Jesus!" she shrieked as she looked into the kitchen at Sonny's lifeless body.

Coco looked up at Mrs. Warren, her eyes glassy, and said simply: "I killed him."

43

Today was a day for lovers, and Audra couldn't even get hers on the phone. Or her ex-lover, rather. She'd been trying since she got back to call Lewis's cell phone, and he still wasn't answering. She was hoping to catch him before he went home. She'd tried him since she returned home, but he still never answered. He owed her some explanation. "The bastard didn't even have enough thought to call me," she mumbled as she slammed the phone down again.

"That's because he's with his wife."

Audra jumped. She turned around to see Miss Bea standing in the doorway to her kitchen.

"Are you eavesdropping on me?" she snapped.

"Ummm, no, I'm taking care of your child, remember? I can't help it you're in here talking to yourself."

Audra instantly apologized. "I'm sorry, I didn't

mean to snap at you." She'd been in such a rotten mood that Andrew had asked to spend the night at Miss Bea's last night.

"I understand. If I was being used and abused, I'd be a little jumpy, too." Miss Bea walked over to the coffeepot.

"Miss Bea, you don't understand . . . ," Audra began.

"Don't understand what? Loneliness? Hmph. When is the last time you heard my floorboard creaking at night?" She pushed the button to brew the coffee, then walked over and sat across from Audra. "You think because I'm old, I don't have wants and desires? Even if for nothing more than companionship. But guess what, the Lord ain't saw fit to send me nobody. And I'm not just gonna take any old thing. Besides, I believe God has me doing my calling, taking care of your son."

Audra narrowed her eyes. "Are you trying to say I'm not a good mother?"

"I'm not saying that at all. I told you before, I think you're a good mother."

"I know because everything I'm doing, I'm doing for Andrew," Audra said forcefully.

"So you're allowing yourself to be Lewis's mistress for Andrew?"

"It's more complicated than that, Miss Bea." She

didn't know what she was to Lewis anymore. Part of her wanted to believe that Michelle was messing with her, trying to get under her skin. The other part told her to wake up and read the writing on the wall. Lewis was nothing but a liar.

"Is it so complicated?"

"He doesn't really want to be married to her." Audra knew her words were unconvincing. At this point she wasn't even convinced herself anymore.

Miss Bea looked at her in complete doubt. "How many cheating husbands across America do you think are saying that right now? And I'd be willing to bet my left ovary, if I still had it, that his wife would tell you an entirely different story. I think there's this part of you that's holding out hope they'll break up, even though they just got married."

"Would that be such a bad thing?" Audra was surprised Miss Bea was reading her so well.

"Number one, you know the majority of men that do leave their wives never end up with the woman they were cheating on their wives with. Number two, if he cheats on her, what in the world makes you think he wouldn't cheat on you?" Miss Bea got up and fixed them both cups of coffee. Audra watched her in silence. Miss Bea was saying the same things she'd been telling herself. "Baby girl, I know you're lonely and I know you think this is the man that God sent to you, but God don't operate like that. This may be who the devil sent for you. In fact, I'm sure that Lewis is the devil in disguise. Ain't nothing good about what that man's bringing to the table. Yeah, he's paying some bills, sending that annoying mutt that drives everybody crazy, but what price are you paying? Forget adultery, which I ain't even gon' get into with you. I'm talking about you denying yourself the opportunity to meet your real soul mate. You might have passed him in the grocery store last week, but you're so blind behind Lewis that you didn't even see him."

Audra didn't realize she was crying until she saw a tear fall off her cheek. Miss Bea took her hand and lifted Audra's chin. "Baby, you're better than that. You've been looking for love in all the wrong places. You're not going to find your soul mate at the club, and truth be told, nowadays, you're not even going to find him at church. Honestly, I think you need to just stop looking. Let him find you. You're using all your energy trying to figure out how to snag a man. For what? So Andrew can have a daddy? He's better off with a good mama than a no-good man. Take that same energy you're using to snag a man and go back to school, get more training. Focus your energy on you."

Audra was about to respond when the phone rang.

Miss Bea gave her a weary look. "That's probably the call you're waiting on. I just want you to ask yourself, are you prepared to believe the lie he's going to tell you? And as he's telling you that lie, I just want you to ask yourself, 'Do I deserve better?'" She looked meaningfully at Audra before turning and walking out of the apartment.

Audra glanced at the phone, which had stopped ringing. She swallowed hard, then walked over and picked up the phone. It had been Lewis. She was just about to redial his number when the phone rang again.

She took a deep breath and answered. "Hello."

"Okay, why aren't you answering your phone?"

"Hello to you, too, Lewis."

"I just called and it rang and rang."

"I—"

He cut her off before she could even finish her sentence. "Don't tell me you're sitting up celebrating Valentine's Day with some other man."

Audra had to laugh at his audacity. "What do you want, Lewis?"

"Well, I was calling to apologize for bailing out on you, and I wanted to wish you a happy Valentine's Day."

"It's ten o'clock at night. Eleven your time. Valentine's Day is almost over."

"Well, I, uh, see, I had, I got a little bit busy."

"Yeah, I'm sure."

"Audra, you know I am a busy minister . . ." She couldn't believe he was acting like nothing was wrong. Audra knew Michelle had told him about their conversation by now.

As he talked, all Audra could think was, *I deserve better*. The words seemed to echo like a roar in her head. "Whatever."

"Well, what's the big deal? I'm calling now."

"Where's your wife, Lewis?"

He let out a frustrated sigh. "She's upstairs 'sleep. Why?"

"So you snuck downstairs to call me after your wife went to sleep?"

"Aaaw, here you go with that?"

Audra let out a cracked laugh. "Yeah, here I go."

"I know what this is about," he said, like a light had just gone off. "You're mad because I didn't send you a gift."

"No gift. No flowers. No card. No call," she said flatly. "And oh yeah, let's not forget, you had me fly all the way to Atlanta for nothing!"

"I can't help that I got called out of town. And I'm calling you now. Good grief, I paid your rent, gave you money for groceries, bought your kid a dog. That ought to be gift enough."

The sad part was he thought buying her off was enough to negate how he'd hurt her.

"But look, if it makes you feel any better, I'm sorry. I would've sent something, but honestly, I'm not too good with that stuff. Usually my secretary remembers to do stuff like that, but I couldn't very well ask her to send you something, could I?"

Audra sighed. "Save it, Lewis. It doesn't even matter anymore."

"What does that mean?"

"It means I'm tired."

He had the nerve to raise his voice. "Am I not good to you, Audra? You know I'm staying in the marriage and trying to build this church so we can have a future together."

"So *we* can have a future, huh? Let me ask you something, Lewis. When you do get this church built up to where you want it, you and the first lady, just how would I fit into the picture? I mean, can you honestly tell me that you would then kick Michelle to the curb and bring me in as first lady?" The reality of what she was doing set in more and more with every word that she spoke.

"You make it sound so harsh," Lewis said.

"I'm just trying to get an understanding of how all of this is going to play out."

He sighed like he was irritated. "What do you care as long as I'm taking care of you? I told you I wanted you to move to Atlanta. I would set you and Andrew up in a nice apartment nearby, buy you the finest clothes. Would I do all of that if I didn't want to be with you?"

"I didn't question whether you wanted to be with me."

"Well, what's the problem?"

"The problem is I don't want to move to Atlanta to be somebody's mistress!" Audra caught herself and lowered her voice. "Stop with the lies, Lewis. I talked to your wife."

He didn't reply, and she couldn't help but laugh. He really was going to try to play this all the way out.

"And guess what, not only was the woman I talked to when I called your house *not* the same woman that called me, but your wife kindly informed me that she didn't, nor would she ever, pick up a phone to call her—and I quote—husband's whore."

"Audra, I can explain."

"Can you? Really? I think I can, too. You had some little floozy, who you obviously pay to do your dirty work, call me pretending to be Michelle." Just verbalizing it made her stomach turn. "Did you two get a good laugh at my expense? Did you say, 'This dumb, desperate chick will fall for anything'?" Audra felt like sobbing now. All the pain she had endured over the last few months came rising to the surface.

"Audra, it's not like that—"

"Stop lying!" she screamed. "For once in your life, stop lying."

He took a deep breath. "Okay, fine. I did have someone call you. But only because I knew you wouldn't give us a chance otherwise."

Audra pulled the phone back and looked at it. She thought she hated Chris. Lewis was giving him a run for the money.

". . . never meant to hurt you," he was saying when she put the phone back up to her ear.

"Lewis, you are a low-down, no-good, dirty dog."

Her words must've gotten to him, because his voice suddenly took on a cocky tone again. "Look, you knew what you were getting into from jump. Now, all of a sudden, you got a problem with it."

Audra was seeing the real man. It was as if someone had hit her over the head, knocking some sense into her. "No, Lewis, I'm finally coming to my senses. I am finally realizing that I'm settling. By being with you, I'm blocking my blessings."

"Oh, so I'm not a blessing?" he said snidely. "If it weren't for me, you and your kid would be out on the street. So if you ask me, I'm a huge blessing in your life."

Audra laughed again. By this time all the sorrow she'd felt had drained away. "You can't possibly believe that. Good-bye, *Reverend* Jackson." She hung the phone up, then took a deep breath. That felt good. And what would feel even better was her sticking to her guns and finally letting Lewis go.

Before she turned to walk away, the phone rang again. She inhaled. Maybe she needed to tell Lewis that if he didn't stop calling, she would be calling his church, his father-in-law, and anyone else she could to get him to leave her alone. She snatched up the phone. "Lewis, let me tell—"

"Audra!" It was Nita, and she sounded like she was crying. "It's Coco, she's been arrested!"

"What?" Audra exclaimed. "Arrested? For what?"

"They said she killed Sonny. He attacked her and she killed him. Me and Davis are on our way downtown."

All thoughts of Lewis fled as Audra's heart began racing. "I'll meet you guys there." She threw the phone down, grabbed her purse, and headed out the door.

44

Nita puffed a cigarette as she paced back and forth across the waiting area. She hadn't smoked in six years, but with everything she'd been through this past week, she needed a hit to calm her nerves.

Four hours had passed since her nosy neighbor called her on her cell and told her the "police are taking Coco away in handcuffs." Nita couldn't make out much of what the woman was saying except, "I think she killed her boyfriend."

Nita thought she meant Davis, and she immediately called him. Her heart was racing, but when Davis answered the phone, she knew there had to be some misunderstanding. Then Nita had called downtown and was told Coco was indeed in jail. Like a black stroke of doom, the realization of who the "boyfriend" was hit her. Sonny had reappeared.

Nita had arrived home to find his body still lying in her kitchen. A team of crime-scene techs were scattered throughout her condo. They'd questioned her, then let her grab a few items before making her leave. She'd been tempted to call Marshall, but instead she headed downtown to find out what was going on.

"Will you put that thing out before you get us kicked out?" Audra said. "And when did you go back to smoking anyway?"

"Since my life started spiraling out of control," Nita replied. Nevertheless, she took a long drag, then dumped the cigarette butt into her foam cup.

"Do you think she really killed him?" Audra asked as she sipped her lukewarm coffee.

"If she did, who can blame her?" Nita said bitterly.

"But murder?"

"He had to have done something to make her snap." Nita looked around. "Where's Davis?"

"Here I am," Davis said as he came around the corner. "I was finally able to get in touch with one of my friends who is a police officer. He did some checking, and Coco is being interrogated on suspicion of murder."

Nita shook her head in disbelief. She had been hoping this was all some big misunderstanding. "I knew it."

"Murder, Davis?" Audra said. "Are they sure? I mean, why do they think she did it?"

Davis looked puzzled, like he was trying to make sense of everything. "Because when they arrested her, they had to pry the knife out of her hand."

Audra's eyes filled with tears. "This doesn't make any sense. Coco is not a killer."

"After you've been beat long enough, you can turn into anything," Nita snapped, her eyes watering up as well.

"Beat? What are you talking about?" Davis asked. "Sonny beat her?"

Audra and Nita exchanged glances. Evidently, Coco hadn't shared the details of her past relationship with Davis. They didn't want to sell their girl out, but at this point, he needed to know. If Coco was being charged with murder, all the cards needed to be on the table.

"Sonny Fuqua is a lunatic who thinks that he has carte blanche to hit her whenever he pleases. And if she stabbed him, he had to have attacked her," Nita said.

Davis leaned against the wall, mouth open in shock. "I knew about her parents, but she never mentioned she'd been abused herself." He shook his head in disbelief. "One time, she seemed like she was about to tell me something serious about her past relationship, but then she dropped it. I didn't press her. I just left it alone."

"Don't feel bad. We left it alone, too," Nita said, eyeing Audra. "Against my better judgment. I told Coco a long time ago she needed to do something about it."

Davis looked hopeful. "Well, once the police see the reports she filed, they'll let her out."

"No, she never filed a report," Audra said. "Because he was a pro player who was already on the verge of losing his contract, she felt sorry for him."

"This is unbelievable," Davis mumbled.

"Tell me about it," Nita replied. "So, when can we see her?"

Davis shrugged. "I don't know how long it will take."

"Well, I'm going to find out," Nita said, stomping toward the front desk. "Excuse me, ma'am. But do you have any idea when we'll get a chance to visit our friend?"

The policewoman looked up, not bothering to hide her boredom. "What's your friend's name?"

"Coco—Cosandra King. She was booked earlier tonight."

The woman punched the keyboard on the computer before turning back to Nita and raising an eyebrow. "Sweetie, y'all might as well go on home. Ain't no talking to Ms. King tonight. She won't even go before a judge until tomorrow. And it'll be tomorrow morning before all her paperwork is processed."

Nita sighed heavily, causing the woman to soften. Nita lowered her voice and said, "Just between you and me, do you think they'll give her bond? I mean, they say they caught her with the knife. But if she did kill him, it's because he's been beating her."

The policewoman looked around. "Look, I shouldn't be saying anything, but I know Sonny Fuqua, and he's a prick if I ever seen one. I know someone who used to date him, so if your friend did kill him, I don't doubt he had it coming. But I can tell you now, she's going to have a hard time, because she kept muttering, 'I killed him.'"

"Well, I'm sure he hit her or something. Has she had a medical examination?"

"I'm sure he hit her, too," the policewoman said, still looking around to make sure no one was listening. "But she doesn't have any visible bruises, and she's not demanding to go to the hospital. She's just sitting back there catatonic. You guys need to get her an attorney ASAP. Unless she's visibly hurt, they're not going to take her to the hospital. I overheard some cops talking, and they think she's playing the victim to cover up her murdering him."

"That's crazy."

The policewoman leaned back. "Look, I've already said too much. Just get your girl an attorney quick, because they will eat her alive in here." She straightened up as another officer walked toward the desk. "Ma'am, you'll just have to check back tomorrow on the status of your friend's case," she said in a professional tone.

Nita nodded in thanks before returning to her friends. They needed to find a lawyer—tonight. Nita knew she wouldn't be able to sleep until Coco had an attorney to help her out of this mess.

45

Nita slammed the phone down and let out a frustrated scream. "I can't believe Houston's jacked-up judicial system! They're talking about they can hold Coco forty-eight hours before charging her."

Audra looked around Nita's living room, trying to imagine the fear Coco must have felt. She pictured Sonny charging toward Coco and her friend just snapping. She glanced over at the spot where Sonny died. Nita had had a cleaning service come in this morning and scrub the place from top to bottom. The condo reeked of Pine-Sol, but Audra still didn't see how Nita would be able to continue living there.

"They got all kinds of criminals roaming the streets, but they want to act like Coco is some menace to society." Nita continued ranting. She'd just hung up the phone with Davis, who had called to break the news that Coco probably wouldn't be arraigned until tomorrow.

"Well, didn't Coco's attorney tell the cops about her being abused?" Audra asked. They'd lucked out— thanks to Davis once again—and gotten a friend of a friend who was an attorney to come down to the jail last night. Joel Wright had been up all night and most of today trying to get Coco out of jail. Audra had finally left around six to go check on Andrew. Then she showered, changed, and met Nita back at her place.

"He told him, but the judge didn't believe it because he said there was no proof—no police report, no pictures, nothing. As far as the judge is concerned, she could be making the abuse story up to cover her crime." Nita shook her head. "You know that woman was convicted last month of killing her husband. She claimed self-defense, but they later found out it was planned so she could run off with her boyfriend. Well, the attorney said because of that, the district attorney isn't taking any chances, so they're going hard after Coco."

"Did the attorney at least get her to a hospital?"

"Davis was trying to get that taken care of."

Audra shook her head. "This is ridiculous. Can't we just tell the cops she was being abused?"

Nita began removing her clothes. "It's not enough. I told her she should've filed a report, gone to the hospital, something. But she was always making excuses. Now look where it's gotten her. For once, I hope Sonny did some kind of internal damage."

"Nita!" Audra exclaimed.

Nita turned to her. "What? That's the only thing that's gonna save her. They said she didn't have any visible bruises. How are they gonna believe she was being abused if there's no proof?"

Audra sighed heavily but didn't answer as Nita stomped into her bathroom. "I'm going to change. Then we need to go to the attorney's office."

Audra thought about how Coco was doing, and she wondered if her friend was scared, sitting in that cold jail cell, probably fending off the advances of someone named Big Bertha. Audra wanted to cry, but she'd shed so many tears over the past few days that she didn't think she had any left. She flopped back across Nita's bed, exhausted. That's when she noticed Nita's hot pink journal lying on the nightstand. She absentmindedly picked it up. She knew Nita kept a journal, but she'd always wondered if it was up-to-date, because Nita still didn't seem like the everyday journaling type.

Audra flipped the book open, hoping to get her

mind off Coco's dilemma. She smiled halfheartedly as she thumbed through the pages. Nita would have a fit if she knew Audra was peeking through her journal, but since the shower had started running, Audra took a look anyway.

She turned toward the end and immediately began reading. She hadn't planned to get into it, but it was written so well, with so much detail, that it read like a juicy novel.

"Girl, I didn't know you had it in you," Audra mumbled as she read a passage about Nita's pain over losing Marshall. "Dang, this is good," she muttered, flipping the pages forward.

She leafed back to another entry, dated June 13, and began reading.

I don't know what to do about Coco. We had lunch today and she had another black eye. You'd think a woman would get tired of getting beat up, but for some reason she continues to take it. It's to the point now, she doesn't even try to lie about what he's doing, she's gotten so used to it. It's crazy. I'm scared one day he's going to kill her. If I don't kill him first.

Audra stopped reading, and her eyes grew wide. She quickly turned more pages and found another entry describing how Sonny had dragged Coco by her hair from a party. Audra jumped off the bed and raced into the bathroom. "Nita! Nita!"

"What?" Nita asked, stepping out of the shower. "Why are you screaming like you're crazy?" She wrapped a towel around her as her gaze dropped to Audra's hand. "And what are you doing with my journal?" she said, snatching the book away.

"Okay, don't get mad, but I peeked."

"Why is your nosy a———"

"Let me finish," Audra said, cutting her off. "I saw in there you wrote about Coco."

"*And?* I write about everything," Nita said, tucking the book into a bathroom drawer.

"You write *in detail* about Sonny abusing her. You have dates, times, everything."

"I'm a detailed writer. I told y'all. I'm gonna write a blockbuster book. What's your point?"

"My point is, that"—Audra pointed at the drawer—"could be just the proof Coco needs."

Nita's mouth dropped open as she realized what her friend was saying. "Oh, my God. You think this could really be proof?"

"It would back up everything she's saying."

"Then what are we waiting for?" Nita said, reaching into the drawer to retrieve the journal. She raced out of the bathroom. "Let's go take this to her attorney right now."

Audra followed Nita and waited anxiously as she dressed. Could this be what they needed to get Coco out? Audra sure hoped so, because she knew her friend wouldn't be able to last much longer behind bars.

46

Nita waited with bated breath. The portly, blond-haired man placed the phone on the receiver, then wrapped Nita in a big bear hug. "You are brilliant!" he said.

"So, it's going to work?" she asked.

"Yes! This is what we in the legal profession call the smoking gun. The district attorney accepted it because this basically corroborates Cosandra's testimony. Plus, the exam showed she had internal bruises on her ribs and the back of her cranium, so they're not going to press charges." The lawyer was so excited, like he personally knew Coco.

"Yes!" Nita said. They'd gotten the journal to Coco's attorney last night, but it had been too late to turn it over to the DA, so they'd returned first thing in the morning and had been waiting for hours as

Mr. Wright personally walked the journal over to the DA.

"Thank you, Jesus." Davis bowed his head.

"No, thank *you*, Miss Reynolds," the attorney said.

"Nita, I know we've always given you a hard time about journaling, but thank God you didn't listen," Audra said.

"Y'all know I wasn't fazed by your teasing."

"I'm sure glad you weren't."

"So how long before she gets out?" Davis asked, cutting their conversation short.

"Well, some paperwork still has to be processed, but she should be out by five."

"I wish it could be earlier, but I'll take what I can get." Davis promptly stood up. "Let me go call her mother. She's been a nervous wreck ever since I called to tell her what happened."

Audra and Nita looked at each other. Neither of them had thought to call Coco's mother. In fact, Nita wondered why Davis had bothered her mom with all this in the first place. He must've been reading their minds, because he said, "Coco called me last night and asked me to call her mother and tell her what happened. They have this thing where her mother checks in every evening, and she didn't want her mother worried when she couldn't get Coco."

"Well," the attorney said, clasping his pudgy hands together, "I do know it'll be a few hours before she gets out. Why don't you all go on home and get some rest? I have some business I need to take care of. I'll contact you once I have an exact release time."

Audra and Nita stood, thanked the attorney, and followed Davis out.

"Ladies, I'll catch up with you later," he said.

They waved good-bye. "So, do you wanna go get something to eat until we hear from them?" Audra asked.

Nita shook her head. "Nah, I got something I need to do, so I'll just drop you off at home."

She was grateful that Audra didn't ask questions. "Okay, I'm exhausted anyway. Maybe I can catch a couple of hours' sleep."

They made small talk on the drive home. Neither of them talked about their love lives, probably because they would only grow depressed.

Nita dropped Audra off, then headed toward her destination. When she arrived, she sat in the parking lot, wondering if she should get out. Yes, she was using Coco's release as an excuse to talk to Marshall, but whatever worked, she was willing to try. Marshall hadn't given her the time of day, and she was trying to give him some space, but giving him an update on Coco was a way to get them talking.

Nita had just stepped out of the car when she saw Vera and Lucy coming out the church's side door. *Did these women have radar to know when she was in the vicinity?*

"May we help you?" Vera said, quickly stepping in front of Nita as she made her way up the sidewalk.

"No, you may not," Nita said, walking around her.

"Haven't you done enough damage? You ought to be ashamed to show your face around here," Vera said.

"And you ought to be ashamed to have a face like that." Nita tossed her hand at Vera and kept walking. She wasn't here to get into a fight with them. She just wanted to talk to Marshall. She knew he was here because he always spent Tuesday afternoons in his office doing administrative work.

"Reverend Wiley isn't here," Vera announced.

"Yeah, didn't he take that lovely young widow, Marva Lawrence, to lunch?" Lucy threw in.

That stopped Nita in her tracks. She debated whether to turn around, but she knew they were trying to get a rise out of her, so she kept walking.

When she reached Marshall's office, it was locked. She kicked herself for not at least checking for his car in the parking lot. Nita took a deep breath, then made her way back out to her car. Vera and Lucy were leaning against it, satisfied smirks on their faces.

"Excuse me," Nita said, motioning to her car.

"Told you he wasn't here," Vera snapped.

"Will you please get off my car?"

Both women moved out of the way. "We read about your murdering friend in the newspaper," Lucy said. The story had been on the front page of the paper this morning.

"A harlot and a killer," Vera said. "Birds of a feather."

Enough was enough. Nita spun around, and the fierce expression on her face caused Vera to jump. "I am so sick of your self-righteous, holier-than-thou ass!"

Vera's hand went to her chest in shock.

"You stand in judgment of anyone who doesn't meet your standards, yet you want to act like you are God's designated assistant. You don't know nothing about me or my friend. And the more I see you, the more I see that you sure don't know anything about God."

"How dare you?" Vera spat. "I know God!"

"If you did, you'd know He wouldn't approve of your hateful ways. It's hypocrites like you that give the church a bad name." Nita flung her car door open. This was the last time she was going to let these women get to her. "But don't worry. Marshall and I are over. So you win. I'm sure God is pleased."

Nita slammed her car door, not missing the distressed look on Vera's face. Maybe she should've put things in a spiritual perspective for the woman a long time ago. Or maybe, she couldn't help thinking as she pulled out of the parking lot, she should've trusted that God would work things out in her relationship with Marshall. Unfortunately, it was a little too late for maybes.

47

Sunlight had never felt so good. Coco felt like she'd been locked up for three years instead of three days. It had been a nightmare behind bars. Between the unsanitary conditions and the constant ogling she was getting from the manly looking women, she couldn't wait to be gone.

The deputy had returned the last of her things, then opened up the gates to let Coco walk out, when she spotted her friends standing outside the Sheriff's Department. Audra saw her first and came running toward her. "Coco!"

Davis and Nita quickly followed. "Hey," Coco said to all of them. The three of them came up to hug her, and although she wanted to throw her arms around them, the fact that she hadn't bathed in three days made her a little leery.

"Are you okay?" Davis asked, hugging her anyway.

"Yeah," Coco replied. "Just tired."

"Well, girl, come on, we're going to get you home and give you an evening of pampering," Nita said.

Davis pulled her to him, being careful not to squeeze her too tight. "I'm sorry, ladies, but I'm going to have to put my foot down on this one," he said firmly. "Coco is coming with me."

Nita and Audra exchanged glances. Davis brushed Coco's cheek with his hand as she looked up at him. "I know you all are used to being there for her, but she has me now, and you are more than welcome to be there for her when I'm not, but I don't foresee that ever happening."

Nita looked like she wanted to protest, but the expression on Coco's face stopped her. "He's right," Coco said, turning her attention to Nita and Audra. "I love you two, and I appreciate everything, but Davis is right, I need to stop shutting him out." Her eyes filled with tears as she looked back up at him. "I'm sorry I didn't tell you about Sonny."

He leaned in and kissed her. "Don't apologize. Just know you can tell me anything. We all have done things we're not proud of, so no one is in a position to throw stones."

She dabbed her eyes. "Are you all okay with me going with Davis?"

Davis had a firm look, like it didn't matter whether they were okay with it or not. But Audra and Nita smiled. "Of course we are. We just want you to be happy."

"I am happy now that I'm out of that place." She looked back at the jail.

"Yeah, thanks to Nita, the DA could see it was a clear-cut case of self-defense," Audra said.

"Mr. Wright told me about your journal," Coco said to Nita as she reached over to hug her. "Thank you so much. You're a lifesaver, literally."

"Girl, I'm just glad it helped."

"Well, if you all don't mind, I'd like to get her home," Davis said.

"Go on," Nita said. "We'll get with you later. Boy, do we have a lot to fill you in on."

"Are you sure you're not upset about me going with Davis?" Coco asked worriedly. She'd been through hell, and she knew her girls wanted to be there for her.

"Yes," Audra answered. "Remember our cardinal rule—your girls can be dumped at any time for a good man."

All three of them looked at Davis. "And he's a good man if I've ever seen one," Nita added.

Coco smiled as she waved good-bye and let Davis

lead her to his car. She wanted to go to his house and rest, put this nightmare behind her.

Once they'd arrived at Davis's house and gotten settled, Coco let out a deep sigh. She couldn't believe everything that had gone on. She'd been locked up for what seemed like a lifetime. She didn't know how real criminals handled their time.

Davis massaged her feet as he looked at her lovingly. Coco couldn't help it. She had to ask him something that had been on her mind the whole time she was behind bars.

"Davis, you know, you told me before how you felt about divorce."

He looked away like he knew where the question was going.

"So you really think a woman should stay no matter what?"

He gently ran his hand over her leg. "Cosandra, you know how I feel about the sanctity of marriage."

She looked at him, astonished. "With everything you've seen my mom go through. With me being hurt like I was"—she pointed toward her ribs. "Granted, Sonny and I weren't married, but if we were, you really think a person should work through this?"

He put his finger to her lips. "Sssh. If you would let me finish."

She stopped talking but glared at him. "I believe in the sanctity of marriage, but I also know that God wants us to be well and happy." He tapped his fingers pensively on her foot. "And someone . . . someone beating you, well, that can't be in God's plan. You know I believe divorce should only come from abandonment or adultery. But I guess an abusive man who refuses to change his behavior *is abandoning his marriage.* He's abandoning the vows he made before God, as well as his ordained role in the relationship. So, I guess what I'm saying is, you're right."

Coco felt tears well up in her eyes. She so needed to hear that. Davis wiped away the tear that had started trickling down her cheek. "But I promise you, you never have to worry about anything like that with me. The only thing I want to do is love you." She sat up and hugged him hard, holding on tight. She needed to hear that even more.

48

Audra watched as Andrew chased his puppy around the park. He'd named the dog Zack Ster after some show he used to watch on the Disney Channel. The dog was the one good thing that had come out of her relationship with Lewis. She had wanted to give it back so that she could be completely through with him, but her son would never give his new pet up, so she'd let him keep it.

"Andrew, be careful," she called out when she saw him climbing on the jungle gym, the puppy nipping at his feet.

Audra got comfortable on the park bench and opened her Jacquelin Thomas novel *Redemption*. She needed some of that in her life. And maybe the book could give her some inspiration. Audra was proud of herself so far. Lewis hadn't given up in his quest to get her back, but she was standing strong. She'd even threatened to call the board of his church and tell him she was filing harassment charges.

Audra hadn't read very far when she looked up to see one of the most gorgeous men she'd ever encountered standing over her.

"Excuse me, pretty lady," he said, catching his breath. He looked like he had been running. He had on Adidas track pants and a sleeveless Adidas T-shirt, displaying his chiseled arms. "You know what time it is?"

"It's three-fifteen," Audra said, checking her watch.

"Thanks," he said, exhaling deeply. "Whew, time flies when you're having fun, I guess." He hesitated like he was waiting on her to invite him to sit down. When she didn't, he sat down anyway. "Hi, I'm Marcus," he said, extending his hand.

Audra knew exactly who he was, but she wasn't about to let him know. "Hi, Marcus," she replied, flashing him a tight smile before turning her attention back to her book.

It seemed like he didn't know how to take her blowing him off, because he leaned down and pretended to tie his shoe, even though Audra could clearly see it was already tied.

He returned to sitting upright. "Beautiful day, isn't it."

"Yep," Audra replied. She was proud of herself that she wasn't fawning all over him. After all, he'd been one of the top picks in last year's NFL draft. She knew he was from Houston, even though he played for Kansas City. But if anyone had ever told her she'd be sitting on a park bench next to him, pretending she didn't know who he was, she would have thought they were crazy.

"Well, I can see you're into your book, so I'm going to let you go," he said, standing up.

"Okay. Nice to meet you," Audra said casually.

Marcus clearly wasn't used to this kind of reception. Audra could see out of the corner of her eye the confused look on his face. Even if he wasn't a star football player, he was handsome enough that he could turn anyone's head.

"Do you mind if I ask, are you married?"

Audra closed her book and looked up at him. "No."

"Are you seeing someone?" he asked, like he was trying to figure out why she wasn't interested.

"No, I'm not."

He stood there for a moment, then said, "Are you gay?"

"Why? Because I'm not falling over myself to talk with you?"

He smiled. "I'm sorry, that did sound kind of bad, didn't it?"

Audra nodded. "Yeah, it did."

"It's just that . . . shoot, let me stop beating around the bush. I think you're beautiful and I would love the opportunity to take you out to dinner or something."

Audra smiled, this time genuinely. The old Audra would have given her right kidney to reel in someone like Marcus Mayberry. But the old Audra had been through a lot, and as Miss Bea said, she had a lot of work to do on herself before she could find happiness with a man.

"You know, Marcus—you did say your name was Marcus, didn't you?"

He nodded.

"You are every bit as handsome as you think you are," she said. "And I mean that in the best of ways. Another time, another place, I would've absolutely loved to have gone out with you. But I'm not in that place right now."

He continued nodding. "I guess I can respect that."

"I guess you'll have to," she replied, still smiling.

"You take care of yourself, pretty lady," he said. "Maybe we'll meet again."

He winked as he took off jogging.

"Maybe we will, Mr. Mayberry, maybe we will," she mumbled as she went back to reading her book.

49

Nita absolutely, positively hated begging. Even worse, she hated begging a man. But at this point she would do whatever it took to get Marshall to forgive her. Right about now all her pride was out the window.

She took another deep breath and rang his doorbell again.

Marshall swung the door open and leaned against it. "Yes, Juanita?"

"Can we talk?" She shifted nervously. She'd worn her most conservative dress and had her hair pulled back into a flattering ponytail. She wanted Marshall to see her in a different light.

Marshall sighed heavily, like he'd rather not, but he stepped aside and motioned for her to come in. "Fine, we can talk. Although I don't know that there's anything for us to talk about."

Nita stepped inside, gave him time to close the door, then quickly said, "Marshall, I miss you."

"I miss you, too," he said sincerely.

"Then why won't you give us a chance?"

He stared at her without any emotion. She couldn't stand that look. She was used to his adoration. This was uncharted territory, and Nita was surprised at the pang it brought to her heart.

"Juanita, I've been around a lot of people in my life, good and bad. I try to live a righteous life and not stand in judgment of others. That's why, as much as it hurt, I'm not standing in judgment of you. But I can't be with you."

Nita felt tears begin to fall. "But you're the one always preaching about forgiveness, and you can't even forgive me."

"Number one, I forgive you. That doesn't mean I take you back, but I do forgive you. Number two, more than anything, the reason I can't be with you is your casual reference to 'that God stuff.' My relationship is not some casual thing, and the woman in my life has to be in tune with what God wants for her and for us. I knew from the very beginning that we weren't spiritually yoked, but I prayed on it and I hoped that you would be led to see Him like I do."

"So because I'm not some religious fanatic, I'm suddenly not good enough?" she asked.

He shook his head. "That's not what I'm saying at all. And you know that. You are good enough. You're better than good enough. The problem is, you don't recognize it. I was being led by my heart and not my head, and I wasn't listening to God, because He told me that we were spiritually out of tune with each other."

"Well, He told me that we were supposed to be together," she said mockingly.

Once again he looked at her pityingly. "So He talks to you now?"

"Yeah, He talks to me," she snapped.

"Do you listen?" he asked. When she didn't answer, he said, "That's what I'm talking about. You just throw it out there like God is only there to give us what we want. He's not a name-it-and-claim-it God. I want a car, so He gives me a car. I want a man, so He gives me a man. You haven't found the love you want because God knows your heart."

She dropped her hands. Was what he was saying true? Audra had said she was spending her time learning to love herself. Was that what Nita needed?

"Juanita," Marshall said, taking her hand, "you're a good woman, and I have no doubt that you will eventually find the happiness you want. But I'm a firm believer that everything happens for a reason. The day before those pictures were plastered all over the church, I prayed to God to send me a sign that you were indeed the woman for me."

She wiped the tear that was trickling down her cheek. "I guess you got it."

He nodded knowingly. "I did." He wiped her face. "I'm going to keep you in my prayers. I only ask two things."

"What?" She sniffed.

"That you learn to pray for yourself. And that you take your hands off the wheel. God is a pretty good driver."

Nita weighed his words. Miss Bea said that all the time. Maybe they were both right. Maybe she should just let go and let God. Maybe it was time to try something different, because her way definitely wasn't working.

Epilogue

Y ou look beautiful."

Audra teared up at the sight of her best friend. Coco was a vision of loveliness. "Doesn't she look great, Nita?"

Nita had turned away and was peering into the mirror. "She does," she gently said, her voice shaky.

"Are you crying?" Coco asked, a huge smile across her face.

"Girl, please." Nita sniffed. "You know I don't cry." She dabbed her eyes. "It's this ol' cheap mascara that makeup artist is using."

"Excuse me," the makeup girl, who was sitting at a dressing table applying makeup to one of the brides-maids, said. "That's M.A.C., I'll have you know."

Coco waved her off. "Tasha, don't pay my friend

any attention. She's crying because she's happy for me. She just doesn't want anyone to know it."

"Whatever," Nita said.

"My baby does make a beautiful bride, doesn't she?"

Coco smiled at her mom, who had walked in the room looking the best Coco had ever seen. She seemed happy, in a way Coco hadn't seen in a very long time. "Mama, you look good."

"Tell me something I don't know," her mother joked.

"Mrs. King, you got a weave?" Nita said, feeling Coco's mother's long, curly hair.

"No, darling. This is all my hair."

"What?" Coco said.

"It sure is. I paid for every inch of it." She laughed.

"Look at you," Nita said. "I ain't mad at you. Trying to get your groove back, looking twenty years younger."

"Well, it's the new me."

"I like the new you," Coco said.

"So do I," Mrs. King said as she did a little wiggle. "Georgia agrees with me. Well, I'm going on out so we can get this show on the road." She took in Coco's appearance one more time. "My baby is getting married."

Coco grabbed her mother's hand before she walked away. "Mama," she said, pulling her to the side, "do you think I'm wrong for not inviting Daddy?"

The smile left her mother's face. "Baby, this is your day. This ain't about me. This ain't about your daddy."

"I didn't want any drama. And you're doing so much better. I just didn't want anything to . . ." She paused and glanced down.

"Set me back?" her mother asked, finishing her sentence. "Sweetheart, it took me a long time to gather up the strength that I needed, but now that I have, there's no going back. You know, a lot of times, we don't know it, but we serve as an inspiration to people. I never thought my daughter would be the inspiration I needed to make such a drastic change in my life."

Coco smiled through her warm tears. "So you don't think I'm bad for not inviting Daddy?"

Her mother gently wiped her face. "No, baby. It's your day, and even if your dad had shown up here, he loves you too much. He wouldn't have ruined your wedding."

"But everyone is going to wonder why Uncle Aaron is giving me away."

"Then everybody needs to mind their own business."

Coco's father had called her numerous times. At first he had been still trying to find out where her mother was; then it was to apologize. The last phone call had sounded so sad and pitiful that she was almost tempted to call him back, but when she finally confronted the issue, she knew she wasn't ready.

"Eventually, you'll have to make peace with him and forgive him. I've forgiven him, and eventually, you should do the same," her mother told her.

"Maybe I'll call him after all of this is over."

"I think that's a good idea. But you also need to forgive yourself. It's been a year since Sonny died. You didn't face any charges. His family forgave you. And it's time for you to let it go," her mother said.

"I know, Mama." That had been the hardest part of the last year, coping with what had happened with Sonny. She had thought his family was going to hate her, but the day before the funeral, his mother had come to visit her. Naturally, she was devastated about the loss of her son, but she told Coco she didn't blame her, saying Sonny's father had had a horrible temper. It had cost him his life when he got into a fatal barroom fight.

Her words had made Coco realize there truly were

generational curses. She wished more people would understand the trickle-down effect of dysfunction. That's why she was glad that Audra had made peace with her single life and resolved that Andrew would no longer see an array of men coming in and out of her life. And she was definitely glad that she'd broken the abuse cycle.

"In the meantime, dry those tears," her mother said. "You look too beautiful to ruin that makeup. You are about to marry a man that you don't have to worry about. Davis is a good man. I feel it in my spirit. And you will know happiness."

"Thank you, Mama."

Her mother kissed her gently and walked out.

Andrew came running in. He looked adorable in his ring bearer shorts and jacket.

"Hi, Auntie Coco. You look pretty," he said.

Davis's daughter stood next to him. She was adorable as well in a white, fluffy dress and a wreath around her head. Coco reached down to hug them.

"Crystal said she's gonna be my cousin. Is that true?" Andrew said.

"It is. Crystal is about to become my daughter," Coco answered. Crystal flashed a big, toothless grin at her. Angie had agreed to let Crystal come live with them. She'd been doing everything she could to keep her lifestyle under wraps, but she said now she wanted a chance to live her life freely and thought the better environment for Crystal was with Davis and Coco. Coco was just fine with that. Instant motherhood was another perk of being married to Davis.

Miss Bea appeared in the doorway, with the wedding coordinator standing behind her. "I told you they would still be back here," Miss Bea said.

The coordinator quickly clapped her hands. "Come on, everyone. It's showtime."

Everyone left the room except Miss Bea, Audra, Nita, and Coco. "Ummm, can we get a moment?" Nita asked Miss Bea, who had folded her arms and didn't look like she was moving.

"I'm tryin' to make sure y'all hurry up. It's already six-fifteen. This shindig was supposed to start at six."

"We are well aware of the time, Miss Bea. Now, please?" Audra motioned toward the door.

Miss Bea huffed as she spun around. "Y'all holy rollers need to roll on up out of here and get this show on the road. Hmph. Black folks can't never start nothin' on time," she mumbled as she walked out.

Nita and Audra laughed as each of them took one of Coco's hands. "She's right. We need to go, but we just wanted to tell you we love you and we're so proud of you," Audra said.

Nita brushed a strand of hair from Coco's face. "Look at you, about to go get your man."

"Yeah, I guess my rollin' days are over." Coco smiled gingerly.

"Well, I'm nowhere near marriage, but my man-hunting days are over also," Audra said. "I'm going to have to let my man find me."

Coco gently squeezed Audra's hand. "I'm proud of you." She turned to Nita. "Are you okay with Marshall marrying us?"

Nita shrugged nonchalantly. "Hey, it is what it is," she replied. Coco had hoped that Marshall would find a way to forgive Nita. He'd been cordial to her at the wedding rehearsal, but that was as far as he'd gone.

Vera and her crew had been happy about Nita and Marshall's relationship ending and the fact that they had managed to drive Nita away. She no longer attended Higher Elevation, but the good news was, she'd found another church and was going regularly. Like Audra, she'd stopped looking for Mr. Right, but unlike Audra, she hadn't stopped fooling with Mr. Right Now. Coco told herself Nita was still a work in progress, but she was confident her friend would be all right.

The wedding coordinator stuck her head back in

the door. "Ladies, please, there's an anxious man up front."

"Okay, here we come," Nita said. They hugged Coco one last time, then raced to get ready to start the wedding march out.

Left alone, Coco turned to survey her reflection in the full-length mirror. What she saw made her smile. Looking back was a strong, confident, beautiful, God-fearing woman. A woman who, when she stopped looking, had finally found true love.

Readers Group Guide

Holy Rollers tells the story of three lifelong friends—Coco, Audra, and Nita—and their quest to find true love. The three women have endured their share of heartache: Coco is abused by her boyfriend, Sonny; Audra is a single mother who seems to meet only unreliable men; and Nita can't get over a married man who wants to keep her as his mistress. Deciding to take fate into their own hands, the three women attend a conference for ministers, hoping to meet men who are God-fearing and wholesome. The results are varied, but the experience with the church changes the lives of these three women in this hilarious and heartbreaking story.

DISCUSSION QUESTIONS

1. The novel opens with the three friends discussing Sonny's latest abuse of Coco. Nita says, "That fool needs to die. I'm talking an acid-in-the-face, burning-in-the-bed, slow and painful death." Do you agree? Did this opening scene provide a sense of foreshadowing for Sonny's eventual demise? Did you have any inclination it would be Coco, not Nita, who would be brave enough to stand up to Sonny?

2. Miss Bea is the voice of reason throughout the story. How does she advise Audra and her friends? Do you have the sense she is speaking from experience? Is she a judgmental character, or a helpful one? Miss Bea instructs Audra, ". . . you need to stop looking for love period, and let love find you." Do you think Miss Bea is right? Does Audra?

3. Compare Coco, Audra, and Nita. How are they alike? How are they different? Do you sympathize with one more than the other? Does one need a chance at love more than the others?

4. It seems that all of the women have reasons for turning away from the church. Nita discusses what happened to her mother as a result of being a part of the church. Do you think her background informs her present? What about Coco and Audra—what are their reasons for leaving the church? Do you think all the women have a justified reason for walking away from God? Why or why not?

5. A possible theme of the novel emerges when Coco sings: "After you've done all you can, just stand." In light of this quote, think about the ways in which the characters in the story "just stand" when they've reached the end of their rope. Discuss Coco, Audra, Nita, Coco's mother, and Marshall in your response.

6. Consider the structure of the story. What effect do the three narrators have on the story overall? Whose story is this? Is it more Coco's or Audra's or Nita's, or do you think it's about all of the women? Whose point of view did you enjoy the most?

7. How would you define Lewis's character? Did you see him as sympathetic before the ending? Did you like him? Did you hate him? How did Audra see him? How did Nita and Coco? Consider these questions in light of the fact that we never get Lewis's point of view directly and come to know him only through his relationship with Audra. Did the revealing of his "true colors" surprise you? Why or why not?

8. "Having a piece of the man was better than not having a man at all." Here Audra is describing her rationalization for going to see Lewis in Atlanta after she has discovered his marriage to Michelle. Do you agree with her statement? Why do you think Audra went? Do you think it was out of loneliness, or was there another reason? What did you make of her decision?

9. Discuss Nita's relationship with Marshall. Do you think Nita loved Marshall, or was he filling a void for her? If she was in love with Marshall, how does Neil come into play? Can Nita's actions be forgiven? Do you think Marshall loved Nita, or was he also looking to fill a void?

10. Coco tells Nita that she is enjoying her "newfound relationships"—both with Davis and with God. Do you think the author is connecting pure, unadulterated love with a spiritual relationship with God? What role do you think Christianity plays in the story overall? Do you think all three of the women have a changed relationship with God by the end of the story, like Coco does? Why or why not?

11. Much of the story centers on good versus evil, temptation, and the choices we have in the face of temptation. The women battle constantly with making the "right" choice versus following their hearts. Discuss the different forms of temptation the women face in the novel. As a starting point, turn to page 205 and consider the following quote: "And while she cared for Marshall deeply, Nita actually was looking forward to reaching the point where she loved him as much as he loved her."

12. Love, a difficult word to define, is debated throughout the novel. How do the women define love? How would you

define it? Do you think the women share the same idea of love, or not? Do you think anyone can share the same idea of love? Use Nita's quote on page 137, beginning with "Don't weep for me," to begin your discussion.

13. Discuss Coco's murder of Sonny. Do you think Coco has finally broken the cycle of violence in her life? Although it was a sad and violent scene, do you think the consequences of the death—Coco moving on, her mother finding the courage to leave her father—outweighed the sadness? Why or why not?

14. Did you find any irony in the title *Holy Rollers*? Do you think the title is meant to be comical, serious, or both? In the end, what group of women were the "holy rollers"?

ENHANCING YOUR BOOK CLUB

1. *Holy Rollers* tells the story of three very different women all searching for the same thing: a chance at love. Nita, Coco, and Audra all represent different "types" of women, to whom we can relate. Compare and contrast the characters to your favorite television show or movie featuring strong female leads. What are the similarities? What are the differences? Who are you most like?

2. "Y'all women so busy running around trying to snag you a man, make him fall in love with you. You need to be falling in love with yourselves. You're trying to drive your life into the direction you want it to go. But sometimes, you got to take your hands off the steering wheel and let

Jesus take the wheel." Here Miss Bea is encouraging the three women to stop trying to force love. She thinks the women should put their trust in God and everything will turn out well in their lives. Have your group come up with a song that contains the same message as in the book and share it.

3. Have a movie night with your book club and rent *Enough* (2002) with Jennifer Lopez. Discuss how Jennifer Lopez's character in the movie learns the same harsh lessons as Coco in *Holy Rollers*. What parallels can you find between the two stories? What are the differences between the book and the film?

4. Didn't get enough of ReShonda Tate Billingsley's work? Have your book club do a series on her. Read any of ReShonda's novels—*The Devil Is a Lie, Can I Get a Witness?, The Pastor's Wife, Everybody Say Amen, I Know I've Been Changed, Let the Church Say Amen,* or *My Brother's Keeper.* What themes do you notice in her work? What message do you think ReShonda is sending to her audience? Which of these books was your favorite? The favorite of the group?

GALLERY BOOKS

proudly presents a sneak peek of

WHAT'S DONE IN THE DARK

by

ReShonda Tate Billingsley

Felise

I never knew Jack Daniel's could be so comforting. I'd been sitting here crying for the past thirty minutes, and since I knew I wasn't much of a drinker, I'd been taking it slow. But the whiskey had me realizing one thing for sure—I was sick and tired of my husband.

Fourteen years of begging for affection. Fourteen years of an obsessive workaholic. After fourteen years you'd think I'd be used to it, but all I was was tired. I'd begged Greg to make more time for me, to give as much to our marriage as he gave to his job. And he'd try, and succeed for a while, but then he would go back to normal.

I needed a new normal.

Don't get me wrong. I had no plans to divorce my husband. At least I didn't think I did. He'd been the one who had repaired my broken heart when my one true love chose another. It's why I'd hung in for so long. But I knew that if something didn't change, a change of address would be in my future.

"Felise?"

I turned around to the voice behind me. I immediately smiled at the sight of Steven, my dear friend and Paula's husband.

"Hey, pretty lady," he said, hugging me. "What are you doing here?"

I raised my drink. "Drinking," I replied with a giggle. I wasn't surprised that he was here. The Four Seasons bar had some of the best drink specials in town. "What are you doing here?"

"I had a meeting with one of my frat brothers. He's trying to get me on board with this business venture. It sounds promising, but it may take me away from the family more, and I'm just not sure that's something I want to do."

That made me smile. Greg wouldn't have even considered his family.

"Good ol' Steven," I said, raising my drink to him in a toast. With the stretching I almost slipped off the chair.

"Whoa," he said, catching me. I could see the wheels turning in his head as he assessed my condition. "Okay, what's really going on? What are you doing here?"

I released a strained laugh. "What does it look like?"

"It looks like you're drinking"—he cocked his head and studied my drink—"whiskey."

I saluted him. "You're good."

A light went on in his eyes, and his face changed. "Felise, what's going on? Isn't today your anniversary?"

I couldn't help but laugh. Steven remembered it was my anniversary, but my own husband didn't.

"Where's Greg?"

I immediately lost my smile. "He's at home, cleaning up."

"What?" Steven said, confused.

"He's vacuuming up the rose petals I had laid out for our romantic evening."

"What do you mean, 'vacuuming up'?"

I took a deep breath and set my drink down. I needed to leave that bourbon alone. It was starting to make my head spin. "You know my husband," I said. "He's cleaning. On our fourteenth anniversary. I know it sounds unbelievable. But that's my husband, good ol' Greg."

"Hey, man, can I get you anything?" the bartender asked, approaching us.

"Bring me something a little lighter," I said. "Apple martini."

"Should you be mixing liquor?" Steven asked.

"Should you be all up in my business?"

Steven smiled at that. He knew he couldn't push

me too far. He turned to the bartender and said, "You know what? Bring me a cranberry and vodka." He slid onto the barstool next to me. "You don't mind me sitting here and having a drink with you, do you?"

I shrugged indifferently. What I was thinking, though, was that right about now I'd rather sit with him than just about anybody else.

When the bartender placed the drinks in front of us, Steven said, "Okay, tell me what's really going on. You and Greg have a fight?"

I took a deep breath, sipped my martini, then relayed the whole sad story.

"Wow," he said when I was finished.

"Yeah." I leaned in. "So tell me, Steven, if I recall, didn't you whisk your wife away for a weekend in Puerto Rico for your fourteenth anniversary?"

Steven held up a finger to stop me. "Ah, not quite. That was the plan, but remember, Paula bailed on me."

I nodded. "Oh, yeah." I remembered thinking Paula was out of her mind that day. Steven had called and asked her to meet him at the airport. He'd planned a surprise weekend trip for their anniversary, arranged for child care and everything, and Paula wouldn't go because she said they "couldn't just drop everything and jet off somewhere like we were single." I'd felt like Paula and I needed to switch spouses.

It was a feeling I quickly brushed off, even though

Steven had been mine before he was Paula's. But that was a long time ago. Back in college when he and I were best friends who crossed the line. And when he'd gone to DC for grad school, I'd hooked him up with Paula, my best friend since high school, who had gone to Howard University and was now making her home in DC. I'd just wanted her to show him around. I never expected them to fall in love.

But the one thing I knew about Steven, he was a hopeless romantic. He would make up for that fourteenth-year fiasco this year. No way would he let his fifteenth anniversary go by without some grandiose celebration.

Steven took a sip of his drink, then sadly said, "I don't know if we'll even make it to fifteen."

"What?" I asked in shock. I knew Paula had been unhappy, but I had no idea Steven was feeling the same way.

"Sometimes I feel like marrying Paula was the biggest mistake I ever made," he candidly admitted.

Immediately, I started feeling butterflies in my stomach. I tried to tell myself it was the liquor, but my heart wanted to believe that maybe, just maybe, Steven was thinking about us. As horrible as it seems, at that very moment I hoped that he was. Then I would know I wasn't the only one who still had unresolved feelings.

Felise

It's true that liquor brought out the real you. Because I had just asked a question that, had I been in my right mind, I would've never dreamed of asking. But I repeated it anyway.

"You can be honest. It won't hurt my feelings," I said. "Do you ever think about us. That's a yes or no question."

I was on my third apple martini. Couple that with the bourbon I'd had earlier and I was feeling pretty courageous.

Steven was nursing his third drink—since joining me—so I could tell he had a little buzz, too. Still, he said, "Come on, Felise, we agreed that was a chapter that was closed."

I playfully stuck my bottom lip out. "I know we made the right decision. We're too much alike."

"Yeah, and don't forget, you fixed me up with Paula."

"Yeah, I did and here we are." My heart ached as I thought of their beautiful wedding. I loved Greg. I really did. But he was frugal and had considered a big wedding a waste of money, so we'd been married in a simple ceremony by a justice of the peace. The bad part was Paula was simple, too. She couldn't have cared less about a big wedding. But Steven was from a prominent family and his mother would've died if she'd been denied the opportunity to see her son married in a huge ceremony. And talk about huge! They'd had ten bridesmaids (including me), ten groomsmen, and two hundred fifty guests watch them exchange vows in a historic Catholic cathedral, followed by a reception for four hundred at an elite country club. Yep, I'd gotten a dirty courtroom at the courthouse and Paula had gotten my dream wedding.

When the minister had said if anyone sees any reason why the two of them should not be married, the only thing that kept me from speaking up was the one-twentieth of a carat ring on my finger. Of course, Steven had pulled out a four-carat diamond that had made everyone gasp.

"Hey, are you still with me?" Steven waved his hand in my face.

I tried to laugh, but a distorted cry came out instead. "Sorry." I covered my eyes with the palm of my hand.

"Hey, hey," Steven said, scooting closer.

I turned my head as I tried to ward off the tears. "Sorry. It's just that sometimes I wonder about my marriage."

He sighed like he could relate. "You're not the only one. It's like, I love Paula, I really do. But after she became a mother, she changed. I try to do my part to help. I tried to hire a nanny, but Paula refused. I did what I could to make life easier for her. But it's almost like she's happier wallowing in pity."

I knew all too well what Steven was talking about. I knew full well how miserable Paula was. I talked to her about her negative attitude on a regular basis.

Steven was about to say something else when his phone rang. He pulled it out of the holder on his hip, glanced at it, and said, "Speak of the devil. This is Paula." He pressed Talk. "Hello." He paused.

"Naw, I'm still here," he said into the phone. "I am not drunk . . . Yes, I had a few drinks." He rolled his eyes and pulled the phone away from his ear as Paula's loud voice broadcast from the phone. He put it back to his ear. "Look, don't start with me, Paula. I told you I was going to be out late . . . I asked you to come. You're the one who wanted to stay at home . . ." He gritted his teeth. "Oh, don't give me that. Your mom was there. Why is she living there if you don't ever want to leave the kids with her?" He paused again and I could tell Paula was going off. "You know what, I told you about calling me out of my name . . ." His brow was furrowing and I could tell he was getting upset. "I don't think so! I pay the mortgage. I wish you would put my sh—" I put my hand on his arm to calm him down and remind him where he was. He took a deep breath and said, "Stop threatening me with divorce. If you're going to leave, then leave . . . I wish you would put my stuff on the lawn!"

More muffled roars came from Paula's end, then finally he said, "You are deranged! I was meeting with Kevin, not another woman! Why would I invite you if I was planning on meeting another woman? . . . I didn't think you'd refuse. You know what? You're being ridiculous, as usual. Don't call me to rush me. I'll be home when I get home! You . . . Hello? Hello?"

He tossed the phone on the bar. "Uggh!" He flinched as, unexpectedly, he grabbed at his chest.

"Are you okay?" I asked. Paula had mentioned he'd been having some chest pains, but she had just chalked it up to stress from his demanding job.

Steven stood deathly still for a minute, then relaxed, before saying, "Yeah. That woman gives me heartburn." He signaled for the bartender and I relaxed. "Excuse me, can I get another drink? This time, skip the cranberry and make it a double!"

I knew Paula wasn't happy, but I had no idea their marriage had reached this extreme. "What was that all about?" I asked. I definitely noted he hadn't told her that he was with me.

"I swear, that woman! I just don't know how much longer I can do this. She's always accusing me of cheating! Felise, as God is my witness, I've never cheated on her, but for as much as she accuses me, I might as well be."

"Don't say that," I replied as the bartender set a double shot glass in front of us. "Your wife loves you."

"I'm just tired." Steven took his drink and downed it in one extended gulp. "See, you're not the only one who's unhappy."

"Can I ask you a question?" I said.

He managed a smile. "Ask away."

"Why didn't you tell her you were here with me?"

He shrugged, not looking guilty. "I don't know. She didn't give me a chance before she started going off. It's probably best anyway. With the rampage she's on, you don't need to be dragged into our drama."